Praise for

Brooklyn Girl

"*Brooklyn Girl* is a well written, gritty exploration of how poverty and disadvantage, coupled with poor adolescent choices can spiral out of control. The sympathetic characters pulled me in and made me root for them the entire way. *Brooklyn Girl* is a compellingly dark novel."

—Lisa Wayman, author of *Longing for Home*

"If ever there was a novel crying out for a continuation, this one is it. Ronald Belfort's *Brooklyn Girl* is the heart-wrenching tale of an adolescent girl whose broken family is debilitating and dysfunctional. Her absentee, recovering-alcoholic father is almost angelic when compared to her bi-sexual, drug-addicted, crack-whore of a mother. Belfort skillfully uses descriptive images to portray the teenager's destructive journey into drugs, debauchery and despair. Relating her painful experiences in the first person effectively adds to the intimacy of the story. This book is hard to put down, and will likely have readers clamoring for a sequel. Well done."

—Rich Schiesser, author of *Shattered Hearts*

"*Brooklyn Girl* takes us to places in a young girl's life that is best observed in a book rather than in person. It has been said, "We learn more from our mistakes than our successes." Belfort does an excellent job in providing an opportunity to engage in the mystery, excitement, and outcome of a life being educated in the school of poor choices."

—Dr. Ida Baty, Human development Professor (retired),
and Licensed Professional Counselor and
Certified Rehabilitation Counselor

"Belfort presents a darkly introspective story of a dysfunctional teen struggling with drugs, alcoholism and childhood neglect."

—Betsy Ashton, nominated for 2016 Library of Virginia Best Novel.

"In this era of fiction novels, it is difficult to find a book that truly captivates the reader from beginning to end. *Brooklyn Girl* is not the case. The colorful characters draw you in right away, and by the end, you feel as if you have become a character in Lonnie's escapades. Lonnie's tale is truly a must read"

—Samantha M. Chapman

"Absolutely singular! A reverting, brutally honest and heartfelt roller coaster ride that delivers a brilliant message. Read *Brooklyn Girl* and you will understand the harsh realities of physiological and substance abuse while battling peer pressure to fit in."

—Steve V

"Ronald Belfort is wonderful storyteller. *Brooklyn Girl* is an enrapturing tale of heartbreak and moral redemption."

—Christopher Bowron, author of *Devil in the Grass*

Brooklyn Girl
by Ronald Belfort

ISBN 978-1-63393-228-9

This is a work of fiction. The characters are both actual and fictitious. With the exception of verified historical events and persons, all incidents, descriptions, dialogue and opinions expressed are the products of the author's imagination and are not to be construed as real.

Published by

köehlerbooks™

210 60th Street
Virginia Beach, VA 23451
212-574-7939
www.koehlerbooks.com

Brooklyn Girl

RONALD BELFORT

VIRGINIA BEACH
CAPE CHARLES

This book is dedicated to my beautiful wife, Lorena, without whom this project would have not been completed. Thank you for all of your love and support over the years. Also, to my wonderful children, Diego and Dominique, all that I do, I do for you.

Chapter I

There was nothing I could do, no one I could talk to. I had no idea where my mother was. More than likely, she was out on the street, getting high and turning tricks as usual. My father wanted nothing to do with me and stopped taking my calls a long time ago. My best friend, Lia, had moved away. I was abandoned by everyone who I thought cared about me. My grandparents were the only ones who showed up for my arraignment. Sitting in the back row of the courtroom, they didn't seem like they wanted to be there either. I could see the disappointment on their faces. It was official; I had alienated every important person in my life.

I rose from my seat when the judge entered and took the bench. As he began going through the long list of charges, my mind slowly started drifting. *How did I get to this point in my life?* I thought. *I'm seventeen years old. The biggest problem most girls my age face is algebra homework or which dress to wear to the prom.* But as for me, I was standing in a New York City courtroom facing felony drug charges. Seven years have passed since that day, and I still struggle with the question. How did I end up in here?

Unofficially, I'd say it started when I was twelve and my mother introduced me to beer. I quickly developed a love for alcohol, and ever since then it had contributed to a litany of poor decisions. It might be hard to imagine how a mother could do that, but if it didn't happen to me I might not believe it. Looking back, my life was dysfunctional from the beginning.

I didn't grow up in the all-American family, the kind with two working parents and two-and-a-half kids. We didn't live in suburbia in a house with a white picket fence. I have never been on a family vacation or sat down to a family dinner. My parents were not high school sweethearts, and I am not a product of their love.

Growing up, my father was a bit of a ladies' man. A tall, angular guy with big brown eyes and curly hair. He had a round chest and a strong physique. He was popular with the girls in the neighborhood, including my mother. She hung around him a lot, but despite her best efforts, he barely noticed her. Then one night in the summer of 1988, she discovered the key to his heart— booze. That night, after she bought him several rounds of beer—something she later regretted because she would go on to support his habit for the next five years. They ended up in a nearby schoolyard and had drunken sex. Many years later, I attended that very same junior high school.

Surprisingly, their relationship lasted a while, but it was five years of lying, cheating, and emotional distress. However, somewhere in-between all the fighting they managed to have a baby—me, Lonnie. When my father learned that he was going to be a parent, his reaction was unenthusiastic. The responsibility frightened him. He told my mother he wasn't ready for a child and asked her to have an abortion. She refused, saying that it was against her religion. Ironically, a few months after I was born, she became pregnant again. This time, however, she ran down to Planned Parenthood without giving it a second thought.

So much for religion.

. . .

I was born March 8, 1991 on a Friday afternoon while my father was sleeping off a hangover. On the eve of my birth, he and my mother got into a huge fight and she threw him out of the house. This was not a big deal to him, for he had long since grown accustomed to it. By her third trimester, they were arguing constantly.

The fighting was always about the same things—his drinking and the fact that he couldn't keep a job. My father drank all day, every day. Even in the final days of her pregnancy, my mother often had to take care of him when he got drunk. On more than one occasion she had woken up to find him passed out with a lit cigarette in his hand or asleep on the toilet. His drinking had become too burdensome for her. So when things got out of control, she'd make him leave.

After leaving my mother's house that day, my father ended up at some other woman's house, where he overindulged in alcohol and sex. He was nowhere to be found when my mother went into labor the next morning. After frantically calling everyone she could think of, she finally got a hold of him some time before noon. But it was too late. By the time he made it to the hospital, I had already been born.

My mother was not innocent in all this. The only time she managed to stay off the streets herself was during the nine months she was pregnant. As a junior in high school, she worked at a drug store in her neighborhood—the only legitimate job she ever held in her life. She attended an all-girl Catholic school, the foundation for her lascivious behavior. All Catholic schoolgirls certainly are not promiscuous, but if there's a hint of truth to this stereotype then my mother was living proof.

After my arrival, my mother insisted on making up for lost time. She hit the streets with a vengeance, drinking, smoking, and partying. Oddly enough, my father came from out of nowhere and began to develop a sense of responsibility. While she paraded the streets, he stayed home and took care of me. For a brief period he even stopped drinking. But soon my mother's lewd behavior in the streets started to cloud his judgment. Consumed by allegations and hearsay, his desire to be a father suddenly faded. I got dumped off on family members, or anyone who would babysit me, while the two of them roamed the streets together.

Their fighting never stopped and my father's drinking resumed. Finally, after about a year of fighting, breaking up and making up, my mother left him for good. She moved in with a girlfriend and soon the two of them became lovers. Shortly thereafter, my mother lost interest in me and stopped coming around. I became my grandmother's responsibility.

My father continued to come around two or three times a week. But his visits were usually brief because of my grandmother's nagging and complaining. She had a habit of talking to herself and in doing so she'd bad-mouth everyone. She talked about my father out loud as if he wasn't there—even though he was in the next room. She didn't like him. In fact, no one on my mother's side cared for him; they all knew he was a drunk.

My father tried not to let my grandmother discourage him. He'd come by and take me to the park or the zoo or the arcade or other fun places. He never had money and always showed up empty handed. This infuriated my grandmother. Trips to the park and the playground may have been nice, but what she felt I needed most were essential things such as food and clothing. She couldn't understand how he could have money to get drunk yet he couldn't provide for his baby. What she didn't know was that my father could always find some naive young girl and charm her out of all her cash, which he used for beer and cigarettes. He was also running tabs in just about every corner store in the neighborhood.

To his credit, on a few occasions my father tried to clean up, but each time he failed. He enrolled in college but barely finished the first semester. He tried to find work but without an education or work experience there weren't many career opportunities. Any minimum wage or odd job he landed was usually short lived because a forty-hour work schedule interfered with his drinking.

At age twenty-five, he had nothing to show for himself except a bad reputation. Everyone but his mother had written him off. He spent the next year living in a state of despair, feeling sorry for himself and looking for answers at the bottom of a bottle. When he finally got sick and tired of the insults and criticism, he decided to leave New York City.

In March 1996, he joined the United States Navy and disappeared. Seven years later, in the summer of 2003, my father showed up on my doorstep. I didn't know much about him other than what my mother had told me. She didn't talk about him much, and when she did it was never anything nice. But despite what she said about him, I still wanted to get to know him.

Chapter 2

My father wanted to take me to California, where he lived and worked. I had never been anywhere outside of New York City except for the time I went on vacation to Florida with my aunt and her two kids. Incidentally, this was a trip I did not like. My father's family was nice, but they were not my kind of people. They were from a Long Island suburb and I was from Brooklyn. My aunt was a strict disciplinarian and didn't tolerate nonsense. My cousins behaved and were well mannered. I was a spoiled brat from Brooklyn. I was used to having things my way and doing just about anything I wanted. The word *discipline* was not in my vocabulary.

The plan was for me to live with my father for the summer, while my mother tried to get her life together. My mother had some issues that she was dealing with at the time. After a series of bad jobs, including stints as a phone-sex operator, a dominatrix, and a drug runner, she felt compelled to change her life. The decision came after her lesbian lover decided to go back to men and kicked her out of the house.

After their break up, my mother moved back in with my grandmother and me. The three of us shared a tiny space we rented from an Indian family who charged much more than it was worth. For starters, the space wasn't even zoned for renting. It was actually the second floor of their single-family house. It was old and dilapidated, rife with mice and cockroaches. The floors throughout were damaged. The walls were dingy and dirty and every window was either cracked or broken. It got so cold in the winter sometimes I thought I would freeze to death.

My grandmother was a terrible tenant. She only paid the rent when it was convenient for her and when she did the amount was usually short. After her husband, my grandfather, walked out her home life fell apart. Her career suffered and eventually she stopped working.

My mother assumed the burden of paying the bills. Her source of income was a monthly welfare subsidy that was barely enough to support me, let alone pay rent and utilities. The Indian family wanted to have us evicted. We were able to live there rent-free while the case dragged out in court. But when justice was finally served, we were forced from our upstairs dwelling that had been home for twelve years.

We moved to the fourth floor of an old apartment building in a nearby neighborhood. The place was an overleveraged, graffiti-scrawled, rundown building made up of low-income families in rent-controlled or subsidized apartments.

The neighborhood was as mixed as New York was diverse. On my street, teenage boys and aging gangsters congregated in cliques in front of buildings and on porches. A few streets over, at least three Middle Eastern families were crammed into every signal family home on the block. Old guys playing dominos could always be found down by the corner store. And then there were the crack addicts roaming the streets looking to score a hit.

At first the tiny one bedroom seemed nice, but soon it became cramped with my grandmother's possessions. She had an obsessive need to acquire a significant amount of things, but always failed to use or dispose of them. Our house was piled with boxes of books, bags of clothing, cookware, old VCRs, and every kind of Virgin Mary statuette imaginable. The apartment became an unsanitary hazard.

My grandmother spent most her days complaining to herself and cleaning up dog shit, which was about the only thing she was willing to throw away. The dog was a gift from my grandfather. It was something I thought I wanted until I realized the responsibilities that came with it. Walking her, feeding her, and bathing her were not things I wanted to do. So I didn't, and my grandmother got stuck doing it instead. Somehow though, I didn't think the old woman minded. After all, she didn't have anything else to do and frankly, I think taking care of the little dog gave her a sense of purpose.

Once my mother moved back in, the apartment seemed to get even smaller. Forced to share my room with her, I lost my space and privacy. My room was the only place in the house where I could find solace, but now it had become her dumping ground as well. My mother was as much of a slob as her mother.

My personal possessions got pushed into a corner to make room for her dominatrix paraphernalia. She was still in the business of dominating men when she had moved back in. So boxes of paddles, handcuffs, chains, floggers of every kinds, clamps, slave collars, and other deviant devices were now crammed into the room. At first I was bitter, but then rooming with her proved to be an interesting experience.

. . .

My mother's candidness about sexuality got me interested in sex and men at an early age. Where she lacked as a mother, she made up for it as a friend. She let me stay up late, smoke cigarettes, and watch pornographic movies. She told me all about sex, and not just the clean classroom biology version. At age twelve, I knew all there was to know about oral sex, anal sex, BDSM, erotic spanking, golden showers, and much more. In my eyes, she was the coolest mother in the world, because she let me do anything I wanted. But what I later realized was that all the things she exposed me to were things she should've protected me from.

My mother was a lot more excited than me about me going to California. I was nervous and I had a lot of questions, but to her it just meant one less mouth to feed.

"What do you mean you don't want to go?" she asked when I tried to express my concerns.

"What am I supposed to do in California?" I replied. "I don't have any friends in California. What am I going to do there?"

"The same thing you do here."

My mother stopped to compose herself, I could tell she was getting annoyed with me and was about to say something else.

"You don't have to do anything," she said behind a fake smile. "Just be a kid, enjoy yourself, and get to know your father."

"What if he doesn't like me?"

"He already likes you, sweetie. That's why he wants to take you to California—so he can get to know you better."

"Okay, but what about his wife?"

"What about her?"

"What if she doesn't like me?"

"Look, Lonnie, you're reading too much into this," my mother responded, looking frustrated once again.

"I need you to go to California," she said after a long pause. "It will be a good opportunity for you to bond with your father. But more importantly, it will give Mommy a chance to get things in order here. I'm out of work and under a lot of pressure these days. I need you to do this, Lonnie. It will make things easier on me."

I will admit, there were a few good reasons to go to California, but there were also good reasons not to go that left me ambivalent. I enjoyed the freedom I had living with my grandmother and mother and feared that I wouldn't have that living with my father. The most conflicting thing, however, was that Lia and I would be separated.

Lia was my first cousin on my mother's side and my best friend. She was a year younger than me but admittedly a lot smarter. She lived in a two-story, single-family house in the East Flatbush section of Brooklyn just a few miles from me. Lia's house was nice; it wasn't crummy and rundown like my apartment. It was a colonial-style home, nestled around big trees in a quiet and clean neighborhood. The three-bedroom house was nicely decorated with modern furnishings that were a lot more comfortable than the dated stuff I had in my apartment.

Being nearby gave us the opportunity to spend a lot more time together. There wasn't a day that went by that we weren't together. I was protective of her as she was of me. I knew everything about her and she knew everything about me. We were inseparable, and the thought of being apart made the decision to go that much more difficult. In the end, I decided to go. I figured that Lia and I had a strong friendship and there was no way a little time apart could ever damage that. But more importantly, I wanted to get to know my father.

Chapter 3

Joining the navy was the best thing for my father. It changed him for the better, but it didn't happen right away. The navy didn't make him stop drinking like he thought it would. Instead, it gave him more avenues and opportunities to do so. Long deployments and overseas port visits only seemed to glorify the partying and drinking. He went from being a drunk on the street to being the stereotypical drunken sailor.

Irresponsible drinking in the navy wasn't without consequences. He was no stranger to trouble, but still, he continued to drink. It wasn't until he was facing administrative discharge that he decided to quit. Determined to change, he went through a two-week outpatient alcohol treatment program and got sober.

Now that he had stopped drinking, my father wanted me to be a part of his life. My father lived with his wife, Jenna, in a beautiful three-bedroom condominium in the Mira Mesa section of San Diego. The two of them went through a lot of trouble to make sure I was comfortable. They bought me a gender-neutral bedroom set, which suited my taste just fine because I wasn't into girly stuff. I got a television set, a stereo system, video games, and other luxuries I didn't have in Brooklyn. They also took me on a shopping spree and replaced my dusty old clothes with the latest trendy fashions. For the first time in my life I had every material possession a teenage girl could ask for. More importantly, I was in the company of responsible adults who seemed genuinely concerned for my welfare.

The first two weeks I was there were terrific. My father took off from work and gave me a grand tour of the city. We visited every theme park and amusement park San Diego had to offer. We went to the zoo at Balboa Park, we petted stingrays at Sea World, and we came face-to-face with giraffes at Wild Animal Kingdom. We spent the entire two weeks just doing fun stuff.

It was great getting to know my father. He was a lot nicer than my mother gave him credit for, and I couldn't believe the uncanny resemblance between us. I was also surprised that we had a lot in common. We liked the same foods, the same music, and we both shared a love for art. Jenna was nice too, although at times it seemed like she was trying too hard. I could tell she didn't have much experience with kids, but she was trying for my father's sake.

I overheard them talking one evening.

"I just don't think she likes me," Jenna said to my father.

"No, I'm sure she likes you," my father replied. "She just needs time to warm up to you."

"No, she doesn't, I can tell," Jenna insisted. "I am not good with children, I never have been. I don't know what to say to them, I don't know how to act around them. Kids make me nervous."

Jenna took a deep breath.

"I know how important this is to you," she continued. "And I'm trying really hard, but I'm afraid I don't have what it takes to be a stepparent, and I'm going to let you down."

"You won't let me down," he assured her. "Just be yourself, and everything will be fine, I promise."

Jenna said okay, but she didn't sound too sure of herself.

At the end of the two weeks, my father went back to work and I enrolled in summer day camp, a local program organized through his work. At first, I welcomed the idea. I had never been part of a summer program before and I thought it would be fun. But to my surprise it was incredibly dull.

This so-called summer day camp was more like a daycare center. We spent most of the day in a big open room playing board games and watching TV. Once in a while we'd go on a field trip, but it was always someplace boring, like a nearby park to play soccer or to toss a Frisbee.

The kids ranged from ages seven to about thirteen. I was not the oldest, but I was certainly the biggest kid there. I was twelve years old, five foot four, and a hundred and fourteen pounds. I felt awkward being the tallest—and the only black girl there. Nevertheless, I was grateful to be tall and slender like my father and not short and stocky like my mother. Despite the awkwardness, I tried to stay positive and befriend some of the girls my age. They were very nice and took a liking to me right away. The problem was I didn't like them. They were cultured, refined, and well behaved. They didn't curse and weren't into boys like I was. I didn't have anything in common with these *California* girls.

The routine was the same every day. I'd spend eight excruciating hours at day camp, followed by a really dull evening at home with my father and his wife. I looked forward to the weekends, although they weren't much better. On the weekends, we might do laundry, clean the house, go grocery shopping, or do other things people normally do on weekends. Sometimes on the weekends we'd take a trip to the mall or go out to the movies. Whatever it was, we did it together. I had never been under so much supervision. The only highlight of my week was being able to sleep in on Saturdays and Sundays.

It didn't take long before I became homesick. I missed the freedom I had back in Brooklyn—the luxury of coming and going as I pleased. Being chaperoned everywhere by my father or his wife annoyed me immensely. They were nice people and San Diego was a nice place. But the palm trees, the sandy beaches, and moderate weather wasn't for me. I missed the tenement buildings, the trash-filled alleyways, and drug-infested neighborhoods found throughout Brooklyn. But above all I missed my cousin, Lia.

After only a month of being there, I told my father I wanted to return home.

"But why?" he asked, looking surprised.

"California is too big," I told him. "I don't like not being able to walk anywhere when I want to. Everything is so far away."

"Jenna and I can take you anywhere you want to go."

That wasn't the point, and I don't think he understood.

"I also don't know anyone. I don't have any friends here. I miss Lia."

"Don't worry, honey, in time you will make lots of friends."

My father had an answer for everything. But before I could tell him that I wasn't interested in making friends and that I only wanted my best friend, he got on his soapbox.

"I know you're homesick, honey," he said. "But you have to trust me when I tell you that you're better off with me. You will have better opportunities living with me as opposed to your mother. Your mother has a lot going on right now, and it's best if you stay here."

That might have been true, but it wasn't necessarily what I wanted. As the days went by I became more and more depressed. I continued to complain and he continued to ignore me. One evening after a long, uneventful day at camp, I tried talking to him again and got the usual response.

"Don't worry you'll come to love this place in no time," he said nonchalantly.

Having heard that too many times, I lost my temper.

"I don't like this place, Daddy. I want to go home."

"You have to calm down, honey."

"No, I don't want to calm down, I miss my best friend."

I stormed off and locked myself in my room.

My father felt bad. To comprise he said I could have Lia come for a visit. It was a great idea. Seeing my friend again would have certainly cheered me up. I got on the phone right away and told Lia the good news. She was so excited she dropped the phone and ran screaming for her mother. A few minutes later, Lia's mother picked up the receiver. She said it was a nice gesture, but she would have to give it some thought. I nearly dropped the phone in shock. What was there to think about? Did she not understand that I haven't seen my best friend in a month? Apparently, she didn't know the importance of this visit, because the next day I learned that Lia would not be coming to California. Her parents didn't like the idea of her traveling cross country by herself. My father offered to pay for the trip, but Lia's mother still refused.

Disappointed, I became angry and my emotions got the best of me. I took it out on everyone around me, mainly the kids at camp. On more than one occasion, my father received complaints from camp counselors about my ill temperament and the physical threats towards the other kids. It got to a point where none of the kids would play with me and the counselors couldn't leave me alone. This created an uncomfortable situation for my father and his wife, as counseling reports and phone calls became an everyday occurrence. My behavior put a lot of stress on their already suffering marriage. They argued a lot and mostly about two things—how I had become a nuisance and Jenna's desire to go home.

. . .

A native of Australia, Jenna came to the United States after falling in love with my father. The two met a few years earlier when my father was on assignment in Perth, Australia. After he left they continued to have a long-distance relationship, and before long Jenna quit her job, left her friends and family, and moved to San Diego to be with him. But soon after, she realized that although she loved him she hated living in the states. She complained about it as much as I complained about California. She wanted my father to leave the navy and move to Australia, but he wouldn't hear of it.

America had already been a culture shock for Jenna and dealing with me was the last thing she wanted. Jenna dreaded the idea of being a stepmother, even though I never considered her anything more than my father's wife. They tried to conceal their fighting, but the walls were thin and I could always hear them in the adjacent room. One evening as I was running up their phone bill making calls to New York, I heard them fighting.

Jenna was angry because she had to leave work early to pick me up from camp. I was misbehaving once again. I was climbing up a tree after a counselor had told me not to and slipped and twisted my ankle. Apparently, she was very busy that day and when they couldn't get hold of my father they called her, as she was the secondary point of contact.

"Lonnie is your responsibility," she said, yelling in her Australian accent. "I didn't come here for this shit."

"I know and I'm sorry," my father replied, trying to neutralize the situation.

"I had a lot of work to do today, but instead I got stuck here taking care of your kid. Where the hell were you?"

"I was out of the office. I promise it won't happen again."

"It better not," she threatened.

"It won't," my father said, still trying to keep the peace. "Why are you so angry anyway?"

There was a brief silence. I told Lia that I would call her back and continued to listen.

"Just forget about it," she said, finally.

"Come on, talk to me," he insisted.

"I'm not cut out for this. I'm trying, but I'm just not good with kids and your kid is especially difficult."

"She's just having a hard time adjusting," he differed.

"No, she is not. She is purposely misbehaving so that you'll send her back. She doesn't appreciate anything we have done for her. Honestly, I for one would love to see her go."

I called Lia back right away and told her what happened. She was excited at the thought of me coming back. In fact, we both thought that I would. We spent a long time talking and making plans for when I got back. I couldn't wait to see her. I missed her terribly, for she was the only one who understood me.

Later that evening my father knocked on my door and asked if he could talk to me. My heart raced as I jumped off the bed and opened the door.

He walked in, staring strangely at my clothes scattered about. I thought I was going home so I starting packing. I probably shouldn't have been so presumptuous. Still looking around the room, he finally asked how my ankle was. *My ankle is fine. Just get to the point*, I thought.

"I'm fine, Daddy. Are you okay? You seem troubled."

"Well, it's funny you ask," he replied, smiling awkwardly. "I'm a little worried that you might not be happy here. I know you're homesick, but if you just give this place a chance I'm sure you'll come to love it."

"California is okay," I said, sparing his feelings. But what I should've said was, *I hate this place and I want to leave now.*

California was nothing like I had imagined. I had a preconceived notion that it was this humongous gang-infested, black hole environment made up entirely of graffitied aqueducts, dirty sidewalks, crack houses, and oppressed minorities. But the California I discovered was nothing of the sort. My father lived in an upscale housing community that encompassed acres of scenic beauty. Surrounding neighborhoods were made up of luxury homes and condominiums with manicured lawns set to backdrops of canyons and hiking trails. I saw few minorities except for the Mexicans who came around to cut the grass and trim the hedges.

"I'm glad you think so," he continued, "because I really love having you here. You're very important to me, and I've missed you over the years. I would like for us to get to know each other again."

I wasn't sure what to say. Guilt had left me speechless so I just nodded and smiled. To make matters worse he reached over and gave me a gentle, soft kiss on the cheek. That night I went to bed confused. Deep down inside, I knew staying with my father would be best. He could provide for me, protect me, and love me.

There was nothing in Brooklyn for me except a dysfunctional home and lots of negative influences. Somehow though, I couldn't help but feel like I was missing something. I loved Brooklyn and that was where I wanted to be.

I loved the small neighborhoods made up of diverse cultures. I loved taking the bus and riding the subway. In Brooklyn, I didn't have to drive across miles of highway just to go somewhere, as I did in California. I missed being able to walk to the store at one o'clock in the morning to buy ice cream. I missed hanging on the corner with my friends. I missed the pizza parlors, the Chinese restaurants, and the cute boys hustling drugs on street corners. I missed everything that was the essence of Brooklyn and I didn't want to give it up, not even for a loving relationship with my father, a great house, and perfect weather.

Chapter 4

The next day I told Lia what happened and she was not happy. Admittedly, I was disappointed too, but mainly with myself. I should have told my father how I felt and insisted he send me back. Now it was too late. I had already committed to his request to try harder and give California a chance.

I tried to explain to Lia that it would just be for the summer, but she wouldn't listen. In a melodramatic outburst, she told me to wise up.

"It's never just for the summer," Lia warned. "The summer will turn into fall, fall will turn into winter, and before you know it you're there permanently."

"No, that's not true," I said.

"It is true. Think about it. If it was just for the summer then why did he have you bring all your things? And why did he buy you such a great bedroom set, huh?"

"I don't know. Because he's trying to provide for me," I said, not sure what to think.

Lia was convinced we would never see each other again. I wasn't sure I agreed with her, but the thought of being so far away from my friend made me sad. I cut the conversation short and hung up the phone.

That evening, Jenna prepared one of her vegetarian meals—an eggplant lasagna recipe she tried to force on me. At the time I didn't even know what an eggplant was, and as far as I was concerned lasagna without meat wasn't lasagna. She got mad when I wouldn't eat and got more upset when my father took me out for some New York-style pizza. The pizza was terrible. There was nothing New York about it. It wasn't thin, wide, and foldable like the hand-tossed street snacks found throughout the five boroughs. Now I had one more reason to be homesick.

Later, I called Lia back and told her what happened.

"Are you kidding me?" Lia said in shock. "She's not even your mom, and she's trying to tell you what to do?"

"I know right, luckily my dad came to my rescue."

"You see, this is why you have to come home," Lia continued. "There's no telling what else she's going to force on you."

"I know. I want to leave too, but I told my dad I would give this place a chance. I can't go back on my word."

"You don't have to," Lia said. "I have an idea."

"What idea?" I asked.

"Didn't you say Jenna got really pissed off when she had to leave work to come and get you?"

"Yeah, so," I replied, unsure where Lia was going.

"What if we piss her off some more? Continue being difficult. Be as miserable as possible and be especially rude to Jenna."

"What's that going to do," I asked, still confused.

"Jenna doesn't like being there either. She's probably looking for an excuse to leave, just like you. So if you pushed her far enough, she might threaten to leave and force your father to choose between the two of you."

"I don't know, Lia. That seems really mean, and what if it doesn't work?"

Lia was convinced it would work, and my father would choose his marriage over me. I argued differently, believing that he had a genuine desire to be a part of my life.

"Trust me, Lonnie. It will work. My mom does it to my dad all the time. Every time she doesn't get her way, she threatens to leave and my dad always gives in to her demands."

"Okay, if you think it will work, I'll give it a shot."

I wanted to leave, but ironically, it bothered me to think that my father would choose this woman over his own flesh and blood. I got angry. I let my temper run away with me and condemned my father before the facts. I was pretty nasty to him, but Jenna got it much worse.

She had the responsibility of taking me to camp in the morning. My father couldn't do it because camp started at eight and he had to be at work by seven-thirty. Jenna had to be at work by nine. So every morning in order to piss her off I made sure I woke up late and took my time getting ready. It drove her crazy. But not as much as when I tried on her makeup and ruined her imported cosmetics. I rearranged her work files. I scratched her music CDs and used her silk blouse to wipe down the kitchen counter.

I could tell Jenna was near her breaking point and was about to lose it. She complained over and over, even pleaded with my father to be more assertive with me and to instill some type of discipline. But his idea of discipline was begging me not to do it again.

. . .

Every day Lia and I thought of new ways to annoy Jenna. One evening after one of her weird vegetarian meals, which my father was making me eat at this point, I decided to go outside. I had a crazy idea that I could drive out of California, and I took Jenna's keys on my way out.

I sat in the car for several minutes trying to figure out how to turn it on and which of the three pedals would make it move. I turned the key. I pushed every button and turned every knob, and still nothing happened. Finally, I released the emergency brake, thinking that might have something to do with why the car wouldn't start. The engine didn't start, but the car did begin moving. The car slowly rolled down the driveway. By the time I realized it, the back end had cleared the sidewalk and was heading towards a parked car on the opposite side of the street.

My first reaction was to jump out, but the car had started gaining momentum and I panicked. I tried turning the steering wheel to change its direction, but it was incredibly stiff. I held my breath watching the parked car get closer and closer from the rear window. I froze, awaiting the impact. Then suddenly I heard the sound of tires screeching against the asphalt followed by a loud honking sound. I turned just in time to see an oncoming vehicle slam into the passenger side of the car. The force launched me in the air and my body ricocheted inside the cabin. I blacked out.

When I finally woke up my father was kneeling over me doing chest compressions and Jenna was beside him shouting hysterically at the 911 operator. I couldn't believe what I had done. I closed my eyes and prayed that I was dreaming, but this was no dream. I quickly came to when my father began shaking me gently.

"Wake up, Lonnie," he said, nervously. "Wake up."

I gasped and threw my arms around his neck, nearly choking him as I cried into his shoulder. By now a crowd of spectators had gathered. My father made me lay back down and told me to remain calm. Too embarrassed to look at anyone, I kept my eyes closed as we waited for emergency services to arrive. My father held my hand and said comforting words to me, but I just knew once we got home it would be the end of me.

The ambulance finally came after what seemed like forever. Two men strapped me to a gurney and took me away. I pleaded with my father to take me back in the house, but he said I had to go to the hospital. They needed to run some tests to make sure I was alright. Four hours later, after a CT scan and some other tests, a doctor cleared me to go home. The ride home was very awkward. I pretended to be asleep in the back seat while my father tried to make small talk with Jenna.

"I'm certainly glad no one got hurt," he said.

"Yeah, me too," she replied, looking out the window.

"I'm sorry about your car."

There was a long uncomfortable pause. Jenna didn't respond and continued staring out the window. I could tell she was furious.

"Maybe tomorrow you can take the day off," my father suggested.

"I don't want to take the day off," she replied with a hint of anger. "Can you stop the car please? I need a cigarette."

"You had a cigarette right before we left."

"Well, I need another one," she said, curtly.

My father sat behind the steering wheel rubbing his temples looking incredibly stressed, while Jenna smoked two cigarettes back-to-back. Afterwards, we drove home in complete silence.

. . .

The next day, Jenna stayed home to take care of the insurance proceedings. Too afraid to face her, I hid inside my room all day. I wanted to annoy her, but not like this. I felt bad about what I did, especially considering how much money it cost them. That evening I heard them arguing and she didn't hold back.

"That's it, either she goes, or I go," she yelled.

"Come on, you're being unreasonable," my father pleaded. "Didn't you ever do anything stupid when you were a kid?"

"Not like this," she said. "Have you seen this estimate?"

"I know—" my father started to say.

"Sixty-five hundred dollars," she yelled, cutting him off.

"Can you please calm down, I'm aware of the damages."

Both the front and rear window on the passenger side shattered into a thousand pieces. The side panel was crushed beyond repair and both doors had to be replaced. The car that slammed into me suffered severe damages as well. The entire front end was mashed—the front bumper, headlights, fan belt, and radiator were all pushed back into the engine. Both the driver and passenger side airbags deployed.

Jenna paused for a moment. There was no way she was going to forgive me. If my father didn't send me back after that, I would've had to run away. There was no way I would've been able to face her.

"Do you know what this is going to do to our insurance?" she continued. "I mean it, either she leaves, or I leave."

It was a hard decision, but in the end, just as Lia had predicted, my father chose his marriage over me. It was heart breaking for him but bitter-sweet for me. Finally, I was going home. Still, I couldn't help but feel remorseful. I hurt someone who really cared about me simply because I was selfish, closed-minded, and afraid of change. I had a strange feeling that my actions would somehow come back to haunt me.

Chapter 5

I arrived on a Friday late in the evening. Excited about finally going home, I barely slept the night before. Walking across the jet bridge, I yawned and stretched my aching muscles. A flight attendant escorted me and two other unaccompanied minors into the terminal, where my grandfather, my grandmother, and Lia were waiting. Lia and I were both giddy with excitement upon seeing each other. It was like we had been apart for years.

Outside, I took a deep breath, inhaling the many diverse smells of the city. The August heat was unbearable and the humidity made my skin moist. As we walked to the car, I couldn't help but think about my father and his wife. I wondered what kind of impact my antics were going to have on his marriage. I prayed that Jenna didn't take the anger she felt for me out on him. When all was said and done, he was a good person and I appreciated what he tried to do.

I was happy to be back and not surprised to see some things hadn't changed. My grandmother was still her usual nagging self. She complained the whole ride home, and as always no one listened to her.

My grandfather shook his head inattentively as she rambled on. Once in a while he'd interject with an unenthusiastic "uh-huh," "yeah," or "I know" to make it seem like he was listening. I caught his reflection in the rear-view mirror and the expression on his face was one of pure agony. He didn't like being around her, but he pitied her situation and tried to help out in any way he could. Even though they were divorced, he lived a few blocks away and he came around from time to time or whenever she called him to complain about my mother. Doing little things like picking me up from the airport or giving her a few bucks once in a while helped appease his conscience for leaving her in the first place.

I couldn't wait to get home and show Lia all the great things my father purchased for me. Unfortunately, I couldn't bring the television and stereo with me, but I got to keep the video games and all the new clothes. Lia suggested that I keep my new things at her house so my mother wouldn't get her hands on them. She had a habit of wearing my clothes and trashing them before I could enjoy them.

My mother was under the impression that my clothes made her look young and more appealing. I didn't mind keeping my things with Lia since I spent most of my time at her place anyway. Besides, I preferred to share my clothes with her rather than have my mother ruin everything I owned.

In all the excitement of seeing Lia I had completely forgotten about my mother. I asked my grandmother where she was and she quickly changed the subject. Later, I found out that she was trying to keep my mother's whereabouts from my grandfather. She didn't want him to know that my mother had gotten arrested.

. . .

I don't know how she did it but in the little time I was gone, my mother managed to screw up her life even more. Shortly after I left for California, my mother got arrested for assaulting a woman in the street. The story I heard was that she was having an affair with the woman's husband. When this woman confronted her, my mother allegedly hit her, claiming the woman tried to rob her. Other sources claimed that my mother was high and she was the one doing the robbing. After getting released from jail a week prior to my arrival, she went on a cocaine binge, and no one had seen her since.

My mother finally dragged herself in Monday morning around seven. She flopped down in the bed beside me, reeking of alcohol, tobacco, and some other pungent smell I couldn't identify at the time.

She looked absolutely terrible and I couldn't stand the sight of her. She fell asleep right away and began snoring, interrupting the little bit of sleep I had since the weekend. When she woke up twelve hours later, she called me in the room and asked for my father's phone number. She didn't ask about my time in California or why I had returned; she just said she needed his number.

She called my father and gave him some sad, depressing story about falling on hard times. She said she couldn't find a job, even though she hadn't looked for a job since high school. She went on to add that we were late on the rent and facing eviction. I watched in amazement as she lied skillfully and sobbed over the phone.

I didn't know my father could be so gullible. He promised to send her money in addition to the child support payments. This came as a surprise to me. I did not know my mother was receiving money on my behalf. This whole time I thought she was barely getting by on her welfare subsidy. I started to question her character and wondered what she was doing with the extra money. To me, child support meant money that should be spent on the child. *This was odd,* I thought. *She had extra money and she never once bought me school supplies, new clothes, or anything I asked for*. This angered me, not necessarily because I wanted to go to school, but because it seemed wrong.

. . .

There was only one aspect I liked about school—art class. It was the only thing I excelled in. I was fortunate to have inherited my father's artistic ability. But other subjects, math, reading, and writing, gave me a hard time. I was in the seventh grade but I wasn't reading and writing at a seventh grade level.

The only other thing that kept me interested in school was the boys. Boys showed me a lot of attention, and because I was developing rather quickly, I also received attention from some of my male teachers. Their eyes were always lingering over me, friendly and suggestively. I was just a girl, but I looked like a woman.

I didn't see myself as pretty, but I received lots of compliments on my caramel complexion and long dark hair. I had thick, curved eyebrows and big brown eyes with lashes so long they'd make a giraffe envious. I had a perfectly symmetrical nose and mouth and skin that my mother said was gorgeous. But perhaps my biggest asset, or at least what got me the most attention, was my trim, athletic figure, flat stomach, and adult curves.

. . .

I was glad Lia spent the weekend at my house. We had a wonderful time. We stayed up late eating junk food, trying on clothes and talking about boys.

I was green with envy when I learned that she had made out with a boy and got felt up. I was even more jealous when she told me that she lost her virginity too. I couldn't believe eleven-year-old Lia, who was only a year younger than me, was already having sex. She was on the fast track to becoming a major slut. By the end of the summer, she had three boyfriends she frequently fooled around with. I had always thought that I'd be the first to lose my virginity since I had developed a lot quicker than she did. I got my first period when I was ten, and by age eleven I was already wearing a size 32B bra.

Now that I was twelve, I figured sex should be the next sequence of things to occur. I cursed my father for dragging me out to California. Had I been back in Brooklyn I might have gotten some action too. But not long after I got back that summer I lost my virginity too.

My experience with boys began probably the same way most young girls are introduced to sex. It began with the discovery of kissing, the first peck of our lips, surprisingly nice. A clumsy tongue in my mouth was not something I enjoyed, but I craved the experience. First there was kissing and fondling of my breasts. Then there was the ineffable sensation of having a boy's hand over my vagina. I loved it, but the giddiness and new-found pleasure faded quickly and I wanted to experience more. So I lost my virginity at age twelve.

. . .

Within a few months of my deflowering, I had multiple partners. At first, I was having sex with only one boy, a thin, dark-skinned kid who lived down the street from me. He wasn't much of a looker, but he knew how to talk to me and how to make me smile. He was my first crush, my first kiss and the one I lost my virginity to. Lia on the other hand was a lot more promiscuous. She changed boyfriends as often as I changed socks. I wanted to be indiscriminate too, but I was afraid of being labeled. A few months later though, I got my first lesson in love and that changed everything. I had been cheated on by the one boy who I had given myself to and who I thought loved me. Afterwards, I started having sex with anyone who was half-way interesting.

Because there was actual penetration I would define it as sex. But as far as good sex was concerned, it was nothing like I had seen in my mother's porn movies. I didn't know what I was doing and neither did they. But soon enough we figured it out, and Lia and I spent the rest of the summer having sex and drinking beer.

We never once considered any kind of contraception; we were too busy having fun to be responsible. Having sex took some creativity. Sometimes I was able to talk Lia into using her house while her parents were at work, but it took a lot of pleading. She was terrified of getting caught. She didn't want to do anything to annoy her father, and I couldn't say I blamed her. At six foot three, weighing nearly two hundred and forty pounds, he was quite intimidating. She also didn't want to shatter the good-little-girl façade she had created for herself. Her parents were convinced that she was the perfect child. So for Lia's sake we did it wherever we could, usually on the roof of my building or in the schoolyard late at night.

Drinking beer took some getting used to. I didn't like the taste at first, but I didn't let that stop me from getting drunk. Getting alcohol was easy. My mother always kept a six pack of Heineken in the fridge. We didn't even have to sneak it. She just gave it to us, providing we drank in the house. Her logic was that if allowed to drink in a controlled environment then we wouldn't be tempted to do it in the street. Little did she know what she had started.

g under my mother's supervision. There was no gotten away with any of these things in California y father. We stayed in close contact after I left. My . me once a week, usually on the weekends to see ıoing. As far as he was concerned, I was doing great. I w... od health, school was going good, and my grades were up. But they weren't; the opposite was true.

I hated lying, but I didn't want to disappoint him. He had high hopes for me—more than my mother and more than I had for myself. It was easier to lie than to have him worry about me. I can only imagine how he would've felt if he knew I wasn't going to school. More than a year had gone by before my mother even found out.

...

I had left my father's house August 2003. It was now October 2004—fourteen months since I had seen the inside of a classroom. Anywhere else, this would have raised a red flag. But when you live in the ghetto, where the public school system is sub-standard and there is a shortage of teachers, it's real easy to get lost in the system and forgotten about. At first, I'd just skip a class here and there, and eventually I stopped going all together. So, telling the truth wasn't an option at this point. I wasn't sure how he would react.

There were so many things that he was blind to that I didn't have the heart to tell him about. For starters, my mother was a drug addict and the money he was sending her was going to support her habit. I also kept her prostituting a secret and failed to mention how she had turned our one-bedroom apartment into a whorehouse.

Over the summer she had propositioned an undercover cop and got arrested. She spent a week in jail. Following her arrest, she began operating out of our apartment. It was then that I finally figured out what that pungent smell was the morning she got in bed beside me. It was the stink that could only come from a street whore who had a long, busy night.

I didn't care that she was using our apartment to sell sex since I was hardly there anyway. My grandmother, however, thought the men were simply friends of hers. Then again, she might have known and just didn't care. After all, my mother was the one paying the bills.

Somehow I knew not going to school would come back to bite me. But I was having too much fun and simply didn't care. My mother might have figured it out if she wasn't always under the influence.

I wish I had been more like Lia. She had everyone fooled. She was just as bad as I was, but she was better at hiding it. She went to school just enough not to raise suspicion and enough to maintain decent grades. But when it was time to party and there was alcohol and cute boys around, she was right there beside me. I could have followed her lead and gone to school once in a while, but I didn't care. School didn't interest me and no one was interested in me going.

My mother only became interested when the Bureau of Child Welfare finally showed up at our doorstep. I guess I wasn't completely lost in the system, someone finally figured it out after all. A caseworker knocked on the door one morning shortly after my mother had returned from a night of gallivanting. I could tell right away she was not pleased with what she found. As usual the house was an absolute mess. There were dirty dishes in the sink, laundry piled up to the ceiling, and dog shit everywhere. She documented everything, including the conversation she had with my mother and I.

"Please excuse the mess," my mother said, as she held the door open. "I just got off a twelve hour shift from my second job at the factory. I haven't had time to tidy up."

Second job, I thought. *What is she talking about*?

The caseworker replied, "Thank you," and walked through the door.

She took a quick look around the apartment and let out a long breath. I could tell she had seen this kind of stuff before but still hadn't got used to it. We walked to the living room and sat down. She looked at me and smiled.

"Hi, Lonnie," she said.

I returned her greeting with a fake smile of my own. My heart was beating uncontrollably; I knew she wasn't delivering good news.

"I'll get right to the point," she started. "Ma'am, are you aware that Lonnie has been absent from school for over a year?"

"Oh my God," my mother replied. "I did not know that."

"Unfortunately," the caseworker continued, "the parents are usually the last to know."

The caseworker turned to me.

"Lonnie, is there any reason why you haven't been attending school?"

I shrugged my shoulders and looked at the floor.

"Are you uncomfortable at school?"

I shrugged again.

"Are you having problems with the other students?"

I continued to ignore her questions, and that's when my mother snapped.

"Lonnie, you better answer her questions right now."

"I don't like school," I finally said, feeling suffocated.

"What don't you like about it?" the caseworker asked in a calm voice.

"Everyone is so much smarter than me, and I always feel stupid at school."

"Okay, so you were having trouble with your assignments?"

"Yeah, I just told you, I'm stupid okay."

I stormed out of the apartment and slammed the door behind me. I could hear my mother yelling, "Lonnie, get back here right now," as I dashed towards the staircase. I don't know how much longer the caseworker stayed after I left, but my mother did her best to cooperate. Then again, she didn't need much convincing. Once she learned that my behavior and the house violations could have a direct impact on her welfare subsidies, she pledged to fix the problem immediately.

Chapter 6

Bureau of Child Welfare was the startling wakeup call my mother needed. Suddenly, she became interested in my life and well-being. She called Lia's house and told me to come home right away. Realizing she was going to want a good explanation, I took my time getting back. I thought about it long and hard and I couldn't come up with a good reason why I hadn't gone to school in over a year. And I couldn't very well tell her I was busy partying.

She was standing in the living room smoking a cigarette when I finally walked in. She looked upset.

"Get in here and sit down," she said, through clenched teeth.

I sat down on the raggedy old couch covered in dog hair. Feeling nervous, I reached for the pack of cigarettes on the coffee table and took one. My mother turned and rushed towards me.

"You are not grown," she said, and snatched the cigarette from my mouth.

I sat back and looked up at her.

"You just can't do whatever you want," she continued.

"Smoking wasn't an issue before, so why now?" I asked nervously.

"Because you're thirteen years old," she snapped.

"I'm almost fourteen," I corrected.

"You're a kid. You shouldn't be smoking or drinking, and you certainly don't need to be skipping school."

"I don't like school."

"Well, you better learn to like it."

I folded my arms and looked away. I wasn't sure what to say. There was a strong tone coming from her that I hadn't seen before.

"Do you hear me?" she continued with force.

My grandmother was standing in the doorway looking worried.

"Stop yelling at the child," she said. "The neighbors will hear you."

"Shut up, Mother. I don't need your help."

My grandmother walked over and stepped in between us.

"Getting angry never solves anything," she said, and reached for my hand.

My mother didn't budge.

"I said I don't need your help."

She shoved my grandmother aside and continued to tower over me. Feeling trapped and suffocated I started to cry. My grandmother ran, screaming for the phone. She had a habit of calling my grandfather whenever the two of them got into an argument. My mother turned her attention back to me.

"Cry all you want, but you're going to school," she said, reaching for a book of matches on the table.

I tried to get up and leave as she lit her cigarette, but my mother was quicker than I thought. She grabbed me by the arm and shoved me back down.

"Get your hands off me," I screamed hysterically.

My grandmother dropped the phone and rushed back over. She pushed my mother away and got in between us again. This time I jumped up and stood behind her.

"What is wrong with you?" she said. "Violence is not the way to resolve this."

There was a brief pause. Either my mother came to her senses and realized she had gone too far or she didn't want to hurt the old woman. She took a long drag of her cigarette and blew the smoke in my grandmother's direction. Then she looked at me.

"You and I are going down to the school and we're going to get you reinstated."

Her voice was stern and unyielding.

"You're going to go to class, and you're going to go every day. God help you if that woman comes back here and tells me you've been truant."

She grabbed her cigarettes off the table and stormed away. I probably shouldn't have said anything, but I felt angry and confused. After years of being my pal, suddenly she wanted to play mother. I didn't want a mother. I liked my life just the way it was. If I wanted structure I would've stayed in California with my father and his wife. I couldn't believe her audacity. I snapped.

"Is that what this is about?" I said, still crying hysterically. "You're afraid of losing your precious welfare money."

My mother stopped in her tracks and came back. She shoved the old woman aside and grabbed a handful of my hair. She looked possessed. She was the angriest I had ever seen her.

"You ungrateful little shit," she said, pulling my head back as she screamed in my face. "You think food is free?"

"No," I replied, trying to free myself from her grip.

"You think electricity is free?"

"Let me go. You're hurting me."

"You think living here is free? This apartment cost money. Food cost money."

"Okay," I screamed, cutting her off. "I'll go to school."

I couldn't stand to listen to anymore of her everything-cost-money speech. She let me go and walked away once again. I fell to the ground sobbing like a baby, holding my throbbing head. My grandmother helped me up and comforted me until my grandfather arrived. My mother didn't stick around and left before he got there. I should have left too. I hated listening to his long boring speeches about life.

. . .

My grandfather was a lot more level-headed than my grandmother, but he was somewhat of a bigot. Being half white made him feel like he was better than the average black person.

Growing up, he had repeatedly advised my mother to marry a white man. He was convinced she would be better off if she avoided black men. He said white men were better providers. They weren't abusive like black men and marrying a white man would produce better looking kids. On a few occasions he tried to instill his racist views upon me. But his advice went in one ear and out the other. Not only was he a racist, he was a hypocrite as well.

My grandmother wasn't white. In fact, she was a couple of shades darker than he was. No one was really sure why he married her since he had these racial biases about him. But then again, no one was surprised when he left her for a white woman.

I was in the bathroom washing my face when he arrived. I could hear my grandmother talking a mile a minute, giving him every single detail about what happened. After combing my hair and finding my composure, I went back in the living room. I sat beside my grandmother and listened to him lecture about the importance of staying in school, helping out around the house, and respecting my mother. I even got a little bit of his philosophy about white men. I listened to be polite but nothing he said registered with me. They were things I had heard all too often.

Later, after he left, I called my father to get an intelligent perspective on the situation. Surprisingly, he didn't show any signs of anger or disappointment. I got more out of our thirty-minute conversation than from all the nonsense my grandparents had been spewing over the years.

"Why don't you like going to school, Lonnie?" he asked.

"School is hard. I have a difficult time paying attention and keeping up with the other kids. I'm sorry, Daddy, I try but I just can't stay focused. I don't know what's wrong me."

"There's nothing wrong with you, honey," he assured me. "It sounds to me like you might have ADHD."

"Oh my God, is that bad?"

I started weeping.

"No, honey, it's not bad. ADHD stands for Attention Deficit Hyperactivity Disorder. It's nothing to worry about. It simply means you have a hard time paying attention."

"Yeah, it means I'm stupid."

"No, you are not stupid. More importantly, we can fix this."

"How?"

"Well, in order to be certain you have ADHD, you would have to be evaluated by a specialist. But don't worry about any of that right now. Just promise me you'll keep an open mind and you'll do what it takes get through this."

"Okay, Daddy. If it will make me not stupid. I'll try."

My father said he would talk to my mother and have her take care of everything. But little did he know how unreliable she was.

Although nervous, I was looking forward to the evaluation and getting help if I did indeed have a problem. After talking to my father I realized that being smart was a lot better than being dumb, and I didn't want to be the stupid kid anymore.

. . .

My mother went down to the school and spoke to the school officials. She made a bunch of promises and appointments but failed to keep any of them. She did just enough to get my hopes up and enough to keep the Bureau of Child Welfare away. After about three weeks of getting the runaround I told my father of her negligence and for the first time he got angry. He gave her an extensive third degree over the phone to which I received severe backlash. She didn't like that I complained to him. It was one more thing that could have disrupted her cash flow. Feeling the need to rectify things himself, my father decided to come to New York.

Chapter 7

After I left California in the summer of 2003, my father went through a series of marital problems, many of which I was to blame for. This led to a huge downward spiral of arguments and fights with his wife, Jenna. The fighting eventually drove him from their marital bed into the spare bedroom. This caused him to start drinking again. Having missed her opportunity with me, Jenna quickly tried to capitalize on his relapse. Convinced my father could not stop drinking, she decided to leave. Hoping to save himself and his marriage, this time, he checked into a thirty-day treatment program for alcohol dependency.

My father got sober once again. But despite her joy over his new-found sobriety, Jenna still could not find it in her heart to stay. In the end, she stopped making excuses and finally came clean, admitting it was never her intention to live in America or be a stepparent. She told my father that although she loved him it was not enough to make her stay. If he was not willing to move to Australia then there was no way they could be together. Going to Australia was not an option. That would've meant leaving the navy and everything he had worked so hard for. He turned her down and a few months later they sold the condominium. She went back to Australia and my father transferred to a new duty station—a naval air base near Malibu California. Then after getting settled at his new place of work, he came to New York.

It's now January 2005, two months before my fourteenth birthday. A few days earlier a blizzard paralyzed the city with over three feet of snow. I was standing in front of my building staring at the parked cars buried under mountains of snow, anticipating my father's arrival. Worried that the storm would somehow delay his flight, I found myself waiting for him hours before he was actually scheduled to arrive. His plane wasn't due to land until seven in the evening, but I was out there at ten o'clock in the morning.

I thought about my father a lot that morning and how patient he had been with me. Anyone else probably would've disowned me for the terrible way I behaved. He almost seemed too relaxed and I couldn't help but wonder if he was up to something.

As I stood there collecting my thoughts, more snow began to fall. Shortly after, a chilling breeze whipped through the street and shook me back to reality. I decided to go back inside and find some way to occupy my time. Just as I opened the door, I heard someone call out my name. I turned and saw my mother high-stepping through the snow, trying to maintain her balance. She was walking with one of her johns and calling for me to hold the door. As always, she looked horrible and I just couldn't fathom what it was that these men were paying for.

She used to be beautiful, but her destructive lifestyle made it seem like she was aging overnight. Her once-pretty face was now tough and leathery, showing early signs of wrinkles. Her long brown hair began thinning, and the bags under her eyes told the story of a woman in dire need of rest. She was still shapely and had a full set of breasts but that too was quickly fading as she often went days without eating.

She hurried inside and shook the snow out of her hair and off her clothes. Her companion stood beside her, staring at me with bewildering curiosity until my mother finally broke his concentration.

"Hey, she's only thirteen. She's a child," my mother warned.

"Yes, in America," he replied, with a strange accent. "But in my country, she is a woman."

"Well, this isn't Bangladesh, so don't even think about it."

He blushed but continued staring at me lewdly. Suddenly, a feeling of disgust came over me and I couldn't stand to be in my own skin. This wasn't the first time one of her johns had eyeballed me. Normally, they were overweight, middle-aged white men. But this guy, who was in the country illegally, was young and vibrant. More than a customer, he was a business partner as well.

Searching for his path to citizenship, the two of them were planning to get married so that he wouldn't be deported. For her services, my mother would receive her biggest payoff yet—twelve thousand in cash. At this point, nothing she did surprised me anymore. In fact, this was a step up from some of the other things she had done for money in the past.

Luckily, I stopped caring a long time ago and began accepting things for what they were. I gave her a blank look and tried to ignore the Bangladeshi man staring at me. She returned my gaze with a semi look of concern.

"Are you okay, and what are you doing out here?" she inquired.

"I was worried about dad flying in this weather. I came down here to get some fresh air."

"Oh my goodness, is that today?"

She grabbed the man's arm and dragged him upstairs.

"We'll have to hurry," she said. "I have a lot of work to do. Lonnie, you stay down here and play."

I hung out in the lobby of my building until my mother finished her business. On his way out, the Bangladeshi man tried to talk to me, but I ignored him and ran upstairs to my apartment. Inside, I found my mother running back and forth cleaning like a maid on speed. She was scrubbing baseboards, wiping down walls, and picking up dog shit for a change.

When she was done, the apartment was the cleanest I had ever seen it. She even took on a transformation of her own. In the three weeks my father was in town not a signal john came to the apartment. I didn't see her get high once and she attended all of my school appointments. She even set up fake job interviews to give the impression that she was looking for work. As confusing as it was, I enjoyed this new mother of mine. She was kind, loving, warm, and pleasant to be around. I wanted to ask her where she had been all my life. For a brief period, I felt like we were an actual family.

Later that evening, I received a phone call from my father letting me know he had arrived safely. He was staying at his sister's house in Long Island, where he normally stayed when he visited New York, and would drive down to Brooklyn in the morning.

My father didn't waste any time and got to work right away. I was glad he was the one handling things, because there was no way my mother would've accomplished all that needed to be done. Lots of information had to be gathered in order for the doctor to make a diagnosis of ADHD. The information was obtained partly through behavior checklists, questionnaires, and clinical interviews. I also had to undergo a series of psychological and educational tests. Finally, I had a physical examination in order to rule out any medical conditions that could be a factor.

To be diagnosed with ADHD, symptoms in three criteria had to be present. After going through all the tests, it was determined that I had symptoms of inattentiveness, hyperactivity, and impulsivity, thus making me a prime candidate for medication. The doctor told my parents that for the best results, both behavioral treatment and medication should be used. I welcomed the idea and I looked forward to getting better. My father felt the same way. But all my mother cared about was who was going to pay for it. Fortunately, his medical insurance covered things of that nature and it wouldn't be an inconvenience to her.

The thing that worried me most was getting her to commit to the behavior therapy regimen the psychologist prescribed for me. The therapy seemed simple. Its goal was to incrementally introduce new ways of behaving by praising desired behavior and eliminating undesired actions through a structured system of rewards and consequences. It sounded like all she had to do was be a parent.

. . .

My father's visit made a world of difference in my life. Not only did he get me the help I needed, but he promised to stay active in all my academic endeavors. He said if I stayed in school and worked hard, he would do his best to get me into an arts high school, one that offered an arts-integrated academic curriculum and would exploit my artistic abilities. That alone was enough to change my attitude. And the new clothes and school supplies he bought me were an added perk.

I was sad to see my father go, but I appreciated everything he did. When he left, my mother left too—in the sense that she went back to her old ways. The facade she put on for him disappeared the minute his cab drove off. I told myself that I wasn't going to let her lack of parenting discourage me. I made a promise to myself and I was going to keep it.

I took the medication and I went to school daily. My mother wasn't much help, but my father was always on the other end of the phone if I needed help with a math problem. And if he happened to be deployed I could always reach him by e-mail.

With his help, I made up past assignments. I committed to additional assignments. I went in early and I stayed late. I did everything I possibly could and in the summer of 2005, I graduated from junior high school. It was a proud moment for me, but more so for my father who was standing in the audience.

Chapter 8

I was ecstatic that my father came to my graduation. But his visit came as a complete surprise to us all. By not announcing his arrival, my mother was unable to cover up her incompetence and elicit lifestyle this time around. Rather than face him, she disappeared the week that he was in town. He finally got to see things for what they really were as opposed to the lies she had been feeding him.

"How often does your mother take off like this?" my father asked.

"All the time," I replied. "But please don't tell her I told you, Daddy. I don't want her to get mad at me."

"How long does she normally take off for?"

"Usually a few days, but sometimes a couple of weeks."

"A couple of weeks," he echoed. "And where does she go?"

"I don't know, Daddy, I've already said too much."

"Lonnie, I need you to be honest with me. I can't help you or protect you if I don't know the truth."

I let out a long breath. I didn't want to snitch on my mother, but I knew he was right.

"Usually, she's here locally, running the streets and getting high," I finally said. "But sometimes, she leaves the city. I don't know where she goes, but she always comes back with a lot of money. I know because that's usually when she'll throw me a couple of bucks."

My father lct out a long sigh as he rubbed out the creases in his forehead.

"What else does she do?" he asked, looking frustrated.

"She's always bringing strange men to the apartment."

"What strange men?"

"I don't know, Daddy. She says they are just acquaintances and business associates."

"Okay, thank you, honey."

I could tell my father was overly disgusted. He probably wanted to know more but was too annoyed to listen anymore. He could care less that she ruined her own life. But he was extremely disappointed and angry over how she had been raising me. He wanted the very best for me, but my mother was getting in the way of everything he was trying to do. While he didn't say it directly, he did, however, suggest that she didn't love me like I thought she did. He said she didn't have my best interest at heart—something I didn't want to accept at first but was forced to swallow later on.

Despite her flaws and obvious drug use, I still held my mother in high regards. She was the only woman I had to look up to. My grandmother was a pushover and half the time I didn't understand what she was talking about. I honestly thought she was becoming senile by the day. Lia's mother, although she was a caring individual, was somewhat intimidating. She was a broad woman whose serious demeanor made her hard to be around. Then there were my three aunts on my father's side—three intelligent and successful women who I could've learned a lot from. But they wanted nothing to do with me. They didn't have the patience my father had.

Admittedly, I loved being under my mother's supervision, or lack thereof. She wasn't as smart as my father, but she possessed an enormous amount of street savvy. She took to the streets after graduating high school. She's had it rough, but she is a survivor. Strangely, I found her cunning to be more impressive than my father's military training or his undergraduate degree. I never once thought she was a bad person or a bad influence as my father tried to make me think. I simply thought she was being herself and doing what made her happy. So I tried to live by her philosophy. Unlike my father who believed the opposite.

There was a long pause while my father collected his thoughts. It was a bit of an awkward moment, but I knew he had a lot on his mind.

"You know, Lonnie," he finally said, "in life, we don't always get to do what we want. Instead, we have to do what's best for those around us."

I didn't respond because I wasn't sure what he was trying to say. I just nodded and listened.

"I regret not being a bigger part of your life," he continued. "Growing up, I did some stupid things, and I made some poor choices. But after you came along, I realized that I couldn't continue to do what I had been doing."

"I can't imagine you doing stupid things, Daddy. You seem to have everything together."

"That wasn't always the case." He chuckled.

"What kind of stupid things did you do?" I probed.

"That's not important, honey. The point is, the navy wasn't my first choice of careers. But I knew I had to do something if I was going to provide for you. Now, I love what I do, and I'm glad I joined. But growing up, I wanted to make a living as an artist."

I was touched, I didn't know what to say except thank you.

"That's why it's important to stay in school, so you can have more options and do the things you want to do. Stay away from drugs and alcohol and use good judgment, because the choices you make now will impact your future."

"Okay, Daddy."

My father always gave me good advice, but it was not what I wanted to hear on the weekend of my graduation. I sympathized with his frustration. I think he felt that he had to be both my mother and my father. Because unlike my father, my mother was still making poor choices.

After he finally lightened up, he tried to take me shopping, to which I declined. Over the years, he had spent a considerable amount of money on me. And I felt bad that my mother had pawned nearly everything he got me. My video games, my digital camera, my iPod, and even the Japanese katana he send me from Japan had been sold for crack. I didn't want my father to take me shopping. But despite my resistance, he bought me a ton of stuff anyway. It made him feel better knowing that at least I had the things I needed. And truth be told, I had outgrown most of my clothes and needed a new wardrobe. I was now five foot six inches tall, weighing a hundred and twenty-eight pounds. With rounder, thicker thighs standing on long, slender legs, it was as if I had blossomed overnight. A thin waist and a set of 36C breasts made me look more like a grown woman than a teenage girl.

I wanted a new wardrobe, but I wanted to get it on my own. Maybe it was my ADHD medication or maybe it was the euphoric feeling of having just graduated, but I suddenly felt a need to be more responsible. I figured if I got a summer job I could get the things I need and help my mother out with the bills. That way she wouldn't have to sell her body anymore.

My father applauded my attempt to be independent but insisted he still had a responsibility to provide for me. I appreciated the interest he had in me and the constant concern he had for my well-being. Secretly, I wished that my mother had been more like him. Upon leaving, he asked me if I would be interested in giving California another chance.

"By another chance, do you mean come live with you again?" I asked.

"Yes," he replied excitedly, putting his arm around my shoulder.

I took a deep breath and looked for the best way to let him down. I didn't want to disappoint him, but I had no desire to return to California.

"I don't know if that's a good idea, Daddy."

"Sure it is."

"Are you kidding me?" I got up and walked away. "After everything I did, there is no way I could ever face Jenna again. Surely she hates my guts."

"No, she doesn't hate you," he assured me. "And beside, we're not together anymore."

"Oh, Daddy. I'm so sorry. Was it because of me?"

"No, not at all," he lied. "She had been planning this long before you came along."

There was a tone of sadness in his voice and a look of repent on his face. I don't know all that transpired between them, but it was evident that he regretted their breakup.

"Okay, but what about when you go on your long deployments?" I asked, trying to change the subject. "Who will I stay with?"

"Well, I'm glad you brought that up."

There was suddenly a sparkle in his eyes and he was wearing an ear-to-ear grin.

"I've been seeing someone else," he continued. "She is extremely nice, and she's not a vegetarian so you won't have to eat any more tofu quiche."

We both laughed casually.

"Seriously though," he added, "will you give it some thought? I would like for us to be together again."

I promised to give it some thought even though it was the furthest thing from my mind. I was looking forward to only two things: getting a part-time job and spending the summer with Lia. Going to school had put a damper on my social life. I couldn't remember the last time I had a beer or the last time Lia and I got into some mischief. I was looking forward to the time off, but part of me wanted to hang out with my father. He was beginning to grow on me. And frankly, I was worried about him. Each time he said goodbye, he looked sadder and more depressed than the previous time.

"Don't worry, Daddy, I'll be fine," I told him.

He caressed my face and smiled awkwardly as if he knew something I didn't. He left in a hurry to avoid a long goodbye and promised to call me as soon as his plane landed.

. . .

A couple of days after my father left, my mother finally came home. She had been on a drug run. Occasionally, my mother took trips out of state to deliver and pick up drugs. She didn't do it often as there were huge risks involved—only when times were hard, as it was in this case. A few months earlier, she had tried carrying out her plan to marry the Bangladeshi man. He had promised to give her six thousand dollars once they were married. And said he would supply the rest upon starting the initial paperwork for citizenship. But before they could go down to the courthouse and get married his father passed away, forcing him to leave the country with no way of returning.

Unsure if she would ever see the Bangladeshi man again, who

got her pregnant before he left, my mother became desperate for cash. At five months and showing, prostituting was hardly an option anymore. There just weren't many men in the market looking for a pregnant drug addict. In her desperation, she resorted to not only running drugs but other illegal activities as well. It's a good thing my father didn't find out until later, because there was no telling what he would've done.

She walked through the door limping, sporting a black eye with swollen lips, and wearing the odor of smoke and cheap wine. Stained with dried blood, perhaps her own or someone else's, her clothes were frayed and tattered. I was shocked, as was my grandmother who became hysterical immediately.

"Dear Jesus," my grandmother cried. "What happened to your face?"

"It's nothing, Mother," my mother replied. "No need to get excited."

"What do you mean, don't get excited? You walk in here limping, your eye is bruised, your clothes are filthy and I shouldn't get excited. Tell me what happened. Are you okay?"

"I'm fine. This is nothing you need to be concerned with."

"This is not nothing. I'm your mother, don't you lie to me."

"Okay, if you must know, I fell down," my mother finally said.

"You didn't fall down," my grandmother said smartly. "You were fighting again, weren't you? You are thirty-five years old. Why are you fighting in the streets?"

My mother snapped.

"For the last time," she shouted, "this is none of your business. Please, leave me alone. I don't need this right now."

"Fine, I'm going to call your father. He'll get to the bottom of this," my grandmother threatened.

"Mother, please do not call Dad. Jeez, the man left you for another woman, and you're still stuck on him."

My mother lit a cigarette and limped away. She went into the bedroom and slammed the door shut. I was speechless. I looked at my grandmother dialing the numbers and wondered what I should do. I didn't want to listen to my grandfather either, but I didn't want to leave. I was worried about my mother. So I figured I'd stay in case things got out of control. About twenty minutes later, my grandfather showed up at the apartment.

When my mother emerged from the bedroom, she gave my grandmother the nastiest look. I knew how she felt, I hated that my grandmother was always calling him.

"What happened to you?" my grandfather asked.

"Nothing, Dad. I was running for the bus. I tripped and took a nasty spill."

My grandfather took a deep breath. There was a long pause.

"I'm fine, Dad," my mother added, trying to break the uncomfortable silence.

"Your eye looks pretty bad," he finally said. "Did someone hit you?"

"No, Dad."

"Was it that Bangladeshi fellow? You know, white men don't solve their problems through violence. This is exactly why you should find yourself a good, wholesome white man to take care of you."

My mother blew out a long breath.

"I'm sorry, Dad. I can't do this right now. I'm tired, and I need to lay down."

My mother went back into the bedroom and knocked out. My grandmother and I stayed in the living room and listened to my grandfather for the next hour. I should have left too.

. . .

In the days that followed she stayed home, occupying the only bed in the house, which was fine with me. Because once I learned what she was doing in our bedroom, I began sleeping on the old, sagging sofa bed with my grandmother. I wouldn't even sit on the bed, let alone lay my head on it.

I stuck around and helped nurse her wounds. I pitied her, but part of me felt she probably deserved it. My mother was as conniving as they came. There was no telling what she would do for money. I tried asking her several times what really happened, but she wouldn't say. So to move things along I told her about my plans to get a job for the summer. My grandmother didn't like the idea. She thought I was too young. But my mother was thrilled and promised to help me in any way she could. I was grateful to have her support, and I looked forward to her recovery so that she could help me.

Chapter 9

Independence Day is characterized by barbecues, picnics, and family gatherings. But for me, July 4 was a sign that summer was in full swing. And what better way to celebrate than with a barbeque. Lia called me early Sunday morning and invited me to a barbecue that a friend of her mother's was having. Lia's mother, or Auntie Pamela as I call her, loved catering barbecues and parties. I responded with an enthusiastic "yes" and asked if they could pick me up on their way there.

I was glad that Lia had called. After a week of pandering to my mother's demands I needed a break. I went downstairs and waited in front of my building. Outside, it was a perfect summer day. The sky was a crisp blue with only a few clouds in view and a small touch of humidity; there was just enough breeze to offset the midday heat.

They arrived shortly after one in the afternoon. Sitting in the passenger seat of her mother's 1998 Nissan Maxima, Lia signaled for me to hurry up. I jumped in the back seat and Auntie Pamela sped off before I could buckle my seat belt. She drove through the street like a thief making a getaway.

"Mind the trays, Lonnie," she said, as she turned a corner much faster than she probably should have.

I grabbed the three huge aluminum trays of food just before they slid off the seat.

"What's the hurry?" I asked, struggling to maintain my balance.

"Thanks to your cousin here, the potato salad got ruined," she replied, sounding frustrated. "I had to stop what I was doing to make a brand new batch and now everyone is waiting on me."

I could see she was angry, and I wasn't surprised. Lia hated cooking. But her mother had the old-fashioned mentality that if a woman couldn't cook and clean then she wouldn't be able to keep a man. She dragged her into the kitchen every time she prepared a meal. Lia got so tired of it she purposely started messing things up, hoping her mother would drop the domestication efforts.

Afraid to take sides, I just listened while she rambled on and Lia sat there with her arms folded. I caught a glimpse of Lia's face in the side-view mirror and I could tell she was about to lose it.

"Alright already," she snapped. "I said I was sorry, can you please just let it go?"

"Don't you dare give me attitude," my aunt yelled, slamming hard on the breaks.

The car swerved in the road as it came to an abrupt stop. My first reaction was to grab the trays of food, but I couldn't stop myself from slamming into the back of the passenger seat. Her mother quickly turned her attention to me.

"Are you okay, Lonnie?" she asked, checking to see if the food had spilled.

"I think so, Auntie," I replied, getting back in my seat and buckling up this time.

"Oh my God, what is wrong with you?" Lia cried, shaking her head in disbelief. "What if someone had been behind us?"

"No one was behind us."

"But there could've been," she challenged.

"Lia, you better shut your mouth right now, or I will get out this car and beat you right here in the street."

Lia rolled her eyes and looked away. Her mother was always making threats but she never actually followed through on any of them. I couldn't understand why Lia was so annoyed with her mother for trying to teach her things. She had it good and, frankly, I envied her. Her parents were still happily married and they were both employed. She lived in a spacious house; she had her own bedroom, and her mother cared enough to spend time with her. My mother didn't spend any time with me.

. . .

I had wanted to get a summer job to earn some play money, and secretly assert my independence. My mother said she would help me get working papers, but as soon as she got better my mother was out roaming the streets once again. I needed just three little things to start working. I needed the signature of a parent or guardian. That one was easy. My mother signed the forms as soon as I gave them to her. I don't even think she read them.

The other two things were not so easy. I needed a copy of my birth certificate and a physical exam by a doctor. But for some reason, my mother didn't know where my birth certificate was, and as far as the exam, it never happened. My grandmother and I turned the apartment upside down looking for my birth certificate, and all we found were paystubs of old welfare checks, unpaid utility bills, and a bunch of sales invoices from when my grandmother sold encyclopedias.

Not wasting any time, I went online and researched lost birth certificates. I ended up on the NYC Department of Health and Mental Hygiene Office of Vital Records website. It was that simple. My choices were to mail in my request, but the processing time for that was a minimum of thirty days, or for a fifteen dollar application fee I could order it online and I would receive it in seven business days. The only problem was I didn't have a credit card, nor did my mother or grandmother.

I grew angry with frustration, as my mother made little effort to help me. First, she said she would apply for a credit card. Then she said she would borrow one. And finally, she promised to go down to the Office of Records herself and expedite the process.

She also promised to take me to the doctor to get the physical I needed, stating that I was fit to work. But she didn't deliver on that either. My mother was all talk and I was starting to understand what my father meant when he said she didn't have my best interest at heart.

As I sat in the back seat amid the tension between Lia and her mother, I wondered how I could get my working papers without my mother's help. If my father was there I would've been working already. He was one of the few people that cared about my future. But ironically, he wasn't in my life enough to make a huge difference. It was terrible. Here I was trying to do better and I couldn't get support from my own mother. *Why bother*, I thought.

"Did you say something, Lonnie?"

I didn't realize I had been thinking out loud. I also didn't realize that the answer to my problem was sitting right in front of me. Auntie Pamela had been just as much of a mother to me as she was to Lia. I wanted to ask her for help, but I wasn't sure how to go about it.

"Nothing, Auntie," I said, shying away from the opportunity.

I stumbled over my words looking for the right approach.

"Um, I was just thinking about the summer," I finally said.

"What about the summer?"

"I was thinking that . . . "

"Thinking what?" she persisted.

"She wants to get a summer job," Lia said, coming to my aid.

"That's great, Lonnie! Do you already have something in mind?"

"No, not yet. I have to get working papers first, and then I can start looking."

"Okay, where are you with that?"

Still feeling nervous, I leaned back in my seat and took a deep breath. I knew I needed my aunt's help, but I wanted to give my mother the benefit of the doubt. I wanted to believe she cared and that my father was wrong about her. But I was kidding myself. I told my aunt my dilemma and she laughed, insisting I'd be waiting a long time relying on my mother. She offered to help.

"Don't worry, I'll help you get your working papers," she said, looking over her shoulders as she attempted to parallel park.

I was relieved to hear that. Having her on my side, I knew things would get done. She was good at making things happen, just wasn't very good at parallel parking. After running over the curb several times, she gave up and left the car half parked with one back tire on the sidewalk.

We walked towards the house, each of us carrying a tray of food. The house was a Victorian-style, single-family home in the East Flatbush section of Brooklyn. Brightly painted with all its original details, decaying rosebushes and hollies encircled the front and sides of the house. Mildew covered the outer bricks and rotting window shutters showed their age. A flight of squeaky, wooden stairs led to a huge front porch with a hanging swing. The door was unlocked so we walked in and followed the music to the backyard where scores of people were eating, drinking, and laughing.

Most of the people there were in their 30s and 40s; some might have been older. I wasn't sure. There were a few babies and some toddlers too, but no kids our age to socialize with. Lia and I spent the first two hours serving food and retrieving drinks. We ran around so much I started to think that was the only reason I was invited. Later, after waiting on nearly everyone there, we sat down and had something to eat. I told Lia that I resented how her mother was using us, and she made it up to me by handing me a Heineken.

"Just drink it fast," she said, looking around nervously.

"Right here?" I questioned, taking the cold beer from her hand.

She realized it was a bad idea and told me to go to the front porch. A few minutes later, she joined me with a beer of her own. We both downed the beers as quickly as we could and then threw the empty bottles in the bushes. It had been a long time since we drank, and I became silly almost immediately. We sat on the porch and watched as one cute boy after another walked by. I told Lia that we should come back later in the week and try to meet some of them.

"I was already planning on it," Lia confessed.

"And were you going to invite me?"

"Duh," she responded sarcastically, then got up, and went inside.

"Where are you going?"

"I'm going to let my mom know where we are in case she needs us."

A few minutes later, Lia came back with two more beers. We drank them, although not as fast this time. We sat on the porch for a long while until our conversation turned to something other than boys. I told her what my father said before he left and she quickly advised against it.

"If you didn't like it the first time you're probably not going to like it a second time," she told me.

I admitted I didn't like California, but I liked being around my father.

"He cares about me," I said defensively.

"Yeah, I know, but you're never going to have this kind of fun and freedom living with him."

"Come on, Lia. I'm being serious. You don't understand what it's like to be me. You have a great home and loving parents who would do anything for you. I don't."

I probably should have chosen my words more carefully. It was obvious I made her feel bad. Her face went through a remarkable change. She tried her best to smile but it didn't work, because the look of shock was frozen on her face. Her thoughts seemed to be everywhere as she tried to find a reasonable response but couldn't. Instead, she got up and retrieved two more beers. I don't know how she was getting the beers, but I wasn't complaining. By now, I was experiencing a really good buzz.

. . .

An hour or so later, and after six beers between us, the day suddenly became interesting. Out of nowhere, four very attractive and nicely dressed young men stopped in front of the house. They looked around for a minute then walked up to the porch where Lia and I were rocking back and forth on the old porch swing. They looked like they were in their early to mid-twenties. One of them, a tall, slender, but semi-muscular, fellow came forward and smiled, revealing a set of perfect white teeth. Obviously a child of mixed race, he had a copper-colored complexion with big, sparkly teal eyes. With jet black curly hair, he couldn't have been more handsome.

"Is this the Johnson barbecue?" he asked.

Flabbergasted, I just sat there staring with my mouth open until Lia finally answered and directed them to the backyard. I couldn't believe how cute they were. Lia and I jumped up and down screaming like the two schoolgirls that we were. Without giving it a second thought we rushed in after them. Outside, we watched from nearby as they socialized a bit and had something to eat. They had to know we were watching them, because we were pretty obvious about it, practically following them everywhere they went. They were all good looking, but I was especially taken back by the one with the pretty eyes. Incidentally, so was Lia.

"I think he is looking at me," she said.

"Are you kidding me," I responded, almost insulted that she thought he would be interested in her over me.

Lia was cute, but she was a tad thick. To her defense, her mother was a great cook and Lia loved to eat. To compensate, she wore oversized sweatshirts. Still, however, she was beautiful. She had the complexion of rich, dark mocha with dark tangled curls that hung just past her shoulders. Her brown, saucer-shaped eyes masked her perception and cunning. She had an innocent beauty and a warm smile that could light up a room.

Maybe because I was tipsy, or maybe because there were four attractive men standing just a few feet from us, I offended my best friend and I didn't mean to. Her tone quickly changed and she spoke to me in a way that she had never done before.

"Why is it so inconceivable that he could be looking at me?" she huffed.

"It's not. It's just that we made eye contact."

"Well, he made eye contact with me too."

"I can see how it might look that way because we're standing together, but he was clearly staring at me," I said.

"And why do you suppose he was staring at you and not me?"

Lia was getting angrier by the minute. I had inadvertently insinuated that he was more likely looking at me because I looked better. And here she was demanding a straight answer, and I didn't have one. Luckily for me, Lia's mother came over and handed me a twenty-dollar bill. She told us to go down to the corner store and buy a couple bags of ice.

While we were arguing, the four guys had left the barbeque and we failed to notice them walking out. I felt foolish. I picked an argument over some guy I didn't even know and hurt my friend. Truth be told I wasn't even sure he was looking at me. For all I knew he could've been looking at Lia. After all, I was a little drunk. Normally, three beers wouldn't have that much effect on me. But it had been almost a year since I drank and my head was turning like a windmill.

We walked to the store in silence. Lia was probably too angry to say anything, and I was afraid of putting my foot in my mouth again. I wanted to apologize, but each time I looked over she wore an uncharacteristic frown. I had never seen her so angry and I became worried.

"I'm so sorry, Lia. Please don't be angry," I said in an outburst of emotions.

Lia stopped in her tracks when I spoke. I turned to see what she was looking at. The four guys we had been drooling over at the barbeque were standing in front of the store. They were causally smoking marijuana.

"Let's just get the ice and go back to the barbeque," she said.

If only it were that easy. I kept my head down and tried not to make eye contact. But with each step I took I could sense them watching us as we approached the store. I had a strange feeling one of them was going to say something. And one of them did—the really handsome one with the pretty eyes.

He said "Hi" and my heart suddenly started racing and my palms became sweaty. I had never been so nervous around a group of guys before. I told myself it had to be the alcohol.

"What are you guys up to?" he asked, taking a long drag of the marijuana cigarette his friend handed to him.

"Nothing," Lia answered. "We're just getting some ice and then we have to go back."

"Why don't you hang out for a little bit and then we'll go back together?"

Lia told them we couldn't before I had a chance to respond.

"Why can't we?" I asked, pulling her aside.

"Why do you think?"

But I wasn't thinking. Between the alcohol and the infatuation I felt for Pretty Eyes, I lost every bit of common sense I had. The fact that my aunt was waiting for the ice never entered my mind. I convinced Lia to stay for a minute, but she wouldn't smoke any of the marijuana they offered us.

I happily accepted the joint Pretty Eyes handed me and took a long drag. The smoke was harsh. It burned my throat and induced a violent coughing fit. My stomach muscles clenched as smoke expelled from my lungs. Unsure what to do next, I gave it back and walked away. He asked if it was my first time to which I lied. I told him it had been a while. Not wanting to look foolish I tried again, this time taking small short drags. I tried to get Lia to join us, but she refused and looked at me like she didn't know who I was.

I didn't feel the effects right away. But by the time we got back to the barbeque I was high and didn't know what to do with myself. It was a strange new feeling for me. One minute I'd find laughter in everything, and the next, I'd feel scared and paranoid.

When we arrived at the house, I was surprised to find Lia's mother standing on the porch impatiently waiting for us. She demanded to know what took us so long. Lia responded quickly with a beautiful lie. She told her mother the store was out of ice and that we had to walk to a different store a few blocks away.

Lia took her two bags of ice to the kitchen. I took mine to the backyard and dumped them in the cooler like her mother asked. A few minutes later, Lia came over and told me to behave myself because her mother had become suspicious of us. Afterwards, she distanced herself and left me alone with Pretty Eyes. At first I thought she was doing me a favor. But little did I realize she was merely leaving me to hang myself—and hang myself I did.

Pretty Eyes loved to drink and insisted I do so with him. But rather than say no, I went against my better judgment and drank the rum and Coke he fixed for me. Paranoid of getting caught, my hands trembled with each sip I took. My eyes rolled back and forth so much I got dizzy. But after three drinks, I was completely drunk and I didn't care anymore.

By now the July sun had faded and night was upon us. I had managed to elude my aunt for most of the day, mainly because she stayed busy in the kitchen and I had a small sense of control. But now I was drunk and found it hard to keep my hands off Pretty Eyes as I became overly romantic, touching and fondling him in the middle of the barbeque. I insisted he give me a kiss and forced my tongue into his mouth.

"Hey, what are you doing?" he said, trying to back away from me.

"Yeah, what are you doing, Lonnie?" my aunt echoed, coming from out of nowhere.

I stood with a glazed expression, and I remember my aunt yelling at me, demanding an answer, but I don't recall what I said to her. I remember everyone staring at me and feeling sick just at that moment.

A rumbling erupted in my stomach, followed by nausea, dizziness, and the foul taste of bile coated my throat and mouth. It was obvious what was coming next so I walked away. My aunt, not letting up and still demanding answers, grabbed my arm, a terrible mistake on her part as I proceeded to vomit all over her. I threw up and blacked out. But later Lia described it as a "volcano of vomit." Not only did I throw up on my aunt in the backyard but also inside the house on the way to the bathroom and in the car on the drive home.

Chapter 10

The next day I woke up face down on the old sofa bed. But I don't recall how I got there or who undressed me. The last thing I remembered was Lia telling me to behave myself and then having a drink with Pretty Eyes. I had an excruciating headache and I don't think I ever felt worse. At first I didn't know where I was. But as I struggled to lift my head off the pillow, I could hear my grandmother rattling on in her usual annoying tone. I figured I had to be in my apartment. Either that or I had died and gone to hell and my punishment was to listen to her voice for all eternity.

The apartment was stuffy and dark. All the windows were closed and the shades drawn. During the night I must have broken the record for sweating because my pillowcase and the T-shirt I was wearing were saturated. I rolled onto my back, quickly stripping away the bed sheet hoping to cool off. I struggled to open my eyes, squinting desperately as I tried to read the clock on the wall. It was nearly ten in the morning. I sat up in the bed and slowly wiped the dried drool from the side of my mouth and face. I tried to collect my thoughts, but I could scarcely recall the events of the night before. One thing was certain, all the drinking left a foul taste in my mouth. I felt like my tongue had been scraped with cactus dipped in shit.

After I finally found the strength to get out of bed, I crawled to the bathroom and had a shower. Water never felt so good against my skin. I stood in the shower for nearly fifteen minutes before I got out and brushed my teeth. The taste of stale alcohol was almost impossible to get rid of. Afterwards, my grandmother dragged me into the kitchen and tried to make me eat leftovers. She said it would make me feel better. But as soon as she placed the plate down I felt queasy. I shoved it aside and told her to just bring me a glass of water. She got upset and started running her mouth once again. Just then the phone rang and I got up and answered it. It was Lia.

"Hi, Lia. I was just about to call you," I said with my free hand over my ear.

My grandmother's yapping in the background made it hard to hear what Lia was saying.

"Hold on, Lia. Grandma, please. I'm on the phone."

My grandmother took away the plate of leftovers and replaced it with a glass of cold water. She left the kitchen, but I still could hear her talking to herself in the other room. I took a long sip of water and then picked up the receiver. Lia asked if I was alright and by the tone of her voice I had a feeling that something bad happened at the barbeque.

"You mean you don't remember?"

My heart started thumping out of rhythm.

"No, I don't. My grandmother has been talking all morning. But I have no idea what she's talking about. What happened?"

After Lia told me how I made an ass of myself, I broke down in tears. I don't know what I was thinking. Not only did I make a fool of myself but I may have ruined my relationship with my aunt.

"Oh my God. Your mom must be pissed."

"Yeah she is. She hasn't said anything all morning; just been walking around the house slamming doors and mumbling to herself."

The first thing that ran through my mind was goodbye summer job. This had to be the dumbest thing I had ever done. *There is no way she's going to help me now*, I thought.

"Lia, put her on the phone. I need to apologize."

"I don't think that's a good idea," she warned.

But I pleaded with her. I felt like I needed to make amends right then and there. She refused to put her mother on the phone and suggested I wait until she cooled off. But I wouldn't. I started arguing with Lia and even though she told me to stop, I continued, not realizing that her mother had taken the phone.

"Lonnie, you need to stop right now," she said, in a stern voice.

My muscles stiffened. My palms became sweaty. My heart felt like it dropped into the pit of my stomach, and my throat suddenly got dry as I tried to utter an apology.

"Save the apology for someone who cares, Lonnie. You have no idea how angry I am at you right now. How could you embarrass me like this?"

There was an awkward silence. I didn't have an answer.

"Well, what do you have to say for yourself?"

"I'm sorry, Auntie," I cried hysterically.

"I don't want your apology right now, Lonnie. In fact, I'm not sure I want Lia hanging around with you. Don't call back till I've had some time to think about this."

I stood there frozen, listening to the dial tone before I finally hung up. My grandmother came back in the kitchen and asked if I was ready to eat yet. I rolled my eyes and stormed out. I got back into bed and sobbed quietly until I fell back asleep. I was asleep maybe an hour when my grandmother came in shaking me like the house was on fire.

"Get up, Lonnie, your father is on the phone," she said and handed me the cordless phone.

Auntie Pamela must have called my father, who in turn wanted an explanation. He was incredibly calm, which I had come to expect. He did express his disappointment, but his peaceful demeanor and positive outlook on things made me feel a little less terrible about what I did.

"Lonnie, why were you drinking?" he asked.

"I don't know, Daddy. I just wanted to try it."

"I must say, I'm a little disappointed."

"I know, Daddy. It was a stupid thing to do."

"Alcohol is not something you should experiment with. It

is a dangerous drug that can hurt you and get you into a lot of trouble."

"It was just one time, Daddy. I won't do it again."

"It may only take one time. Being a recovering alcoholic myself, I can tell you it's real easy to get hooked. And because I'm an alcoholic, you may be genetically predisposed to it."

"What does that mean, Daddy?"

"It means you have my genes, honey, and you may have my same weakness for alcohol. I made a lot of poor choices because of alcohol and got into a lot of trouble. Don't make the same mistakes I did."

"I'm never going to drink again, Daddy. I don't like this feeling."

"Okay then, let that be a lesson to you."

Afterwards, he asked to speak with my mother. Unfortunately, I hadn't seen her in three days. He got mad and started lecturing once again. My father rarely got angry with me, but he had no problem displaying anger towards my family—my mother in particular.

"This is why you should come back to California," he said in an "I told you so" tone.

I tried to change the subject because I didn't want to have the California talk again.

"I really messed up, Daddy. There is no way Auntie Pamela is going to help me now."

"Don't worry. She'll come around," he assured me. "Just give her some space."

. . .

My aunt never came around like my father thought. She held a grudge for a long time and never did help me get the working papers like she promised.

Lia finally called me after about a week. She told me that her mother was sending her to Guyana for the remainder of the summer. She said her mother wanted her to know her roots. That might have been partly true, but I think the bigger reason was so that we were separated. Although I was heartbroken, I couldn't say I blamed her after what I did.

Chapter 11

A week later, Lia left for Guyana. We missed the opportunity for a face-to-face goodbye because her mother wouldn't let us see each other. We said our farewell over the phone, which wasn't much better because I still cried like a baby.

Over the next few days I became incredible bored. Without a summer job or my best friend to talk to life seemed meaningless. Even my mother, who occasionally gave me a good laugh, was not around. She was back on the streets taking drugs and whoring. The only thing I had to look forward to was sleeping in. And even that wasn't guaranteed with my grandmother around. Just about every morning I woke up to the sound of her rambling about something or another.

I realized it was going to be a long summer if I didn't find some way to occupy my time. I called my father and asked him if I could spend the rest of the summer with him. I figured it would be something to do and it would give me a chance to meet his new girlfriend.

My father was now living in Port Hueneme, a seaside community in Ventura California, located about sixty miles northwest of Los Angles and forty miles south of Santa Barbara.

Hueneme sits south of the Pacific Ocean and is known for its beautiful beaches, surfing, and year-round Mediterranean weather. Like San Diego, Hueneme is a beautiful city and if I hadn't grown up in Brooklyn I'm sure I would've liked it.

My father lived two blocks from the beach in a small two-bedroom condo painted entirely white. The walls were free of pictures or any kind of decorative accessories. Downstairs, there was a TV, a couch, and a computer. Upstairs in his bedroom there was a bed and a dresser. Then there was a second bedroom that also contained a bed and a dresser. The place was cold, plain, and unattractive.

His girlfriend, Lorna, had recently moved in but had yet to give it a woman's touch. Lorna was extremely nice and pleasant to be around. I could tell my father liked her and for good reason. She was shapely and attractive. At five foot five, her Latin features were striking. Her long dark hair fell to the center of her back and complimented her lightly tanned skin. Her intense brown eyes revealed a compassionate and sensitive soul. And unlike Jenna, she didn't seem uptight or appear uncomfortable around kids. She had a natural charm about her and she was easy to talk to.

The time I spent with them was a nice change of pace. As usual, my father showered me with gifts and things he thought I needed and did his best to sell me on California—dragging me to every park, zoo, museum, and other fun places. But after about three weeks I couldn't do it anymore. I had overdosed on fun. He must've thought that if he made California seem like the greatest place on earth then I wouldn't want to leave. Little did he know, zoos and amusement parks didn't interest me anymore. I would've preferred to be back in Brooklyn with my best friend drinking beer, smoking cigarettes, and fooling around with cute boys—it was all I thought about.

I was starting to think that I made a mistake leaving New York. But who was I kidding? There was nothing there for me at the time. And more importantly, I was starting to appreciate more and more what my father was trying to instill in me. I was beginning to see his points of view and how I could benefit from living with him. But then something unexpected happened that threw me for a loop.

Saturday morning, I was in a deep sleep when I heard the soft, subtle knock on the door. It wasn't like my father to come knocking so early in the morning. I thought I was dreaming and rolled over looking for a more comfortable spot in the pillow. I had just found a spot when he knocked again. I sat up, dazed and confused looking around the room. I still wasn't used to the idea of having my own room. Normally, I woke up to the sound of my grandmother's voice.

My father knocked and opened the door.

"Lonnie, are you still asleep?" he asked softly.

"No, I'm up, Daddy," I replied, rubbing my eyes, trying to adjust to the morning light.

"You have a phone call, sweetie," he said, walking into the room. "I'm sorry I had to wake you, but I knew you'd want to take this one."

"Who is it?"

"It's Lia."

My eyes lit up and I nearly fell out of the bed reaching for the phone.

"Lia, it's so good to hear from you. How is Guyana?"

But she wasn't in Guyana. Lia had returned to the states a few days prior. She was unable to acclimatize to the environment and the situations down in South America. So her parents flew her back early. She wanted to know when I was going to come home. She said she missed me and that she had no one to hang out with. There was an unfamiliar neediness in her voice that I hadn't picked up at first.

"I miss you too. But I promised my father I would spend the summer with him."

"But you hate California."

"Yeah, but I like my father. And besides, what was I supposed to do? You left the country and I didn't have anything to do."

"That's fine. But I'm back now, so come home," she pleaded.

Lia didn't understand, nor did she care that my father would be hurt if I left early. She suggested that if he had qualms about me leaving, I could do to Lorna what I did to Jenna. But I didn't want to do—I liked Lorna.

"I think it's best if I stay," I told her, hoping she wouldn't get mad.

"Come on, Lonnie," she whined. "Think about all the fun we could have."

"How? Your mom won't even let us see each other. She hates me, remember."

"No she doesn't. She got over that a long time ago. Will you just come home already?"

I could tell Lia was getting frustrated by the tone of her voice. But I held my ground. I wanted to stay because, for one, I promised. And two, I liked the bond that was developing between my father and I. I tried to explain that to her and I thought she'd understand. But then Lia did something that was completely out of character for her. She mocked my relationship with my father.

"You are not seriously falling for this stuff, are you?"

"What are you talking about, Lia."

"Your father is trying to take you away from your real family, your mom, your grand mom, me, and replace it with some woman you don't even know."

"That's not what he's trying to do."

"I never knew you were so naive, Lonnie. You don't know anything about this lady. Just think, what kind of weird food is this one going to force you to eat?"

"She is not like that."

"Whatever, just don't come crying to me when things fall apart. You know what, I don't even want to be best friends anymore. I don't want any part of your fake family."

I lay back down and stared up at the ceiling wondering what came over Lia. My thoughts were fragmented, turning madly in every direction. There was something out of the ordinary about our conversation—something that I should have picked up on. But looking back, my young mind couldn't grasp the true nature of her worry, nor could I read between the lines.

Later, I learned that Lia's outburst and others that followed stemmed from her parents' marital problems for the past year, and it was starting to take a toll on her.

As a regional manager for Sears, Roebuck and Co., one of her father's areas of responsibility was overseeing several stores. One day on a routine business trip outside the city he met a woman and later began having an affair with her. It went on for several months before he got careless and the ugly details surfaced. In order to work through the ordeal, her parents sent Lia away, who incidentally found out about it just a week before her trip to Guyana.

It was through tears that Lia told me the story.

"I heard them arguing," she said. "I didn't think anything of it. They argued all the time, especially about money. My dad was always complaining about the bills. But this was different and was dragging out a lot longer. I cracked open my bedroom door and listened. I heard crying, so I tiptoed through the corridor. I leaned against the wall and peered into the living room. I saw my father down on his knees looking up at my mom, wailing, 'please don't leave me.' My mom was being really mean. She never looked him in the eye. She just stood there tapping her foot and rolling her eyes. It broke my heart to see my father that way. He probably deserved it, but I wanted her to forgive him. I was disgusted with the whole thing, and I could not stand to see my father grovel any longer. I don't remember how many apologies he made, but he continued crying and begging until finally she gave in and they agreed to work through it."

. . .

The following morning, my father was knocking at the door again. He asked if I was hungry. Still upset with Lia, I replied with a simple head nod. He said we were all going out for breakfast. So I got out of bed and tried to shake the bad feeling I woke up with. On the car ride to the restaurant, I sat in the back staring aimlessly out the window. My father and Lorna did most of the talking and although they tried to include me in the conversation, I didn't say much. Finally, inside the restaurant, he asked me if something was wrong.

"No, Daddy, everything is fine," I lied.

He stared at me, smiling awkwardly. He knew I was upset. I looked away. I twiddled my thumbs, I played with my utensils, I did everything I could to avoid eye contact. I needed a distraction. *Where the hell is that waitress with our food?* I thought.

I looked at the clock on the wall. Two whole minutes had passed. Lorna, sensing my uneasiness, finally said something.

"Are you sure everything is okay?" she asked. "Because you seem a little distant this morning."

Lorna's timing was perfect. She gave me the opportunity I was looking for—a second chance to tell him the truth. But when I looked at him, he was still wearing the same awkward, ambiguous facial expression. I could see he was sad, but he was trying to hide it. I didn't want to hurt his feelings, but I had to tell him that my best friend was upset and I needed to go home. And as much as I wanted to, guilt held me back and I said nothing.

We ate our meal mostly in silence. The ride back was the same. There was an uncomfortable tension in the air that wouldn't go away. Finally, while stopped at a red light, my father did what I had been wishing he'd do.

"You're ready to go back, aren't you?" he asked, looking at me in the rearview mirror.

I smiled and nodded. That alone was enough to lift my spirits. My father looked up in the mirror again. He said we would look online for plane tickets when we got home. Three days later I was in the airport saying goodbye to my father and his girlfriend.

. . .

My mother was supposed to make arrangements to have me picked up. But after waiting two hours at New York's LaGuardia airport, I realized that I had been stood up.

I called her cell phone and got an annoying message that the phone had been disconnected. She obviously hadn't paid her bill again. I called the house phone several times and got busy signal after busy signal. I cursed my grandmother for spending so much time gossiping on the phone. My last hope was my grandfather and unfortunately, he wasn't available either. Finally, I contacted Lia and asked her if her mother wouldn't mind picking me up.

Chapter 12

I walked around the airport feeling excited waiting for my aunt to show up. I was relieved that she wasn't holding a grudge anymore. I kept thinking about what to say to her. Every apology I rehearsed in my head sounded dumb and not genuine enough. I felt foolish. I sat down and thought about the snarl that was my life. I was fourteen years old and I found myself having to make apologies for getting drunk. I couldn't understand how I had gotten to this point or where I was going from here.

I grew frustrated and tried to clear my mind. I stood up and started walking around again, wondering what was taking her so long. It was going on three and half hours since I had been there. I was tired, hungry, and cranky. I asked an old woman passing by for the time. She clutched her purse and walked clear across the other side of the airport. My mouth flew open.

"Maybe she thought you were going to rob her," a familiar voice said from behind me.

I spun around and saw Lia and her mother.

"Welcome home, cousin!" Lia shouted and threw her arms around me, locking my neck in a tight embrace.

She hugged me like she hadn't seen me in years. I hugged her back while staring at my aunt who stared back at me with indifference. I got scared. Lia told me that she had gotten over the barbeque incident. But she still looked angry. I walked towards her with a heart full of fear.

"I don't want your apology, Lonnie," my aunt said with a straight face. "Just give me your word that you won't do anything like that again."

She wrapped her arms around me and hugged me tightly. Finally, relief had washed over me. I nodded and hugged her back.

"I can't stay mad at you, sweetie. I love you like my own."

My eyes filled up with tears.

"God knows somebody has to," she added. "Your mother is not doing a good job of it."

"Speaking of which, do you know where she is?" I asked.

My aunt shook her head. There was disgust on her face. I looked at Lia. She gave a blank stare.

"Let's go home. I'll explain in the car," my aunt said.

No one spoke as we drove out of the airport towards the freeway. The sun was falling just as we pulled onto Grand Central Parkway. Traffic was bumper-to-bumper and my aunt got mad instantly, waving her fist in anger as she cursed a delivery truck that cut her off. I slid back in my seat and dozed off. When I woke up several minutes later the sky was black. I looked out the window and I caught a glimpse at the passing freeway signs. We were on the Jackie Robinson Parkway West heading towards Brooklyn.

I looked at Lia. She was sorting through music on her iPod. I looked at my aunt, her eyes were fixed on the road ahead.

"So, Auntie," I said, still feeling tired and jetlagged, "what happened to my mom?"

"Your mother got arrested again," she replied.

The news took me by complete surprise. I clenched my fists and took several deep breaths. It was all I could do to not get angry.

"Lonnie, are you okay?" my aunt asked.

I shrugged and looked out the window. There was a minivan with a family of four driving by. The cabin light was on. A man in his mid-thirties was at the wheel. In the passenger seat a woman around the same age was reading a roadmap. She was giving him directions and they were laughing causally. There were two kids in the back—a young girl about my age and a toddler, a boy. They were watching a movie on the flip-down DVD monitor. They seemed like the perfect family.

As I was watching them my mind began to play tricks on me. I was suddenly placed in the scene and was watching a more pleasant version of my life. I saw my father driving the minivan and my mother was the one reading the roadmap. She looked beautiful. Her long brown hair hung just past her shoulders. She had a radiant smile and her face was worry free. My father, who also looked content, tapped his fingers against the steering wheel to a tune in his head, while my little brother and I watched a movie in the back seat.

I was happy too, attending the most prestigious art school in the city. I had everything I needed and wanted, as did my little brother. We lived in a spacious three-bedroom condominium in downtown Brooklyn, overlooking the Manhattan skyline. On the weekends my father gave me painting lessons. We'd set up our easels in the living room in front of the nine foot panoramic windows. And as we looked out over the city, my mind would drift off, and I would think about how perfect my life was.

"Lonnie, are you listening to me?" my aunt asked, interrupting my thoughts.

I snapped back to reality. I looked around the car at my aunt and at Lia. Things were still the same, nothing had changed. I had drifted off into some sort of daydream fantasy where I had the perfect life.

"Are you okay back there?"

"I'm fine, Auntie, just thinking about my mom, that's all."

My mother had gotten arrested for shoplifting. She went into Macy's department store and tried on several articles of clothes. She then put her old clothes over them and tried to walk out. She had done this successfully in the past, but this time she overlooked the store's high-tech security cameras and got caught before making it out the door.

She was now seven months pregnant and still hadn't changed one bit. She was still getting high and living a reckless life. I feared for what this could do to her unborn child. My mother smoked when she was pregnant with me. But she had come a long way since her days of smoking marijuana and cigarettes. Crack cocaine was now her preferred drug.

"What about your mom?" my aunt asked.

There was a short silence. I didn't know what to say. I looked at my aunt in the rearview and shrugged. I was at a loss for words.

"Well, I've been thinking too, sweetie," my aunt said.

"Thinking about what, Auntie?"

"Lonnie, your mother is not fit to take care of you. She can barely take care of herself. People like her should not be allowed to have children. I'm sorry, sweetie, but she's a terrible mother."

My aunt's comment surprised me. And although it seemed harsh, it was true. She was a terrible mother. Maybe if she wasn't doing drugs, she'd be a better mom. I couldn't argue. I nodded and listened.

"I think you should come live with us," she continued. "I'll have to run it by your father first. But I cannot stand to see you under that woman's supervision any longer."

. . .

The evening traffic turned what was normally an hour drive into two hours of sitting on the road. We arrived in Brooklyn shortly after ten. Auntie Pamela double parked in front of the building and helped me upstairs with my bags. My grandmother opened the door and showered me with kisses. Irritated, I shoved her aside and jumped on the old sofa bed and turned on the TV. My aunt handed my grandmother some money and then left. She always did that whenever Lia stayed over.

We didn't do much that weekend, as I was jetlagged and tired from the time change. We hung out around the house and in front of the building. Lia and I got reacquainted and she updated me on her parent's situation. It was a quiet weekend. A few days later, my father called my mother to discuss my aunt's proposal. My father and I both thought it was a good idea. My mother, however, said it was the worst idea she had ever heard. She insisted that no one was going to look after me except for her. It sounded good, but I wasn't buying it. She was probably saying that because she was afraid of losing the child support and welfare checks.

I was in the kitchen when they were arguing about it over the phone.

"Lonnie is my responsibility," she said to him. "And how dare you imply that I'm not taking care of her."

"I'm not implying it . . . I'm saying it," my father fired back. "You don't take good care of her."

"And you think because you come around once in a while and buy her stuff, that makes you a better parent. Well, I'm sorry I don't have your kind of money. I can't shower Lonnie with gifts and fancy things."

"This is not about me, this is about taking care of our child."

"And who do you think was taking care of her when you ran off to join the navy?"

There was a short pause; my mother found his weak spot.

"You know damn well I didn't want to leave. But I had to do something, which is more than I can say for you. What have you been doing since then?"

"I've been here keeping things together," my mother said defensively.

"No, you've been running the streets, getting high, and selling your body."

"Sometimes that's what it takes to keep the lights on or put food on the table. Don't judge me, you don't know what I've been through."

"Spare me the bullshit, okay. There are other ways to earn a living. Stop thinking of yourself and put your daughter first for a change. You are setting a bad example for her. You need to be a better role model, or she's going to turn out just like you."

My mother started crying. My father had found her weak spot.

"I don't want her to turn out like me," she said through tears.

There was another brief pause while the two of them composed themselves.

"Look, I'm sorry for yelling," my father finally said. "But I don't want to have this conversation again. Please get your act together or I'm going to have to take drastic measures."

After that my father hung up the phone. My mother went into the bedroom and didn't come back out. Even my grandmother was quiet for the rest of the night. Admittedly, I was worried too. I had no idea what he meant by "drastic measures."

Chapter 13

Shortly before my mother gave birth to my brother, my father tried again to convince her to let me live with my aunt. The navy was deploying him overseas and he wanted to make sure that I was going to be okay. But despite his best efforts to change her mind, their conversation still ended up in an argument. There was no reasoning with my mother. She was too far gone to change at this point. I realized for the first time the seriousness of her addiction.

. . .

Lia had been spending a lot of time at my place while her parents continued to work through their problems. She had been nagging me all week to have a drink with her. But I was too afraid of getting in trouble again and refused. Early one Saturday morning, she asked me to smoke a joint with her. I asked her where she got it. She said it fell out of my mother's pocket two nights before, and she was holding it for a special occasion.

"What's the special occasion?" I asked.

Lia said excitedly that her parents had moved away from the idea of divorce. They were now going through the process of rebuilding the trust that had been lost. She had been scared for some time and I was happy for her. Still though, I didn't want to smoke with her. I was afraid of disappointing my aunt or my father if they found out. But Lia continued to pressure me until finally I gave in. She had that kind of effect on me and could talk me into anything.

We went downstairs to the alley behind my building. The alley was unsightly and reeked of urine and garbage. But it was the perfect place to sneak a morning joint. When Lia pulled it out of her pocket, my stomach fluttered and I became apprehensive. She handed it to me and told me to go first.

"No, you go first," I said, shaking my head. "This was your idea."

Lia put the joint in her mouth and pulled out a lighter from her pocket. She cupped the lighter in her hand and lit the joint. My heart beat heavily as I watched. I didn't want to smoke, but I knew I had to. I gave her my word. But just as she took a drag, I snatched it from her mouth.

"What are you doing?" she snapped.

"Shut up for a minute," I said, lowering my voice to a whisper. "Did you hear that?"

We both stood silently. Lia looked at me like I had lost my mind.

"Hear what," she whispered back.

I had to think about it. I wasn't sure anymore, but I thought I heard my mother's voice. Lia laughed at me.

"We haven't even smoked yet and you're already tripping."

I felt foolish and laughed too. I gave Lia back the joint. But then I heard it again. This time there was no mistaking it. Lia heard it too. I spun around. It came from the window above me. The window was about six feet from the ground, and neither of us was tall enough to see inside. I stepped back and tried to look in through a slit in the curtains. I couldn't see anything. Lia grabbed a plastic milk crate that was sitting in the alley and placed it under the window. We both stood on it and looked in through the slit in the curtain.

I knew I wasn't tripping. She was there, in the flesh, smoking crack with the downstairs neighbor.

Her name was Sharon. She lived in the neighborhood for

years, and for years she had been on drugs. She had two children from two different men that she collected welfare for. She too was once a beauty, but drugs and alcohol had destroyed her good looks. Her brown face now had the discerned look of an addict on the edge.

The two of them were in the master bedroom of her two bedroom apartment. The room was dusty, dirty, and dimly lit. There was a queen-size, four-poster bed in the center of the room and mixed-matched, worn-out furniture poorly arranged around it. On the floor was a large area rug that looked like it hadn't seen a vacuum since it was purchased. And all around the room cheap two-dollar incense was burning.

My mother was sitting on the bed when Sharon walked in. She had curlers in her hair and wore a flimsy bathrobe and flip-flops. She shut the door and walked over to the nightstand. She took out a small jewelry box and set it on the bed. Then she took off her robe and dropped it on the floor. She was topless but had on panties. It was obvious that drugs had ruined her figure. She was skinny, frail looking, and her skin was dry and ashen. She kicked off her flip-flops and sat on the bed. She gave my mother a peculiar look, and she stood and undressed as well. My mother didn't look any better. Her huge, pregnant stomach covered with stretch marks hung over her vagina. And her disheveled hair made her look old and fatigued.

After undressing, she sat back down on the bed. Lia and I turned and looked at each other. I was speechless.

"Are you okay?" she asked in a soft whisper.

I nodded. I took a deep breath and forced myself to look again. Sharon opened the jewelry box and took out a little plastic bag full of crack. Then she took out a glass stem and began packing it with the crack. My mother was practically drooling as she watched Sharon meticulously pack the stem with the tiny off-white nuggets of crack. She packed it several times and then tossed the loose bits back inside the bag. Afterwards, she took out her lighter and lit a flame. She held the lighter under the stem as she rotated it between her fingers tips. Finally, she put the stem to her lips and took a long drag and held it for as long as she could.

My mother inhaled deeply as Sharon blew the intoxicating smoke in her direction. Sharon then handed her the stem and she took a hit of her own. My mother sucked the stem hard then threw her head back as her eyelids fluttered and her body went limp. Grinning cheekily, she blew out a large plume of smoke into the air. She was transformed instantly, looking completely satisfied when she gave the stem back to Sharon.

Sharon took another long drag and held it. She motioned my mother to come closer and then exhaled the smoke into her mouth. The two of them looked hypnotized. They giggled like two schoolgirls then shared an open mouth kiss. Afterwards Sharon got up, put on her robe, and left the room, while my mother packed the stem for another hit. A few minutes later, she came back with two beers and handed one to my mother. She undressed once again, this time removing her panties, and then got on the bed.

They smoked some more, drank some beer, and exchanged some words. But with the window down, I couldn't hear what was said. After a few minutes, Sharon took the stem, the lighter, the jewelry box, and the bag of crack and set them aside. She threw herself onto my mother and the two started kissing and fondling each other. Within a minute, Sharon was on her back and my mother's face was buried in her crotch.

At this point I couldn't watch anymore. A sickening feeling erupted in my stomach. I jumped off the crate. I ran down the alley to the nearest garbage can and I threw up the pancakes I had for breakfast. Lia patted my back lovingly as I hunched over the garbage can puking violently.

"Are you okay?" she asked.

I took a few deep breaths and got myself together. I nodded and wiped my mouth with the back of my hand. Lia stared at me with sympathetic eyes.

"I'm sorry you had to see that," she said.

I shrugged.

"It's all my fault. I wanted to come down here and smoke."

"It's okay," I assured her. "It's nobody's fault. Let's just go somewhere else to smoke."

Lia couldn't believe I still wanted to smoke after that. Actually, I wanted it more than ever. I figured it was the only way to get the horrible image out of my head. We went upstairs to the roof, but first we stopped inside so I could rinse my mouth out. The roof was probably not the best place to smoke. The August heat was intense that day. We smoked quickly and then left. By the time we got back downstairs we were both feeling pretty high.

. . .

It was now noon and it was a gorgeous summer day. I was antsy to go for a walk. Lia just wanted to hang out in front of the building. But that was the last thing I wanted to do. Sooner or later my mother would come out of Sharon's apartment and I'd have to look at her. I wasn't ready to do that yet. I grabbed Lia by the hand and dragged her down the street. I wanted to have some fun. I didn't care what we did. I just wanted to leave the area. I had sixty dollars that my father gave me when I left California. I was going to use it to get my hair done but this was more important.

We went into the corner store and I bought two beers. The man behind the counter was one of mother's customers and I told him they were for her. But it must've seemed suspicious that I asked for two paper bags and two straws because he gave us a funny look. When I put the money on the counter he grabbed my hand.

"It's okay," he said in a Middle Eastern accent. "You can buy beer from me any time."

He had lust in his eyes and was wearing a creepy smile. He caressed my hand gently and then took the money. I should've freaked out, but I was high and we wanted the beer. I gave him the best smile I could muster up and a "thank you" and then we left.

We walked to the train station and caught the Q to downtown Brooklyn where we met Marcus and Anthony. There was nothing special about them, just a couple of Brooklyn boys in baggy jeans and Timberland boots. They weren't even that cute. But they had weed and they wanted to hang out with us.

They were high school seniors and I think that's where most of the attraction lay. Marcus had just turned seventeen and Anthony's seventeenth birthday was only a few months away. We didn't tell them that I was fourteen and Lia was only thirteen. They didn't ask and probably figured we were around the same age. But had they asked we would've fibbed I'm sure. We hung out with them the rest of the day. We smoked some more, we drank some more, we got something to eat, and then we went to a movie.

I don't remember what kind of movie it was or what it was called but it couldn't have been anything interesting because the entire theater was empty. We sat in the back and put our feet up on the seats in front of us. Ten minutes into the movie I fell asleep. Later, I woke up and found Marcus kissing my neck and fondling my breasts. I looked two seats over and saw Lia's head in Anthony's lap. Marcus was obviously looking for the same thing. But by this time I was coming down from my high and I wasn't in the mood. He got mad and walked off.

A few minutes later he came back in and called Anthony over.

Lia came and sat beside me.

"What's wrong?" she asked, looking concerned.

"I don't know. I guess I'm still grossed out from this morning."

Lia sighed. She said she understood but looked disappointed. A few minutes later, Anthony came back over and said they had to go. When we got outside it was dark. The downtown streets were busy with pedestrians and honking taxi cabs.

Marcus didn't say anything to me. He waited on the side while Lia and Anthony exchanged phone numbers. I didn't care. I was down from my high and feeling cranky. While I was waiting for them to say goodbye, my aunt called me wanting to know why Lia wasn't answering her phone. She said she wanted to come by and take us out to dinner.

I quickly motioned for Lia and she came running over. She took the phone from me and we started walking towards the train station. Lia told her mother we were at the store buying ice cream and that she left her phone at my apartment. She told her not to bother with dinner because my grandmother had cooked a big meal. Lia was good under pressure. I, on the other hand, would've choked up. Afterwards, we sprinted to the train station.

Chapter 14

My mother was out and about as usual, and my grandmother was dozing off on the couch when we arrived around ten. We tiptoed inside and climbed into the old sofa bed. We watched TV quietly and fell asleep sometime after midnight. My mother dragged herself in the next morning while the three of us were having breakfast. She looked terrible, even more so than usual. Her musky odor dominated the kitchen. Wearing a soiled shirt and oversized jeans, she grabbed a piece of bacon from the stove. She stood in the doorway chewing with her mouth open while scratching her head. She looked repulsive.

She walked over and gave my grandmother a wad of cash for the August rent. I couldn't help but wonder what disgusting acts she performed to get that money. Images of her with Sharon started flashing in and out of my head. My father was right. She was inconsiderate and selfish. Doing drugs while seven months pregnant was beyond selfish; it had to be criminal. I got angry thinking about it and lost myself in the moment. I wanted to ask her, *Why are you smoking crack when you have a baby inside you? Or why are you sleeping with the downstairs neighbor of all people? Or why are you selling your body for petty cash, and how come you don't care about me like dad does?*

But I didn't. Instead, I made a smart remark.

"You know, roaming the streets and staying up all night isn't good for the baby," I said.

She shot me a cold, dark glare, one that made me think that maybe I had overstepped my boundaries.

"Excuse me," she replied, walking towards me. "And what bills do you pay around here?"

"That's not the point," I said.

"Well, that's *my* point. When you start contributing around here, then you can give your two cents. In the meantime, just get your ass to school."

"I'm on summer vacation. School ended over a month ago."

My mother seemed confused. She had spent so much time in the streets and so little time at home that she didn't know what was going on in my life.

"Lonnie, don't test me," she barked. "I'm not in the mood for you this morning."

There was a short pause. I just looked at her with disgust and anger. If she could've read my mind she would've slapped me.

"When was the last time you heard from your father?" she asked.

I shrugged.

"Daddy is on deployment. I don't know when I'll hear from him again."

"Well, when you do, tell him we need some money around here."

She grabbed a piece of bacon from my plate and walked away. I started to respond with another smart comment. I wanted to say, "Tell him yourself. That money is for me, it's not for you to smoke crack."

Lia kicked my foot under the table. Thank goodness she stopped me. There was no telling what her reaction might've been. I couldn't eat anymore after that, so Lia and I went in the living room and watched TV. A few minutes later, I heard the shower running. She was in there for about twenty-five minutes, probably trying to cleanse herself of the foul things she did the day before. Afterwards, she came out smoking a cigarette. She walked over to the old sofa bed and tossed a pack of cigarettes at me.

"I need to get some sleep. You guys keep it down out here," she said and then went inside her room.

There were five cigarettes left and a twenty dollar bill inside the box. That was my mother's way of saying I care. That was her way of showing me affection. And her way of saying, "I'm sorry for snapping at you."

. . .

The rest of the summer was pretty much the same. Lia and I spent the remaining few weeks sleeping in, sneaking around, drinking, and smoking. Lia had become quite fond of Anthony and the two of them became a pair. Marcus finally came around. He found his manners and we became an item as well. The four of us palled around and had a lot of fun together. But the fun got cut short when Lia learned that Anthony had a second girlfriend. Heartbroken and angry, she had sex with one of his friends. Enraged with jealousy, he threatened to hurt her so she stopped seeing him. Naturally, that created tension between Marcus and I, as we were forced to take sides. Eventually, our friendship dissolved too.

Right around the time Anthony broke Lia's heart, a second bomb fell on her. Despite his promise to end their affair, Lia's father was still secretly seeing his mistress. To make matters worse, she became pregnant from him.

It was the last weekend in August. The afternoon sun was warm and the sky was an inviting blue. Lia and I were sitting on her front porch people-watching when her father came stumbling out of the door holding the side of his head. I didn't see it at first but blood was running down his face as he ran to his car. He fumbled with the keys and opened the car door just as my aunt came out of the house. Barefoot and braless, wearing a tank top and cut-off jean shorts, she was brandishing a half broken beer bottle and screaming profanities.

". . . and stay out you cheating son of a bitch."

"You're crazy," he responded, standing beside his car. "I got a good mind to call the police on you, you crazy bitch."

Lia's face was red with embarrassment as her parents exchanged insults.

"Crazy, you haven't seen anything yet. Step foot in this house again and I'll show you who's crazy."

"Well, you don't have worry about that, because I don't plan on coming back."

"Good. I hope you're happy with the little home wrecker."

"Oh, don't worry, I'll be happy. Anything has to be better than this."

"What do I care, she's a whore and a home wrecker."

"Yeah, but at least she knows how to satisfy me."

His last comment hurt my aunt and enraged her more. She ran towards him with serious intent to do him harm. He jumped in the car and quickly turned on the engine. She reached him just as the car sped off down the street. She stood there and watched the tires smoke the asphalt as the roar of the high-performance engine faded in the distance. He angled the 1995 Acura Legend hard right at the intersection, running clear through a red light as other vehicles came to a screeching halt.

Onlookers stood in silence as she broke down into tears. I looked over at Lia. Her jaw was on the floor. I tapped her arm and she snapped out of it. I walked to my aunt, who was balling like a child. Lia followed.

"Auntie, are you okay?" I asked and reached for the bottle.

She didn't answer but made no effort to hold on to it. I took the bottle and placed it on the ground. Lia grabbed her hand and led her back inside the house.

"It's going to be alright, Mom," she said.

After the incident, I found it hard to be at the house. Auntie Pamela had become extremely bipolar. One minute she was angry and hostile and the next she was an emotional wreck, crying hysterically like a child in pain. Lia on the other hand tried to mask her feelings, but I could tell she was in pain too. I tried getting her to talk, but she avoided any dialogue about her parents. She kept insisting we go back to my house and get drunk.

A couple of days later, Lia's father came back to the house. He was wearing the same blood-stained shirt and slacks. His silk tie was hanging from his pocket, and the side of his head was gauzed and taped neatly. He looked like he hadn't slept in days. His face told the story of a man in pain, a man who had lost everything. He looked defeated.

As he entered the house, Lia ran and threw her arms around his waist. He must've been so tired, she nearly knocked him down. She hugged him tightly and he hugged her back. They stood there for a long time just holding each other. Finally, he lowered his six foot three frame and got on one knee. He stared into her eyes and then pecked her on the cheek. Shortly thereafter, my aunt shoved some money into Lia's hand and told us to go catch a movie. For fear they might fight again, Lia refused to leave and broke down crying. For her sake, they promised not to fight. They assured her that they were just going to talk. Lia and I went in her room while they talked downstairs in the living room.

I felt bad for Lia. Up until then, I had envied her. I had always wished I had her life—a nice home and two loving parents. Now, however, it seemed as though she was worse off. Fortunately for me, my parents separated when I was an infant and I didn't know anything else. I never had to witness anything like what Lia had endured. Finally, after about three hours, my aunt knocked on the door and walked in.

"Your father is lying on the couch," she said. "Go say goodnight before he falls asleep."

Lia wasn't sure exactly what it meant. But she was happy that he was at least in the house.

Chapter 15

Every year millions of people from all over New York flock to Brooklyn's historic Crown Heights neighborhood to partake in the West Indian American Day parade. The parade begins on the corner of Rochester and Eastern Parkway and ends near the Prospect Park Grand Army Plaza entrance. From end to end, the streets are packed with people with roots from Trinidad, Barbados, Grenada, Jamaica, Haiti, and other Caribbean islands. A one-of-a-kind event, the parade consists of hundreds of floats and massive sound trucks with live performances. Hundreds of carnival folks in bright, elaborate customs and dozens of food stands and merchandise outlets make the festival a memorable experience.

This was the first year that Lia and I had attended the parade. In years past we couldn't go because of the sheer chaos and danger associated with this event. I thought that taking her this year would help take her mind off her situation at home. The tension in the house had gotten so thick that she couldn't stand to be there anymore. Forced to watch her parents revel in hurting one another, every little detail of their life and marriage somehow became vital to the bickering as they tried to hurt each other.

The resistance mainly came from my aunt, whose

contemptuous heart wouldn't let her see reasoning or listen to his pleas for forgiveness. She insisted on proving that their marriage had been broken. And by no means did she take it easy on him. I could only imagine how Lia must've felt. She was close to her father.

Lia and I took the Q train to 7th avenue and then walked to Grand Army Plaza. The moment we got off the train she dragged me inside a store and insisted we get beer. Lately, it was all she talked about and the only way she knew how to deal with her situation at home. I, on the other hand, didn't feel like drinking. Not because I wasn't feeling festive but because I wasn't familiar with our surroundings. Sneaking drinks at home or in the alley was one thing, but getting drunk amidst a sea of strangers at a parade seemed a little unsafe to me.

I voiced my opinion, but Lia didn't seem to care. It had been a rough summer for her and all she wanted to do was put it behind her. I sympathized and because I had a hard time saying no to her I grabbed two beers from the freezer. Lia shoved a bunch of money in my pocket and we walked to the counter.

I asked her where she got all the money from. She forced a weak smile. Ever since her parents started fighting, Lia found herself with more money than she knew what to do with.

"They just give me money when they want me to leave the house," she said with a long face. "I guess they don't want me to see them fight. They say they're just talking, but I know better."

Lia sighed. There was a short pause.

"A twenty here, a twenty there, it adds up after a while," she continued.

"Yeah, and from the looks of it, I would say they'd been talking a lot."

Lia just shrugged.

I set the two beers on the counter. The man behind the counter looked at me strangely.

"I'm going to need to see some ID, please," he said.

For a minute, I had forgotten where we were. This wasn't my neighborhood, and he wasn't one of my mother's customers. I froze with fear. I didn't know what to do. I turned to Lia and she was gone. She was standing on the other side of the store pretending like she was reading a magazine.

"Is there a problem?" the man asked.

"It would appear so," I replied, smiling awkwardly as I padded my pockets. "I must have forgotten my ID at home. I do that all the time."

The man shook his head. I could tell he wasn't buying it.

"I'm afraid I can't sell you alcohol without proper identification."

"I understand, sir. But I assure you I am twenty-one."

There was a short pause. The man eyeballed me hard. He surveyed my body and then my face. I was built like a twenty-one year old, but he couldn't seem to get past my baby face and innocent eyes. I should've quit while I was ahead. We could've left the store and tried our luck somewhere else. But having been caught up in the moment, I continued the fruitless pursuit and embarrassed myself in the process.

"What year were you born?" he finally asked.

I was not expecting a test question. I was hoping he'd let me get by on my pretty looks, which was all I had going for me, because I couldn't do basic math to save my life.

"Um, nineteen . . . eighty . . . five?"

The man just shook his head. Lia broke out in hysterical laughter. I thought about it for a second. I should've said 1984. I felt like an idiot. Lia walked by and grabbed my arm.

"You are so dumb," she said as she dragged me out of the store laughing uncontrollably.

Outside, Lia laughed until her sides cramped up. I forced a weak chuckle. But I didn't appreciate her laughing at my expense.

"Come on, you know it's funny." She cackled.

This was the first time I had seen her relaxed since her parents started fighting. So for her sake, I tried not to be overly sensitive. Soon, we were both laughing. People walking by looked at us as if we were high on something.

It was a perfect day for a parade. The September sun burned with intensity, and the electricity in the air was indescribable. The streets were packed with people. The Labor Day crowd was milling about in full force along Eastern Parkway. In a flow of mesmerizing colors, both men and women in revealing feathered costumes lined the streets. The sounds of steel bands and calypso music vibrated our ear drums. And everywhere we turned, the smell of Caribbean cuisine invaded our noses. So we walked to a food stand.

An older, heavy-set woman with a thick Jamaican accent took our order. I got the jerk chicken with rice and peas, and Lia ordered the curry goat with rice and callaloo. When I handed her the money I noticed that she was also selling beer. I saw four plastic trash cans, each one filled with ice water and packed with a different brand of beer. One was filled with Budweiser, and the others contained Corona, Red Stripe, and Heineken.

Lia elbowed me in the ribs. It was obvious what she wanted.

"Is the jerk chicken hot, mom?" I asked the big woman. "Am I going to need a cold one with my meal?"

"Whey yuh want," she asked.

"Two Heinekens, please," I replied, with eagerness.

I got excited. I couldn't believe how easy it was. She snatched the twenty dollar bill from my hand and motioned for the young girl that was helping her.

"Two Heinekens," she yelled, as she pulled out a huge roll of money from her apron and made change.

The young girl stuck her hand inside the trash can and fetched two cold Heinekens. She popped the tops off and placed them in front of us. Lia started guzzling hers right away. I shot her a quick stare.

"Show a little class," I whispered.

She pulled the bottle from her lips and blushed with a smile. A few minutes later, our food came and we left. We managed to find a spot behind the crowd under a tree on the sidewalk. We couldn't see much of the parade, but we didn't care. We were only concerned with filling our bellies at the moment. We ate and sipped our beers as we watched the mixture of people shuffling back and forth throughout the parade.

After stuffing our faces with jerk chicken and curry goat, we went back and got two more beers before walking the parade. Afterwards, we strolled along the parkway carefree as could be, with beers in hand, smoking cigarettes. Lia said she felt like a grown-up not having to sneak around for a change. I concurred and we stopped at a different booth and got two more beers. It was just as easy. By now we were both buzzing pretty hard, and

Lia started to open up about her situation. She admitted that she was scared.

"Scared of what?" I asked.

"Of my parents getting a divorce," she replied with worry in her eyes. "What will I do?"

"Well, there's nothing you can do. This is something that grown-ups go through sometimes. You just have to deal with it."

Lia pouted and wiped away what looked like a tear.

"I don't want to deal with it."

"It's going to be okay."

Truth was, I wasn't sure if it was going to be okay. But I didn't know what else to say. I wasn't good at consoling a needy friend. I had my own issues I had yet to come to terms with. I had a father who I barely knew. And while he wanted desperately to be in my life, I was craving affection from a mother who half the time didn't know where I slept at night.

"And besides, a divorce will probably work in your favor," I continued.

Lia shot me a look of confusion.

"What are you talking about?" she asked, frowning so hard that the lines in her forehead were showing.

"Because they'll always be buying your affection, you'll make out like a bandit."

Lia gave me a reserved smile, humoring my pathetic attempt at a joke. It wasn't the smartest thing to say, and I realized that I had put my foot in my mouth.

"I'm sorry, Lia, I don't know what to tell—"

Lia cut me off.

"It's okay," she said with frustration in her voice. "I don't want to talk about this anymore. Let's just get some more beer."

But I didn't want any more beer. I was already pretty tipsy and the heat was starting to get to me. It rose from the concrete and clung to me like a wet shirt. My skin was moist and there wasn't a single breeze to offset the humidity.

"Just get one," I told her, as she walked towards another food stand. "We'll share it."

I felt tired. The September sun was making me cranky. I took a deep breath. I rolled up my hair and fanned myself with a flyer someone had handed me earlier. The breeze felt good against my skin. I closed my eyes and imagined I was in a tub full of ice water. For a second I actually felt cooler. I took several deep breathes and continued to fan myself. After a minute, I opened my eyes. Lia was standing in front of me with two beers in hand, but her mouth was wide open. She looked like she had just seen a ghost. A strange feeling came over me. Then suddenly a voice came from over my shoulder.

"Why you standing there with your neck exposed like that," the voice said, softly and seductively.

I gasped. My heart jumped out of my chest. I spun around. It was Marcus.

"You waiting for someone to come and kiss it," he said with a smile.

Surprised and relieved, I threw my arms around his neck in a tight embrace. Anthony was with him. He waved at Lia.

"What's up, Lia, how you doing?" he said with a smile to match his friend's.

Lia looked frightened. She walked over with caution. For a second, I had completely forgotten how things turned out between them. My heart started racing. *He wouldn't try anything*, I thought. *Not here anyway, in the middle of the parade, in front of all these people and police walking around.*

"So, one of those beers for me?" he asked.

Lia sneered. I could sense her anger and he must have too.

"I'm just kidding," he finally said, still smiling.

But Lia wasn't laughing. Not only did he break her heart, but his violent behavior had frightened her and I included.

"Look, we don't want any problems," I said, trying to break the tension.

Anthony stepped forward.

"We don't have a problem with you guys."

The white tank top he wore fit snuggly around his chiseled chest and hung casually over his cotton boxers and loose-fitting blue jeans. Moist with perspiration, his brown skin glistened under the sun. And his eyes, although they were bloodshot and drawn, seemed sincere.

"I'm over that stuff. That was ages ago," he continued.

"It was barely a month ago." Lia huffed.

"Whatever, but I'm over it."

He reached into his pocket and retrieved a five dollar bag of weed. It caught our attention right away—Lia's especially.

"Come on, can't we just hang out," Marcus said, interjecting for the first time.

I turned and looked at Lia. She looked back at me. I was hoping she'd say yes. Marcus looked nice in his Yankees baseball cap and clean white T-shit. I regretted how things turned out between us. He was actually a nice guy and we had a lot in common. How coincidental, I thought, that he was standing there staring at me hungrily.

Lia let out a long sigh. She handed the beers to Marcus and Anthony, walked back, and got two more.

. . .

We then left the main strip and camouflaged ourselves between two parked cars on a side street. We smoked two joints and talked for a while. It didn't take long before Lia and Anthony were all over each other like nothing had ever happened.

I don't recall how long we were there, but by the time we left, the day was turning to night. A blood-orange sun hung over the city and lit up the sky in an array of magnificent colors. After drinking five beers and smoking more weed than I probably should have, I walked on wobbly knees as we headed back to the strip.

The parade was coming to a close. Still, however, there was a lot of activity in the streets. Groups of revelers were still partying and music was coming from everywhere. We walked around trying to find something to eat. But everywhere we stopped seemed to be sold out. Just my luck. I was drunk and high, and I needed something in my stomach, and we couldn't find anything.

My head was turning in circles, and I had a strange feeling we were being followed. I kept looking over my shoulders. But I wasn't sure what I was looking for. It all seemed like some gray and meaningless dream—the music, the people, the strange customs, and the policemen on horseback. I didn't know what to think. Not wanting to walk any further, I suggested we leave the parade and find a McDonald's.

No one commented on my suggestion. Marcus and Anthony looked right through me. Their faces were suddenly hard, and neither one said a word. Lia looked concerned, worried—frightened almost. Something was happening and I hadn't quite figured it out yet.

"What's wrong with you guys?" I finally asked.

"I bet you never thought you'd see us here," a voice from behind me said.

I spun around clumsily to find three guys standing behind me. I had no idea who they were. But apparently Marcus and Anthony did. And judging from their demeanor, I had a feeling they weren't friendly. The guy on the right was shaking his head. He had the most disappointed and disgusted look on his face. The guy on the left wore a similar look of disgust. He was rubbing his knuckles as if preparing for a fight. The one in the center, the one who spoke, kept his right hand just below his navel around his belt buckle. His hand was lightly caressing what appeared to be a weapon. Suddenly, it occurred to me that we had a problem. I grabbed Lia's hand, and we backed up slowly and moved from in-between them.

"What's going on?" Lia whispered.

I shrugged.

"I don't know."

But what we learned later was that Marcus, Anthony, and the three individuals had been business associates at one time. They sold drugs together. But Marcus and Anthony had cheated them out of money in the sum of five grand. Now they were adversaries, and the three of them were looking for payback.

"Yeah, it's a surprise, and not a pleasant one either," Anthony replied, suddenly looking sober and focused.

"So what's it going to be," the guy in the center said, as he lifted his shirt and revealed a snub-nosed handgun.

"You going to pay up, or do we have to do this the hard way?"

Anthony just sucked his teeth.

"You are not that brave," he said, looking incredibly calm.

Lia and I looked at each. I thought to myself, *Is it really wise to mock a man with a gun? Does this guy have a death wish or what?* Lia and I continued inching away.

"So you really going to test me aren't you?" the guy in the center said.

Then in the blink of an eye, he pulled the weapon from his

waist and fired a single shot. Anthony got hit center mass. His chest erupted and blood and sinew flew everywhere. He dropped like a ton of bricks. Lia and I took off running and hid behind a food stand. He fired two more shots after Marcus but missed. The Labor Day crowd went frantic. People were scrambling everywhere. I stuck my head out and looked through the chaos, trying to make sense of what just happened. But it was all too confusing. I couldn't find Marcus, and the gunman and his crew had disappeared into the crowd. The only thing I could see clearly was Anthony lying on the floor in the supine position.

By now, those that hadn't fled started gathering around. Two uniform cops ran to his body. One was already on the radio calling for backup and Emergency Medical Services. The other dropped to Anthony's side and ripped off his tank top immediately. It was saturated in blood and tore off like a wet napkin. He applied pressure to his wound while his partner talked frantically on the radio.

Marcus suddenly reappeared from out of nowhere and pushed through the crowd. He dropped beside his friend and broke into tears. The policeman told him to move, but Marcus was hysterical.

"I said back off," the policeman barked, as he held both hands over the wound.

Marcus refused.

"He's my brother," he cried, although they weren't really brothers.

"Just calm down," the other policeman said. "We're doing everything we can, but you need to back up."

The other policeman grabbed Marcus and held him back. By now Lia and I had come out from hiding and pushed our way to the edge of the crowd. From where we were standing, I could see the whites of Anthony's eyes. He was still conscious but fading fast. Lia grabbed my hand. She squeezed it so hard my knees buckled.

"You think he'll be okay?" she asked.

I shrugged. I didn't know what to say. The whole thing happened so fast I barely had time to process everything.

"I don't know," I replied. "But we have to get out of here."

I heard an ambulance in the background as police cruisers

screeched all around us. About a dozen policemen with batons charged on the scene and started forcing the crowd back. We didn't wait for an invitation, Lia and I withdrew right away. We navigated through the confusing maze of revelers, spectators, and policemen as quickly as we could. We left the Parkway and walked briskly to the nearest train station without ever looking back. On the train ride home neither one of us spoke.

. . .

At the house, I stayed up and watched TV while Lia went to sleep. She knocked out right away as if she had suddenly fallen into a coma. I, however, searched every channel looking for something interesting to watch. But there was nothing on that could take my mind off the shooting. It was the most graphic and violent thing I had ever seen. I kept wondering what might have happened had the shooter missed. It was pretty dumb of Anthony to provoke the shooter in the first place, especially considering we were both in the line of fire. The bullet could've hit one of us had he missed. I could not get that out of my mind.

Chapter 16

Shortly after midnight, my grandmother flopped down on the overstuffed couch across from us. Normally, she slept in the old sofa bed with me, but when Lia was visiting she took the couch. Soon after, I shut off the TV and lay staring up at the ceiling. The room was dark, but a streetlamp poured light in through the window blinds. Outside, the night was dead still. My grandmother's soft, tolerable snoring was the only thing breaking the silence.

I stared at the ceiling for an hour before sleep finally took me. I was asleep maybe an hour before I woke up squinting to a bright light coming from my mother's bedroom. I didn't think anything of it. It was typical of my mother to come home in the middle of the night and fall asleep with the light on. Lia and my grandmother were still asleep.

I got out of bed and walked to her door. I looked inside, but the room was empty. I walked over to the adjacent door and peered inside. She wasn't in the bathroom. I walked back across the living room and into the kitchen. The kitchen was dark and empty, she wasn't there either. I stood scratching my head in confusion. *Where could she be?* I wondered.

As I looked around, I noticed the front door was cracked open. *How could I have missed that*, I asked myself. I opened the door slowly and then hugged the inner jamb. The little hairs on the back of my neck stood up as I gazed outside and listened for a moment. I heard the misty background hiss of two voices arguing. It was coming from three floors down. Curious, I stepped out into the hallway and closed the door behind me. I walked down to the third floor. Now I could hear things a little clearer. One voice was that of a woman, sobbing hysterically. The other was a man, shouting violently.

"You thought you could steal from me and I wouldn't find out," the man shouted.

"I didn't steal from you, I swear," the hysterical woman cried.

I proceeded to the second floor.

"Don't lie to me, bitch. Tell me where the money is."

"I swear, I don't have your money," the woman said through uncontrolled sobbing. "Please, you have to believe me."

Suddenly, fear took over me, the voice sounded familiar. The woman sounded a lot like my mother. Each time the man shouted I froze and caught my breath.

"Tell me where the money is, Tina," he demanded. "Don't make me use this thing."

I gasped. It was my mother. I ran down the remaining flight of stairs into the open lobby. I stopped dead in my tracks when I saw my pregnant mother on the floor and a strange man with a handgun towering over her.

"Lonnie, thank God you're here," she said, looking at me with eyes full of tears. "Help me, please."

The gunman turned in my direction. He was in his mid-thirties, white, around average height and weight with broad shoulders. His hair was light brown, pulled back in a ponytail held together by a rubber band. Sporting a sleeveless, plaid shirt, his arms were defined and covered with miscellaneous jailhouse tattoos. He looked like a has-been biker slash ex-con slash drug addict. When he looked at me I panicked instantly. His eyes were cold and hard, like that of a soulless man who had lost his conscience.

"Don't even think about doing anything," he said with a cocky grin revealing tobacco-stained teeth.

"Don't worry, she's not going to do anything," another man said as he grabbed me from behind.

It was as if he came from out of nowhere and pinned my arms to my sides. I tried to break free, but his grip was tight and I could barely move. My mother begged for mercy. The gunman told her to shut up as he held the pistol firmly in his hand.

"This is the last time I'm going to ask you," he snarled.

He pulled the slide back and chambered a round. He held the weapon to her face and demanded answers. My mother continued to deny her involvement to which he responded, "You're lying, bitch," and fired a shot into her leg.

The flat crack of the shot rang in my ears. But it was nowhere near as deafening as my mother's painful scream. I wanted to help her. I tried desperately to break free, but the man held me tight.

"Please, stop hurting her," I cried.

The gunman ignored me and fired another shot into her leg.

"If you want to do this the hard way, we will," he said, shaking his head. "I have thirteen shots left. What's it going to be?"

"I swear, I don't have your money," she cried.

"That's not what I want to hear."

He fired a third shot into her other leg. Her kneecap exploded into pieces.

"Lonnie, help me, please," she cried in agonizing pain.

He fired a forth shot.

"Lonnie . . . Lonnie, wake up. Help me, please."

My mother stood over the old sofa bed and shook me violently.

"Wake up, Lonnie. I need your help," she said in a low whisper.

I jumped up and gasped for air. My heart was racing. My brow was covered in sweat, and I looked around the room dully, trying to figure out where I was. It took a few seconds, and then my crummy apartment came into focus. My grandmother was on the couch snoring, and Lia was beside me still in a deep sleep. My mother stood holding her stomach, her eyes were bloodshot. I examined her in the dawn light. She looked okay. I was relieved, it was just a nightmare.

"What's wrong?" I asked her.

She doubled over the sofa bed.

"I think the baby is coming," she said, forcing the words through clenched teeth.

Not giving it a second thought, I jumped out of bed and sprinted for the phone to call a taxi. But before I could punch one number on the keypad, I was on the floor, flat on my back and dizzy. I drank one too many beers at the parade. My head made a loud thump when it hit the floor. My grandmother finally woke up.

"What's going on?" she inquired.

I got up slowly and leaned against the wall.

"Mom is going into labor," I told her as I began dialing for a cab.

My grandmother jumped up and ran over, asking numerous questions. After I got off the phone, we helped my mother to the couch. Then my grandmother and I ran around the apartment trying to prepare her things. Meanwhile, Lia was still in bed sleeping. After gathering my mother's things, I stripped off the bed sheets and dragged Lia out of bed. She woke up and dressed just as the cab driver phoned in.

. . .

At the hospital, a doctor examined my mother and started her on an IV. After about three hours and two bags of fluid, she was barely contracting. So, hours later she was moved to the postpartum ward where she spent the remainder of the day.

My grandfather showed up with flowers and balloons. He and my grandmother did most of the talking while my mother pretended to be interested. After about three hours of his nonsensical spewing, he left and shortly after, my mother started feeling uncomfortable for the first time. Around seven, a nurse came and checked on her. She had dilated four centimeters, so she was moved to labor and delivery.

Within the hour, painful contractions started coming in waves. My grandmother got excited, probably because she was about to get another grandchild, but Lia and I were nervous and scared. My mother looked like she was in a lot of pain. Lia grabbed my hand and squeezed it each time my mother moaned in agony.

“I’m never going to have a baby,” she said, looking uneasy with the situation.

“Yeah, me neither,” I agreed.

The nurse gave her some narcotics for the pain and made her drink a full cup of water so she wouldn’t get nauseous. But whatever the nurse gave her, it didn’t help. She started vomiting shortly after. She threw up three times. Finally, after about forty-five minutes, they decided to give her an epidural.

My mother was hysterical and insisted we stay for support. I wanted to stay, but I knew Lia had a weak constitution and wouldn’t make it. Upon seeing the five-inch needle, her stomach fluttered and she bolted to the lounge. The epidural took effect quickly, but it didn’t seem to improve her situation. She was still in a lot of pain and now appeared bloated. The nurse put her on a fast IV drip because her blood pressure kept declining. She fell in and out of sleep and continued to vomit periodically.

. . .

Outside in the waiting room, my grandmother took my phone and started calling everyone she knew. I looked around for Lia and found her lying on the couch. She was staring up at the ceiling. I called her and she sat up. She had just gotten off the phone with Marcus, and her face was filled with shock.

“What’s wrong?” I asked her.

“Anthony is dead,” she said without emotion. “He died in the ambulance on the way to the hospital.”

My reaction was about the same. I can’t say I was surprised. He didn’t look very good lying on the ground. I had a feeling he wasn’t going to make it. I asked Lia if she was alright. She just shrugged and not much more was said after that.

. . .

After what seemed like forever, my mother was fully dilated and ready to give birth. But the doctor told us that the baby was mal-positioned. It had turned ninety degrees and was facing sideways rather than facing down towards the mother’s back, which would’ve been normal. Talk of a cesarean made my mother hysterical. She insisted that she didn’t want to be cut and began to cry. They got her to calm down, and the doctor explained that a cesarean would be a last resort.

They had her turn on her side and push, but that had little effect. Finally, they had her lay on her back with her knees against her chest and made her push some more while the doctor rotated the baby manually. Twenty minutes later, the baby was properly positioned and began to crown. After a little over an hour, the shoulders passed through and the baby was out.

Chapter 17

I really thought the baby was going to be born with some sort of birth defect or abnormality, considering my mother's elicit lifestyle. But despite the drug use, she gave birth to a healthy baby boy. He was, however, a low weight at just under five pounds. But it was nothing abnormal or a cause for concern, the doctor said. He said that sometimes low birth weight can be caused by smoking, drinking, drug use, or poor nutritional habits. Naturally, my mother denied any drug use or mistreatment of her unborn. She accepted the belief that some babies are just small and happen to weigh less.

My mother remained at the hospital for two days, just long enough for them to monitor the baby and make sure there were no complications. Once he was on a normal feeding schedule and his weight leveled off , mother and baby were released.

To make her homecoming more comfortable, I cleaned the house from top to bottom. I swept, vacuumed, and disinfected every inch of the apartment. I wiped down walls, I scrubbed baseboards and did my best to unclutter the place of my grandmother's junk. But she wouldn't hear of it. Everything was important and she refused to throw anything away. So instead, I cleaned my mother's bedroom the best I could. I rearranged her things around a bit and managed to fit in my old baby crib. For the longest time, it sat in the corner of the living room and housed a bunch of my grandmother's old encyclopedias. But after a good cleaning and polish it looked like new.

I could hardly wait for my little brother to come home. I stood in front of my building and waited for my mother's cab to arrive from the hospital. She stepped out of the cab looking absolutely horrible. But I suppose giving birth while going through withdrawal will do that. It was nice having her home for a few weeks. And to my surprise she remained sober. There was even some talk of her entering rehab.

She had been feeding my little brother, who we named Christian, when I walked into the room. Maybe it was because she had been sober for a few days or because she had just given birth and the experience did something to her, but she opened up to me like never before.

"Lonnie," she said, looking more serious than I'd ever seen her. "I haven't been a very good mother to you."

Her dark eyes displayed a peculiar mixture of caution and concern. She was clearly uneasy and trying hard not to show it. My mother and I seldom had serious conversations and her words took me by surprise.

"Whatever do you mean, Mother," I said with a hint of sarcasm. But thankfully it was over her head.

"It is every mother's dream that her child succeeds in life," she continued. "Not only have I not given you the attention you deserved over the years but I've failed to provide you with the tools you need to succeed. My life is practically over."

"That's not true, Mom," I interrupted. "It's never too late to start over."

She forced a weak smile through misty eyes.

"It's easier said than done, Lonnie."

"Daddy said, 'You can do anything you set your mind to. The only limitations we have are the ones we set for ourselves.'"

My mother sighed and looked away. There was a short pause then our eyes met again. She was tired, I could tell. Fatigue was evident in her weary eyes.

"Your father is a smart man," she said. "But he doesn't know what I've been through. I've burned too many bridges and pissed off too many people. You on the other hand have your whole life ahead of you. Don't make the same mistakes I've made."

She took a deep breath. Choking over her own words, she fought back tears from flooding her eyes. An expression of sincere sympathy took over my face. I felt sorry for her for the first time.

"But your father is right though," she said after a long pause. "You can do anything you set your mind to. Take advantage of his wisdom. You could learn a lot from him. Matter of fact, you really should consider moving back to California with him. He can give you so much more than I can."

"Yeah, but I don't need anything."

"I beg to differ, Lonnie. You need a lot of things—good parenting above all."

I started to get annoyed. I felt as though my mother was trying to get rid of me again. The addition of my little brother was certainly going to put a strain on her finances. So what would be better than to ship me off to California and have one less thing to worry about?

"You could be a good parent," I said, trying to keep my cool. "Just be around more."

My mother shook her head. She got up and placed my little brother in his crib.

"You don't get it do you, Lonnie?" she said, turning to me.

But I did. I understood a lot more than she realized. I understood that she didn't have all the best opportunities and that the choices she made weren't always the wisest. I understood perfectly that she had a drug addiction. But what she didn't understand was that I needed her to do better. She didn't realize just how much I needed her love and affection.

"Okay then, what about rehab?" I asked bluntly.

My mother just nodded.

"Yeah, it's a thought," she said causally.

And that's all it was—just *a thought*.

After about a month, her friend Sharon, from the first floor, began showing up at our apartment. And before long, my mother was roaming the streets again, leaving my grandmother to raise my little brother—just like she did me.

Chapter 18

Everything was brand new—a new school year at a new school. I had new clothes that my father bought for me and a new attitude to go with it all. There was only one disappointing thing—I wasn't able to get into any of the arts high schools that I applied for because of my poor grades. My father did, however, find me a NYC school with a remedial program that specialized in talented kids but who had problems fully understanding math, English, and writing.

At first I didn't like the idea because remedial classes are often looked upon as shameful. But my father helped me to see the positive side of my situation. He explained that remedial classes didn't have to be embarrassing. They can in fact be a useful tool for getting a complete grasp in difficult areas. They act as a safety net for struggling students and allow them to work at a level they are comfortable with, rather than fail because they are not at the level of the rest of the class. He assured me that the program would be a positive environment for me. There would be no hurry or pressure to understand a subject, and I could learn at my own pace.

My father was great. He always knew what to say to make me feel better and motivate me. And the program was simple;

do it for a year, bring up my grades, and then I could reapply to the arts high schools the following year. If only it were that easy.

. . .

The moment I arrived, I knew I wasn't going to make it. The school was located in Midtown Manhattan a few blocks south of The High School of Art and Design, a school that had rejected me.

From the train station, I walked four blocks to what looked like an old abandoned factory but was in fact my school for the next year.

I walked through a giant metal door to an open lobby where I found a security guard half asleep at his post. He was an elderly man with gray hair and a frail body. Reclining back in his chair, he had his feet up on the desk and his security cap tilted over his face. I walked up to him, wondering if I should wake him or not. I decided not to. I looked up at the directory between the two elevator doors and tried to figure out where I needed to go.

"Take it to the ninth floor," the old man said, suddenly waking from his slumber.

Startled, I stepped back and looked at him oddly.

"Excuse me."

"Are you here for orientation?" he asked.

"Um, yes," I replied, unsure what to say.

"Ninth floor," he echoed. "The rest of them are already up there."

On the ninth floor, I stepped out into a long corridor with rooms aligned on both sides. A woman pacing the long hallway spun around as I emerged from the elevator. She was quite stunning—Hispanic perhaps. She wore a pair of vintage, black, big-rim glasses and her hair up in a bum. Her bright-red lipstick made her lips appear larger than life and jump out against her tan complexion. The grey pinstriped business suit she wore looked professional but also screamed sexy. She reminded me of that horny librarian you see in cheap porno flicks.

She walked up to me with clipboard in hand and asked for my name.

"Lonnie," I said, staring at her size double D breasts.

I didn't mean to, but she was a tall woman wearing three-inch heels and her boobs were practically parallel to my face.

Her eyes scanned the clipboard.

"Ah, here we go, Lonnie," she said, and scribbled something next to my name. "You're in room 905."

She escorted me to the far end and then continued pacing the hallway. I walked in and another woman, this one middle aged, about average height and weight, asked for my name.

"Lonnie."

"Welcome, Lonnie," she said with a pleasant smile. "Come on in and have a seat."

I walked to the rear of the class and sat in one of the empty seats in the back row. I took a deep breath and gazed around the room at some of the other students. There was something strange about the class that I couldn't quite put my finger on. There were twenty-eight students a lot like me—inner-city kids from throughout the five boroughs. And like me, they were probably there because they were scholastically challenged.

As I sat looking around, two more students came in. They were both girls, one of them Hispanic and the other African American. Suddenly, it dawned on me. The entire class was made up of minority students. There wasn't a single white student in the class. I started wondering if I was in one of those state-funded programs designed for impoverished, underprivileged minority kids whose parents were either on drugs or had abandoned them.

. . .

The name *Mrs. Livingston* was scribbled across the blackboard. This woman was standing in the hallway just outside the door looking towards the elevators.

"Alright, class, I guess that's everyone," she said, finally coming back inside after standing there for several minutes.

She walked over to her desk and picked up a stack of papers.

"Good morning, class," she said with a great big smile. "My name is Mrs. Livingston, and I'll be your homeroom teacher for this semester. The first thing I'm going to do is hand out your individual class schedules and program syllabus. So listen up for your name please."

"Cassandra Abbott . . . "

A chubby black girl with braids in her hair raised her hand.

"Maria Alzado . . . "

A Hispanic girl wearing heavy makeup raised her hand.

"Amanda Armstrong . . . "

A skinny black girl with glasses and a mouth full of braces raised her hand.

"Hilary Anderson . . . "

Another black girl.

"Sophia Arnaz . . . "

Another Hispanic girl.

Just as I had suspected, every student in the class was a minority. I continued to listen as she went through more names. But by the time she got to the Bs, my mind was somewhere else. I didn't even hear my name when it was called.

Mrs. Livingston walked over and handed me a schedule and syllabus. I looked through it briefly while she continued calling out names. The schedule seemed simple. A few classes in the morning, an hour lunch break, followed by a few more classes in the afternoon. My last class ended at two-thirty. After handing out the last class schedule and syllabus, she got back in front of the class.

"Ladies," she shouted. "Your attention, please."

The class went silent. Mrs. Livingston started going over the syllabus, but I wasn't listening. I was still stuck on the word "Ladies." I don't know why I didn't see it at first. But every student in the class was female. *There is no way*, I thought. *This can't possibly be an all-girl school.*

I had to be sure. I raised my hand and asked Mrs. Livingston if I could go to the bathroom. She said it was past the elevators on the right. I walked slowly along the corridor, nervously looking inside each classroom I passed. The first one I looked into was full of girls, and not a signal guy in sight. The same was true for the second one and the third and the forth and the fifth. I leaned up against the wall and listened to my pounding heart. *Dear God*, I thought. *Please, don't let this be an all-girl school.*

I walked into one of the classrooms. I just wanted to see one boy. Even a male teacher at this point would've been a good sign. The Horny Librarian was standing in front of a class full of nothing but girls. She turned to me.

"Are you lost, sweetie?" she asked.

I didn't respond. I couldn't get the painful thought of an all-girl school out of my mind.

"Lonnie, right?"

She had a good memory.

"You're in room 905, sweetie."

I nodded and left the classroom. The bathroom was two doors over. I went inside. A girl was at the sink washing her hands. She smiled at me in the mirror.

"Where's the boy's bathroom?" I asked her.

She turned and gave me a crazy look.

"Why do you need a boy's bathroom?"

I didn't reply. *Why do I need a boy's bathroom?* I thought. I didn't. I just didn't want to believe that I was in an all-girl school. *Maybe I'm on the girl's floor*, I told myself.

"This is an all-girl school," she continued. "So, ah, I doubt there is a boy's bathroom anywhere around here."

I let out a long sigh. She gave me an awkward look. She walked over to the paper towel dispenser and started drying her hands. I could see her in the mirror trying to figure out what was wrong with me. At this point, I wasn't sure what was wrong with me either. *Does it really matter that it's an all-girl school?* I asked myself.

"Okay, thank you for the info," I said, finally.

"Anytime," she replied and added "weirdo" under her breath as she left.

I walked over to the sink and ran the cold water. I cupped a little bit in my hand and splashed my face. It was all I could do to keep from getting discouraged. This was not how I had imagined my first year of high school would be. But I had to deal with it. I had to accept the fact that my father had condemned me to an all-girl school for the next year. I had to if I wanted to get into an arts school.

High school was not fun, at least not this one anyway. The all-female student body was hard to deal with, and the ride to school was just as discouraging. My commute was about fifty-five minutes by subway. And as luck would have it, I could never get a seat on the train because of the morning rush. Traveling through the outer boroughs wasn't easy and going through

Manhattan was the absolute worst.

Even though I looked into it and everyone I asked said it wasn't a special program, it felt like one. A large number of the students, mostly black and Hispanic, lived close to the poverty line. There wasn't much interaction among the student body, just little individual cliques. And I didn't fit in any of them. I felt like I was in some sort of social limbo. But the thing I disliked most, or the thing that made it feel less like high school, was that there were no interscholastic sports—no basketball team or a football team. I wasn't personally interested in any of these activities, but I knew boys were, and I liked being around boys.

All I really wanted was a normal high school experience. And this all-girl school didn't give me that. I tried to be motivated and stay in school, but the interest just wasn't there. I was kidding myself, thinking I could make it through a whole year. Bouncing from classroom to classroom without anything in-between or anything thereafter to stimulate my teenage senses and needs made high school an incredible drag. Every day, every week, every month was more mind-numbing than the one before. After just four short months at this school, I was already burned out.

Chapter 19

Everything changed when I left for Christmas vacation. Actually, that's when everything started to go downhill. My Christmas break started three days before Lia's. Not having anything to do, I took a train ride to her school and met her for lunch. Lia was always bragging about how great her school was, and I wanted to see firsthand what I was missing.

Edward R. Murrow High School dominates two full square blocks in the Midwood section of Brooklyn. A huge contemporary building made of red brick and glass, it's unlike the conventional high school structured by bells and patrolling teachers. Murrow offered freedom of curriculum through random scheduled classes throughout the day, free periods, and self-paced college courses for the self-directed student. I loved the concept. But not as much as I loved all the handsome young men loitering on campus in-between classes.

I met up with Lia at Midwood field, a sprawling square, block-long football field between East 16th and 17th street. Visible from the BMT subway line, it featured handball courts, tennis courts, and a wrap-around race track. Excitement surged through my body as I walked along the football field towards the bleachers where Lia was waiting. A group of guys running scrimmage plays caught my attention, and I stopped to admire the beautifully fit and muscular players. I watched them with an incredulous expression on my face. *So this is the high school experience I've been missing*, I thought, and let out a long disappointing sigh.

I stared at them for a few minutes before leaving. As I was walking away, someone yelled, "Hey, how about a hand."

When I looked, I saw that their game ball had made its way by me and a player was coming for it. I picked up the ball before he got to it. He put up his hands, indicating he wanted me to throw it to him. But I couldn't throw a football to save my life, so I held it and waited for him.

He jogged towards me. Behind his face mask, I could see his complexion was a soft brown, and his eyes were big, bright, and intense. He examined my face and body before taking the ball from my hands.

He said, "Thank you," with a flirtatious smile as he slowly backed away, still maintaining eye contact. I couldn't help but blush at the obvious attention he'd given me. I was glad I took the extra time to prepare my outfit that morning. I felt very confident in my Kenneth Cole zip-front leather jacket and matching ankle boots. With a cream turtleneck sweater and snug fitting jeans to complete the ensemble, I was looking pretty cute and it had paid off.

He took a last look and gave me one more smile before heading back. I watched him closely and suddenly, I was overcome by pulsing warmth. My face was flushed and my heart started dancing in my chest. I could not take my eyes off his coconut-shaped calves, muscular thighs, and firm buttocks as he ran back to his game. I had gotten aroused just from that brief encounter. It occurred to me then that I was long overdue for some sexual merriment. The last time I had sex was back in the summer with Marcus, before Anthony was gunned down at the Labor Day parade.

I continued to stare at him and began fantasizing about the possibilities when someone tapped me on the shoulder and brought me back to reality. It was Lia.

"What are you doing?" she said, looking at me funny.

"Huh?"

My mind went blank. Before I could form a semblance of a thought, Lia grabbed my hand and dragged me off the field.

"Come on," she said. "I want to introduce you to everyone."

We walked over to the bleachers. Sitting there were two girls and a guy. My first thought was that the guy was gay; there was something about him. His hair was cut in a low Caesar and neatly tapered around his ears and neck. His clothes were neatly pressed and hung off his body as if they were tailor made especially for him. He wore a wool sweater and tight-fitting jeans. His Dr. Martens boots were spit shined and his lips were saturated in lip gloss. I don't know what was shinier, his lips or his boots.

"Hey, guys, this is my cousin, Lonnie," Lia introduced.

Everyone smiled at me.

"Lonnie, this is James."

"Ah, Jamie, thank you," he corrected and rolled his eyes.

Lia just shook her head.

"My goodness, Lia," he said. "You weren't kidding; she is beautiful."

Jamie rose slightly from his seat and shook my hand, but only grabbing my fingertips. It was a very flowery handshake. *He has to be gay*, I thought.

"This is Janette," Lia continued, pointing to a Puerto Rican girl with hazel eyes and Cupid's bow lips.

I nodded and smiled.

"And . . . this is Danielle."

Danielle was about average height and weight, nothing special about her—pretty plain looking in fact.

I said hello and sat beside by cousin, while the others carried on with whatever conversation they were having. Lia was happy to see me and thanked me for coming. But I was the one who was grateful and happy to be there. There were handsome young men everywhere, and I felt privileged to be around them, considering I didn't have that at my all-girl school in Manhattan. Without wasting time, I asked Lia about the guys playing football, in particular, about the one who smiled at me.

"Don't bother," she said. "Those guys won't mess with the likes of us."

"Why not," I asked. "And what do you mean by the 'likes of us'?"

"We're freshmen," Lia said, giving me the "duh" look as if I was supposed to know that. "Most of them are juniors and seniors, and they don't associate with freshmen."

I just stared out onto the field, unaware there were rules and dating protocols about high school.

"Are you sure about that?"

"Yes, why?"

Lia seemed surprised that I didn't take her word for it. I trusted my cousin. It wasn't that I didn't believe her or thought she was lying. It was because of the way he had looked at me. After that I sat there and listened to her blabber about which guys were cute and which were not. I didn't say much because I didn't know who they were talking about. I had gone there to spend time with Lia. But she seemed more interested in her school friends than me.

A little while later, we decided to leave and get lunch. We walked off the bleachers, Lia and her friends in the front and me trailing the rear. As we walked across the field, I heard a voice over my shoulder.

"Hey, hold up a minute."

I spun around and it was him—the football player I had encountered earlier—this time without the football helmet. He was breathing hard from having sprinted across the field. He smiled as he tried to catch his breath. His smile was gorgeous. My blood started pumping quicker when he grabbed my hand and pulled me aside.

"Where are you going?" he asked.

"To get something to eat," I replied, unable to look away from his big brown eyes.

"Why haven't I seen you before? Are you new?"

"No, I don't go to this school."

"That's too bad," he said. "But I'm having a little party this afternoon, I'd love for you to come."

By party, he meant a hooky party, in which a group of school kids skip class and rendezvous at someone's house while their parents are at work. These types of functions usually involved music, drugs, and sex. Lia and I had heard of them, but we had yet to attend one.

"I'm not going to be able to," I told him. "I came here only to hang out with my cousin."

"Which one's your cousin?"

"The one in the gray sweatshirt," I replied and motioned to Lia with a head tilt.

"She's cute. Bring her with you, but leave the other geeks behind."

He smiled and slipped a piece of paper inside my hand. It contained an address and phone number. Then he backed away slowly, staring at me speculatively from head to toe. His eyes were molten with intrigue and arousal. And as his eyes roamed over me, I suddenly become aware of all my female parts. My breasts heaved up to attention. Blood quickly rushed through my body. My loins ached in response to every nuance in his stare and body language. He knew he had done something to me. Still backing away, he hit me again with that wonderful smile of his.

Jamie rushed over.

"Oh my God, is he interested in you?" he asked excitedly. "He is like the cutest guy in school."

Yeah, he is definitely gay, I concluded.

I smiled and just shrugged. I didn't feel comfortable talking about it in front of them. Lia was giving me a peculiar look. I don't think she liked that I was getting attention at her school in front of her friends. At least that's how it felt.

"No, I wouldn't say he's interested," I replied, trying to downplay it as much as possible. "He just wanted to know if I was new here."

As we started walking off again, I grabbed Lia and held her back. I whispered to her what football guy said to me. I asked her if that was something she'd be interested in.

"Are you kidding me?" was her response.

But I wasn't sure what to make of it.

"Is that a yes or a no?"

"*Yes!*" she exclaimed. "Do you realize what this will do for my social status?"

We hurried through lunch and then ditched Jamie, Janette, and Danielle. Lia told them we were skipping school for the rest of the day. But she didn't say why or where we were going. I could tell they were suspicious, but I didn't care. They weren't my friends.

. . .

Soon after we were on the Q train northbound to Coney Island. Football guy, whose name I later learned was Sean, lived in the Marlboro Housing Projects in Gravesend, Brooklyn. We got off at Stillwell Avenue and transferred to the N train. From the N train we got off at 86th Street and walked along West 8th Street into the projects. His apartment was in one of the many high rises along West 11th Street. We entered and took the elevator to the tenth floor.

Sean greeted us at the door. Inside Biz Markie's "Just a Friend" was playing in the background as Sean ushered us through a small foyer and out into the living room. Dimly lit, a thin cloud of gray smoke suspended in the air and stung my eyes as we walked in. Around the room, flavored incense burned throughout, but it wasn't enough to mask the distinct smell of marijuana. The apartment was decorated with dated furniture—two couches that looked like they were manufactured in the 1970s were covered with dingy tapestry, the floor was faded linoleum, and flowered wallpaper covered the walls.

There were ten people in the apartment—six guys and four girls. I assumed Lia and I were invited to balance the ratio between guys and girls. In any case, passing introductions were made. Some waved, some smiled, and a few of them didn't even acknowledge us.

The group was made up of juniors and seniors, which excited Lia being the only freshmen there. She began mingling right away, hoping to improve her social standing in school. I found it rather odd, considering Lia was normally somewhat of an introvert. High school had changed her.

For a brief moment, Sean disappeared into the kitchen and then came back with two beers. It was a cheap, no-frills brand but beer nonetheless.

"Here you go," he said, flashing his smile again.

Lia and I looked at each other.

"Go ahead, have a drink and loosen up," he persuaded, but the subtext was more like go ahead, get drunk so we can really party.

Admittedly, I wanted to loosen up. It had been a long time since I did anything fun and I wanted this. Also, there was chemistry between Sean and I that I couldn't ignore. I grabbed the can of beer from his hand and tossed it back like a jock at a fraternity party.

"YEAH," Sean screamed. "I like your style."

Before I knew it he was handing me another beer and then another and another. Every time I finished one he was there with another one. In no time at all I was buzzing hard and pulling on every joint that got passed around. I lost track of how much I had, but I knew I had overdone it. Things weren't making sense anymore and a sickening feeling was coming over me.

I panned the living room from end to end looking for Lia but she wasn't there. Across from me on the other tapestry-covered couch, a guy and girl were making out. Next to them on a recliner, another couple was going at it, undressing one another. Sitting beside me, Sean was fondling my breasts and the inside of my thighs. Feeling nauseous, I scooted over, but I didn't get very far. Next to us, a girl had her head buried in some guy's lap. For some reason I thought it was Lia.

"Lia?" I called out and tapped her shoulder.

The girl looked up. It wasn't Lia. She gave me an odd look then grabbed his exposed penis and continued. Sean started laughing and pulled me back to his side. He began touching me once again, this time putting his hand down my pants. I liked Sean. And had I not been drunk, things might've been different. But Sean was aggressive and he wasn't reading my body language. The more he grabbed me the sicker I felt. Finally, I pushed him away and stood up but that was a huge mistake. The room spun around so fast I had to close my eyes. An awful rumbling erupted in my stomach and I knew what was coming next. I started heading for the bathroom.

"Where are you going?" he asked.

"I have to go to the bathroom," I replied, trying to look somewhat composed.

But I wasn't. I didn't feel well at all.

"Alright, I'll get you another beer."

I didn't want any more beer, or weed for that matter. I just wanted to find Lia and leave. Feeling hot and uncomfortable, I staggered to a window for fresh air. The window was locked, but outside the sun sparkled off unfamiliar buildings standing side by side. I looked away, wincing in pain as my head started to throb and my stomach fluttered with nausea. Even worse, I started to salivate as that all-too-familiar rancid taste of bile filled my mouth. This was exactly how I felt the night I threw up at the barbeque. I had to find Lia and leave before I made a fool of myself.

I hurried to the back of the three-bedroom apartment and started opening doors. The first room I walked into was empty. I turned and opened the door across from me. And what I saw was shocking. My mouth flew open. I couldn't believe my eyes. Lia was in bed with two guys. The three of them were naked and not holding back. I stood there staring in disbelief. Too busy to notice me, they were doing things I didn't know Lia was into.

I closed my eyes and took a collective breath, and that's when Sean came up behind me. Startled, I turned and faced him. He was holding a beer and smiling again. He was always smiling.

"Why you standing here spying on them?" he said, as he grabbed my waist with his free hand and pulled me close to him.

He took a sip from the beer then put the can to my lips. I tried to turn away, but he tipped the can in mouth and forced me to take a swallow.

"Let's go make our own fun."

He took my hand and led me into the adjacent room. Then he handed me the beer and closed the door behind him. Still feeling sick, I set the can down and sat on the edge of the bed. It was all I could do. Fierce waves of dizziness were hitting me in short intervals. I looked at Sean. He had taken off his shirt and was unbuckling his pants.

I shook my head.

"I don't feel good," I told him, barely uttering the words.

I don't even think he heard me. He exposed his hardened penis and brought it to my face.

"Sean, did you hear what I said?"

Still smiling, he grabbed the back of my head and forced himself into my mouth. My stomach clenched and I gagged for air. I tried to resist but he was too strong. There was nothing I could do to prevent what happened next.

Vomit everywhere, most of it on Sean and his now flaccid

penis. He was in shock, flabbergasted, unable to move. I shoved him aside and bolted out the door. I staggered across the hall to the room Lia was in. I don't recall exactly what I said, but she jumped up right away and started dressing.

"Oh my God, are you okay?" she asked with concern.

I wasn't okay. There was more to come. As I start puking again, Sean emerged from the bedroom and he was angry.

"What the hell is wrong with you?" he shouted.

What could I say? Nothing. I just wiped my mouth with the back of my hand and walked away. I headed for the front door and out to the bank of elevators. I started pushing buttons like a crazy person. It seemed like forever, but finally, one came and just in time. Lia came stumbling out the door, half dressed and out of breath. She jumped in the elevator.

The descending motion didn't agree with my stomach. I vomited again. Outside, the cool December air felt good, and only then did I start to recover a little bit. After a short break, we made our way out of the projects. Not paying attention, we walked in the opposite direction from which we came and ended up on the other side of the projects near Lafayette High School. Annoyed that we went the wrong way, we walked north up Stillwell Avenue looking for a convenience store. Five blocks later, we stopped at a 7-Eleven and got a bottle of water. I rinsed out my mouth and then we walked across the street to the 25th Avenue train station. We took the D train back to Coney Island and then switched for the southbound Q back to my apartment.

Chapter 20

Around my house we didn't make a big deal about Christmas. I remembered as a kid my grandmother would take out the old artificial tree and set it up in the corner of the living room. We didn't have a lot of presents to put underneath it, but we were thankful for the little things my grandmother often reminded us. Perhaps the biggest thing about the holidays was the huge Christmas dinners she'd make. My grandmother was a great cook and nothing was too extravagant. But as she got on in years the dinners got smaller and smaller and soon the tree didn't even come out anymore.

This year Christmas vacation came and went in the blink of an eye. I couldn't have cared less. The yuletide spirit just wasn't in me. The only notable thing about this holiday season was that my father gave me a laptop. It was supposed to be for school, and it was the ideal gift. I could've used it to do homework, write reports, or study for exams. But after the Christmas vacation I stopped going to school. Seeing Lia's school made mine seem unbearable. The laptop just sat around collecting dust until my mother finally sold it for crack.

It was a cold Friday morning when I rolled out of bed hugging myself. There was a chill in the house that would've made a polar bear shiver. *Damn my crummy apartment.* Winter had arrived and it came in full force. During the night, a storm pummeled the city and covered Brooklyn with a blanket of snow several inches thick. It was a sight to marvel at—white sidewalks and leafless, snow-laden trees against a backdrop of monochromatic tones. The cityscape was Norman Rockwell picturesque. I loved New York in the winter. But I hated how the city looked after the snowfall when the perilously unplowed streets turn into pathways of filthy slush.

I was standing by the window when my grandmother came in with my little brother. She sat down to feed him and turned on the TV. The morning news was on. The weatherman was reporting more harsh weather in the forecast. I turned and listened. He predicted another six to twelve inches of wet, heavy snow to come amid blustery winds throughout the day. My grandmother suggested I stay home from school, but little did she know I had been out of school since Christmas vacation.

I called Lia and told her to come over. She packed a bag and took a cab to my place. We spend most of the weekend inside because of the snowstorm outside. We painted our nails and did each other's hair. But mostly we watched TV and played with my little brother. Overall, it was a pretty dull and uneventful weekend.

Lia didn't say anything about her parents while she was there, so I assumed no news meant things were okay. I did, however, want to talk to her about what she did at Sean's party. But each time I tried to I lost my nerve. It was strange because normally we could talk about anything. But this for some reason embarrassed me. And although I was curious, I couldn't bring myself to ask her how it was or if she had done this before and what else she was into that I didn't know about.

Before walking in on Lia, I had never given a threesome any thought. It was something I had only seen in my mother's porno movies—something I viewed as being distasteful. I presumed that ordinary people didn't actually do this, or at least I didn't know any until now.

Walking in on her left me with overwhelmingly curiosity. I began to sink deep into the fantasy of what it would be like—the excitement, the pressure, the control they must've had over her.

I kept wishing she'd bring it up so I wouldn't have to. But Lia never said anything.

. . .

By Monday morning the storm had passed, and the streets were once again busy with pedestrians. I stood by the window as I had done many mornings for the past two weeks, wondering how I was going to spend my day. Normally, I'd ride the trains back and forth or parade the malls window shopping. But now it had gotten cold and I couldn't bear to do that anymore. I got back in bed and rolled myself into the comforter. Just then, my grandmother walked in asking why I was still in bed and not getting ready for school. I just ignored her and pulled the covers over my head.

Later on, I turned on the TV. The weatherman said there'd be more bad weather on top of the bad weather we were already having. *That's just great*, I thought. For a brief second I wondered what the weather was like in California. I went in the kitchen and called Lia. She told me that Sean was having another gathering at his place, and he wanted me to come. Surprisingly, he wasn't as bitter as I thought he'd be. He told her he felt partly responsible for what happened. He admitted that had he not forced so much alcohol on me things might not have ended up the way they did. I was pleased to hear that and agreed to see him again.

After a quick shower, I ate some leftovers my grandmother fixed for me and left. Outside, the temperature was below zero. Most of the heavy snow had been plowed and all that remained were icy walkways. I headed to the train station, walking quickly along frozen sidewalks, trying not to fall on my face. On the train ride over, Lia told me not to drink too much. I wasn't sure how to respond so I shrugged and said nothing.

"I just want you to enjoy yourself, that's all," she continued.

"What makes you think I don't enjoy myself?" I huffed.

"I don't know, Lonnie, maybe because every time you drink you get drunk and puke on someone."

"That's not true." I smiled awkwardly.

"I'm being serious," she said, this time with concern. "I'm worried about you. Maybe your father was right . . . "

"Right about what?"

"Maybe you are predisposed to his alcoholism?"

I laughed at the idea.

"I'm not predisposed to anything. I like drinking. That's all."

"I do too, but I know when to stop."

Lia had touched a soft spot. My feelings were hurt. And rather than embrace the fact that I could be developing a problem, I got angry and went on the defense.

"Well, sorry I don't have the courage that you do."

"What's that supposed to mean?"

"I need a couple of drinks to loosen up, okay. I can't just jump into bed with ten guys like you."

Lia started laughing, which annoyed me more.

"First of all, it wasn't ten guys, it was two. And if you're curious about it, which I know you are, then why don't you just ask me about it?"

It was as if she had read my mind. I was totally curious.

"What made you do it?" I asked eagerly.

"Well, I really didn't have to give it much thought," she answered without care. "After my dad cheated on my mom, and after I experienced the same thing with Anthony, I came to the conclusion that men are liars."

"That's a pretty broad generalization, don't you think?"

"Didn't you say your father did the same thing to your mom?"

Lia didn't get an argument from me.

"My dad did it twice," she continued. "He went back to his mistress even after he promised not to see her again. I realized that I could never trust a man, and I could never give my heart to one. But I like men and I like sex, so what difference does it make if I do it with one or two or ten?" Lia laughed.

What her father did had scarred her emotionally and left a bad taste in her mouth. At the time, I couldn't comprehend the complexity of her problem enough to offer any sympathy or advice. Instead, I probed around for the dirty details of what took place in the room. Lia didn't hold back and after listening to her, I knew this was something I wanted to try more than ever.

. . .

We arrived at Sean's door and Lia knocked a few times. Inside, I heard movement, music, and muffled voices. The chain lock rattled, then the door swung open. Sean appeared wearing his usual charismatic smile.

"I'm glad you could make it," he said, stepping out into the hallway.

He closed the door behind him and asked if we had any money.

"We're a little low on beer, and I really want to keep this party going."

It seemed like a harmless request, so I went into my pocket and pulled out twenty dollars from the Christmas money my father had sent me. Lia dug in her bag and retrieved a twenty as well. Sean snatched the money and kissed us both on the cheek. He told us to go inside and get comfortable and that he'd be back in a few minutes.

The scene inside was much different from the last time we were there. Fourteen people were spread out across the apartment—nine guys and five girls, most of them holding a drink in one hand and a cigarette or joint in the other. A couple of topless guys and girls appeared to be dancing in the middle of the living room. But upon closer observation, it was more like a grope fest, with no two individuals actually moving in unison. No two people seemed to be partnered, all exposed flesh, male or female, was free for grabbing. And all around the apartment, guys and girls were either locked in a kiss or fondling one another.

For a moment, I was frozen. I wasn't sure what to do or what to think. I looked over at Lia. She was already in the crowd mingling. Lia had become quite popular since the last time we were there. I made my way to a chair and sat down. A couple of guys approached me, but I gave them the cold shoulder and told them I was waiting for someone. About twenty minutes passed before Lia spotted me sitting by myself. She came over and kneeled beside me.

"I wanted you to restrain a little," she said, "but I didn't mean for you to hideout in the corner."

I smiled uncomfortably. Without alcohol in my system, I didn't have the courage to be carefree and uninhibited. Lia gave me a sympathetic look and handed me her half-drunken beer.

"Just don't overdo it," she advised.

That day, I realized that I didn't know how to not overdo it.

After that initial half beer Lia gave me, I went on and consumed much more, including quite a bit of the cheap whisky and vodka that Sean brought back from the liquor store. To my surprise, I didn't vomit on anyone. I did that on the train ride home. But my memory of what happened at the apartment was blurry.

I remembered having sex with Sean, my body was limp and almost lifeless. Barely coherent, I had no degree of controlled thought or observation. All my senses were faint and dulled. There were other people in the room, but how many or who they were I couldn't say. I remembered being touched by nearly everyone in the room, several pairs of hands running along my face and body while Sean selfishly rode me until climax. I recalled no pleasure from the experience, just the vague memory of Sean getting up and someone else mounting me. I couldn't say precisely how many times that happened, or how it started or how it ended. I mostly remembered Lia waking me up and helping me dress right before we left the apartment.

On the train ride home, Lia didn't say much. She listened to her iPod and stared out the window at the frozen city flashing by. I, on the other hand, closed my eyes and tried to relax. But the speeding train was making me nauseous. Thank goodness the southbound Q to Manhattan was empty this time of day because I threw up right where I sat. Lia looked at me with disgust but still gave me a sympathetic back rub. When I thought I was done puking, we got up and changed subway cars at the next stop. But once the train started moving again, I threw up again. We changed cars two more times before we got to the Cortelyou Road station and disembarked. Lia walked me to my apartment to make sure I got home safe. But she didn't stick around, just stayed long enough to call a cab back to her place.

When I walked in the house, my grandmother was talking to herself as usual. I had a splitting headache and it was the last thing I wanted to hear. I should've left with Lia, but somehow, I had a feeling she didn't want my company anymore. Instead, I took a long needed shower and then went to sleep.

Chapter 21

The following day I got a phone call from Sean. It started out as a call of concern but ended up with him needing a favor. He told me that he needed a new pair of cleats to play football. He said he had half of the money and was wondering if I could help him out with the other half. I didn't mind. But the funny thing with Sean was that the words *borrow* or *payback* never came out of his mouth. It was always, "Could you help me with this, or could you give me that."

My father had sent me two hundred dollars for Christmas, and I had one hundred left over, forty of which I gave to Sean to buy a pair of Nike football cleats. Afterwards, we got lunch and took in a movie, both of which I paid for. I enjoyed hanging out with him. It was the first time we conversed outside a party environment, and I was not in a drug and alcohol induced stupor.

Sean was charming. And aside from being good looking, he was intelligent and motivated. At just the tender age of eighteen, he already knew what he wanted out of life. His plan was to graduate with honors and accept a scholarship to a major university where he'd play football and study law. During the off seasons, he would do internships at one or more of the law firms in the city. Ultimately, his goal was to work for one of the major firms as a litigator, buy a house in the suburbs, and give his children lots of opportunities.

Listening to Sean, I began to think about my own life. My father had worked very hard to get me into that all-girl school, and there I was skipping class again. But I didn't care. I wanted to hang around with Sean. He said I was his girlfriend. And even though he let his football buddies touch me and have sex with me when I'd been drinking, I didn't mind. As disturbing as that may sound, I had come to accept it; I had fallen for Sean very hard.

Over the next four months, I followed him around like a lost puppy, partying without care or caution, doing anything he wanted. And Sean wanted a lot. He wanted money for football gear, money for sneakers and clothes, money to buy video games, money to go out with his friends. And he wanted money for alcohol for his weekly hooky parties. Every penny I had, or should I say every penny my father gave me, was spent on Sean. I couldn't come up with lies fast enough to keep the money coming. I hated lying to my father, I hated taking advantage of his kindness, but I didn't want to disappoint Sean.

My father understood, or at least he believed that I was growing up and needed a lot more things. And because he couldn't trust my mother, he added me to his bank account and sent me my own ATM card. Every week he'd transfer money into the account so that I'd be able to get the things I needed. He trusted me to be mature and responsible and to use the money wisely for things such as school supplies, clothes, and toiletries. But I didn't. Lia tried to warn me, but I was too caught up to care about anything she said.

. . .

It was now April, the chill and gloom of winter had finally passed. I walked through the front door of my apartment after coming from one of Sean's crazy hooky parties. I was drunk, but it was hard to tell. My tolerance had improved significantly, as I had been drinking a lot more.

My mother was standing in the living room sucking on a cigarette. She was high and I could tell. Her pupils looked like two black olives. I should've known she was angry by the way she was tapping her foot and the way her arms were folded across her chest. But I was fading under the flood of alcohol and marijuana myself and wasn't sure what to think.

She barked something that sounded like, "Why haven't you been going to school?" The words danced around in my head for several seconds before I realized what was going on. My behavior had finally caught up to me.

Two weeks earlier, the caseworker from the Bureau of Child Welfare had called the house to do a follow up. My grandmother told her that since her visit, I had graduated from junior high school and I'd been attending a new all-girl school in Manhattan. The caseworker in turn contacted the school and found out that I haven't been attending class. So she paid us another visit. And as luck would have it, my mother was home the day the caseworker came by, whereas normally she'd be out running the streets selling her body for drugs.

My mother took a final pull on her cigarette. She dropped the butt in the ashtray and blew out a large cloud of smoke.

"You gonna answer me," she yelled, lurching towards me.

I didn't think my mother was going to hit me. The last thing I heard was a loud, hard clap of her hand striking the side of face. I blacked out momentarily. I lost my footing and fell back on my ass. My vision went blurry and my ears started ringing. I looked up, and she was towering over me screaming with rage. I could barely make anything out. All I heard was, "Didn't I warn you?"

I lost my temper. I jumped up and in a clumsy, pathetic attempt to fight back I took a wild swing at her face. I missed. She grabbed my arm and slapped me again. My body went limp and I fell back down. As I hit the ground, a salty, warm, metallic taste invaded my mouth. I touched my lips to discover leaking blood. Short winded, tired, and defeated, I tried to catch my breath as she stood over me yelling again. I knew I couldn't beat her, but I wouldn't give her the satisfaction of submitting. I got up slowly and faced her again. But had it not been for my grandmother's interference she would've put me down again.

My grandmother took me to the bathroom. She tried to help me find my composure, but I asked her to leave me alone. I was a hysterical mess. It was the first time my mother had hit me. The side of my face and lips were swollen from where she slapped me. I was furious. As I stood over the sink, I cried like a baby while cursing her existence. After several minutes, I finally ran the cold water and washed my face.

Shortly after, my grandfather came over. By then, my mother had been long gone. I couldn't say I blame her, his mere presence alone annoyed the hell out of me. And just like the last time, I was forced to listen to him lecture. I had sobered up pretty quickly after fighting with my mother. But still, I couldn't stand to listen to another one of my grandfather's speeches about why I should marry a white man. I told him politely that I didn't feel well and excused myself shortly into his rambling.

I took a long, hot shower and then climbed into the old sofa bed. Still too upset to sleep, I turned on the TV and relaxed for a while. My grandmother brought me a bowl of chicken noodle soup, and I nursed it until sleep finally took me. I was pretty worn out and might've slept through the night if not for my mother shouting on the phone.

"I'm not going to put up with her shit anymore," she yelled at my father over and over again.

I pretended to be asleep and listened while she complained to him about how hard I was making her life.

"She's a miserable child," she continued. "She refuses to go to school, she never helps out around the house, all she does is run the streets and get high all day."

I could hear my father's voice over the receiver. He was speaking with mixed emotions and asked how that was possible.

"With the money you've been sending her of course," she boasted victoriously. "I told you Lonnie wasn't ready for that kind of responsibility."

How on earth did she know what I was doing? And how could she tell him that? *Oh, the hypocrisy*, I thought. It was okay for her to run the streets and get high but not okay for me. I wanted to snatch the phone from her hand and cram it down her throat. But that would've landed me another beating. So I listened a little longer as the two of them went back and forth screaming at each other, blaming one another for what happened. It was hard to imagine that the two of them actually liked each other at one point.

"You won't help me with the bills around here," my mother

said, "but you'll send her money to drink and get high."

"I send her money because I can't trust you. You are her mother, why would you steal from her?"

"I told you, I do what I have to do to keep things together around here."

"You do what you do to stay high," my father said.

"Whatever, say what you want about me. But your daughter is getting high, and you're paying for it. Who's a bad parent now?" my mother taunted.

There was a brief pause. She had found his weak spot again.

"It's your fault she's doing this," he finally said. "This is all you have shown her. I told you that you need be a good example for her, didn't I?"

"It's too late for that," my mother admitted. "You can set the example if you want. I'm not going to deal with her anymore. Lonnie is lazy and selfish. She refuses to go to school, and all she wants to do is drink, get high, and screw around. Honestly, I'm surprised she's not pregnant already."

"What are you saying?" my father asked, sounding confused. "Do we need to get her on birth control?"

"No, not we. You can figure that out yourself. Come and get her before I throw her out of the house, okay. Because if that caseworker comes here again, I'm going to lose my state assistance and then we'll all be homeless."

My mother had given up on me. But thinking back, it's safe to say she never really believed in me to begin with. I was an accident she was forced to deal with, nothing more than an inconvenience. But I was a paycheck from the New York City Welfare Department and from my father, so she kept me around. That night, I gave up on her too. I realized that she was too far gone to ever love me and care for me the way I needed to be cared for, the way my father had been. Finally, after about twenty minutes of yelling at each other there was silence. My mother walked over and pulled the covers from over my head.

"I know you're not sleeping," she said and tossed the phone at me. "Your father wants to talk to you."

I stared at the phone for about a minute, thinking *how am I going to explain this one.* My father had put all his trust in me and I let him down. What could I possibly say? Sorry? My mother was right, I was selfish. I was no different than she was, running around spending my father's hard-earned money on drugs and alcohol. I took several deep breaths then picked up the phone.

"Yes, Daddy," I managed after a long silence.

I don't think I was ever more afraid to talk to my father. But the conversation was brief. There was no, "Lonnie, how could you?" or "What were you thinking?" or "I'm so disappointed in you." He simply said, "You're coming to California."

I wanted to object, but somehow, I didn't think it was up for discussion. I wanted to say sorry and beg for his forgiveness, promise to never do it again. But I don't think it would've made a difference.

"Yes, Daddy," was all I said. Then all I heard was a dial tone.

Chapter 22

In the morning, I called my aunt and told her what happened. She insisted I come over and stay for a couple of days. Auntie Pamela never liked my mother and for years had said she was not fit to be a parent.

She called my father and talked to him, tried to convince him to let me stay in New York with her. She told him she could give me the kind of parenting and mentoring I needed. She bragged how Lia was doing great in school, said Lia was a model child who obeyed curfew and didn't drink or smoke. Lia did a good job hiding things from her parents. I kept thinking, *If only I had taken a page from her playbook and been more discrete. It probably wouldn't have killed me to go to school once in a while rather than stay out for months at a time.* In any case, my aunt got nowhere with my father.

"I'm sorry, Pamela, Lonnie cannot stay in New York," he told her.

"I understand, but things will be different this time," my aunt assured him. "I can give Lonnie the care she deserves."

"I know you mean well, and I appreciate that. But I want to get her out of Brooklyn altogether. She has picked up too many bad habits already, and I have to set her straight. I have to make sure she grows up to be a good and productive member of society. At this rate, she's going to end up just like her mother."

. . .

Sean must've called me about thirty times. And each time he called I gave him a different excuse as to why I couldn't see him. I needed time to let the swelling of my face and lips recede before I could face him. Finally, after the weekend, I went to see him. I met up with Lia at her school and we rode the train to his house.

I was nervous about seeing him after avoiding him for so long. But Sean gave me a great big hug as soon as I walked through the door. My heart sank back into my chest, the butterflies left my stomach, and suddenly things felt right again. I was flattered that he missed me and returned his embrace. I held him tightly for as long as I could. I didn't want to leave Sean, and I didn't want to leave New York.

Finally, he stepped back and looked into my eyes.

"What took you so long," he said, smiling as always. "I did tell you I was having people over, right?"

"Yes, and I'm sorry I'm late," I replied. "I had to help my aunt do some things around the house this morning."

"Alright, that's okay. I'm just glad you're here now. But as I was saying . . . "

I already knew what was coming next. It was usually the first thing he'd asked me.

"People will be here soon, and I should probably get to the liquor store. How much money do you have, sweetie?"

I handed him my last twenty dollars. Sean chuckled.

"I have a lot of people coming over, is this all you have?" he asked, looking disappointed.

He shook his head and mumbled something under his breath. His mood suddenly changed, and I was having a hard time reading him at this point. He seemed annoyed that I didn't have more money. But what could I do? I looked over at Lia. She rolled her eyes and let out a long breath. Lia had stop liking Sean once she saw that he was using me. He didn't care about me, nor did he really miss me like he said over the phone. He only wanted to see me because he needed money to buy booze for his party. Lia dug into her pocket and reluctantly donated another twenty dollars.

Sean snatched the money and walked off, as if the forty dollars still wasn't enough.

"Sean, hold up," I called out, running after him. "I need to talk to you."

"Right now," he snapped.

I couldn't understand why his mood had suddenly changed or why he was being short with me.

"Yes, right now," I said, not shying away.

"Okay, but make it quick," he said.

I told him about the caseworker from the Bureau of Child Welfare and what happened with my mother. Sean just stared at me. He showed very little concern or sympathy. Finally, I told him I was moving to California, and that was when I got a reaction out of him.

"What do you mean you're moving?" he erupted. "You said you'd always be here to help me."

Like a sobering punch in the face, I realized he only cared about one thing—himself. In a brief second, the conversation went from being about me to being about him. Lia was right, Sean never cared about me, and he certainly didn't need my help; he needed my money.

"So when are you leaving?" he asked with frustration in his voice. "Are you leaving for good? Will you be back?"

"I don't know, my father didn't—"

"What am I going to do? I'm starting college in the fall. You said you'd help me."

I couldn't get a word in edgewise. Sean was making this entirely about him.

"Sean, did you hear anything I said?"

"Yeah, I heard you, but did you hear me? I'm starting school in the fall. Don't you remember your promise to me?"

"Come on, Sean, can we please stop talking about you for a minute," I yelled. "I'm in a lot of trouble with father, and I could really use your support right now."

"Oh, like the support you were supposed to give me?"

I took a deep breath and tried to make one last plea with him.

"I don't want to leave," I said. "But my father is making me. I'm sorry I don't have any money right now, but we can work something out."

Sean rolled his eyes.

"How do I know I can trust you?"

"Are you kidding me, Sean?" Lia interjected. "Come on, Lonnie, let's just leave. He is so not worth it."

Lia took my hand and we walked away.

"Go ahead and leave," Sean said loudly. "I don't care. I can get another girlfriend in a minute. You ain't shit, Lonnie. That's why I let all my boys take a turn. I was doing you a favor by letting you hang out with me."

Everyone was looking at me. I stopped and took a deep breath. I had to.

"So go ahead and leave," he continued. "But once you walk out that door, you better not ever come back."

Sean was trying his best to push my buttons. I was really upset, but mainly with myself for being so naive. Outside, Lia stuck a cigarette in my mouth and lit it. I took a long, hard drag and exhaled slowly. Lia asked if I was okay. I nodded my head, took two more drags, and then flicked the lit cigarette at Sean's door.

Outside, we found a park bench and sat down. Lia placed her arm around me and held me close. She didn't say anything, and I didn't need to. She just held me. We sat there for several minutes until I finally broke down into tears. I cried until my eyes burned. I cried until my tear ducts ran dry. I cried until I didn't see the point anymore. And it was at that moment that I understood what Lia meant about not ever giving her heart to a man.

Chapter 23

Two week later, I got a call from my father. He was flying to New York, and he told me to pack my belongings. I had been anticipating his call. In my mind, I went over everything I wanted to say to him. But once on the phone, my throat constricted and nothing I rehearsed in my head came out right. Our conversation was brief and right to the point.

"So, Daddy, how's work?"

"Fine," he replied curtly.

"How was your long deployment?"

"Deployment was fine."

"Are you glad to be back?"

"Yes, but I don't like coming home to bad news."

"I'm sorry, Daddy."

"How could you, Lonnie? You gave me your word you would stop this nonsense."

"I know, I really messed up. It won't happen again. Please give me another chance."

"Absolutely not, you've run out of chances. You are coming to California and that's it. I cannot sleep at night knowing my fifteen-year-old daughter is running the streets of Brooklyn, doing God knows what."

"I swear, Daddy," I pleaded. "I won't do anything like this again."

"Lonnie, this is not up for discussion. For the last time, you are coming to California. So have your bags packed when I get there."

My father hung up the phone without as much as a goodbye.

Ever since my father showed up on my doorstep, I had been fighting to stay out of California. Now it was going to happen whether I liked it or not. Being the stubborn child that I was, I began thinking of all kinds of crazy ideas.

I thought about hiding out at Lia's house. But that was too obvious. I considered running away, finding a job, and getting my own place to live. But as a minor, I couldn't get a job without the consent of a parent or legal guardian. I had already tried that once and failed. I had nowhere to go and no one to turn to. Even Sean lost interest in me now that I didn't have any money.

. . .

My father arrived early Friday morning on a gorgeous spring day. New York had finally recovered from the terrible winter, and the city was alive again. Trees and flowers were in full bloom, old folks were out walking, and little kids were out playing. Summer was on its way and regrettably, I wasn't going to be there for it. My father's visit was brief. He only stayed for the weekend, just long enough to visit his family and then take me back to California.

The plane ride was miserable. My father and I both dipped in and out of sleep during the seven-and-half-hour flight. There was little conversation between us.

The air was heavy with tension. Numerous questions were rolling around in my head but went unasked because I didn't want to piss off my father off again. After the plane took off I went right to sleep. Later, I woke up dazed, staring around the plane's cabin. For a second I had forgotten where I was. Then I looked over at my father sleeping with his mouth open and remembered I was on my way to California.

Still harboring feelings of bitterness, I reached into my carry-on and found my iPod. Music always made me feel better. But just my luck, the battery on my iPod was dead. Desperate for entertainment, I tried watching the in-flight movie but there was nothing of interest on. Frustrated, I glanced mindlessly through the magazines behind the seat. Finally, I got up and went to the restroom.

When I got back to my seat my father was still asleep. I sat back down and looked at my watch. We had only been in the air three hours but it felt like twenty. My father slept for most of the flight back, and when he was awake he said very little. I sat silent, staring out the window into the sky and clouds, thinking.

I forced myself to examine all the things I had done. I started to think that maybe my mother was right. I had been inconsiderate and selfish. I did only what pleased me or what benefited me. I continually disappointed and hurt people who cared about me. I had self-esteem issues that made me slutty. I had sex with anyone who showed me attention, just so I could feel good about myself. I let Sean take advantage of me because I wanted to feel loved.

After I confronted these truths, I began to feel empty and worthless. Even worse, I felt ashamed. I sank into my seat and held my head up, it was all I could do to hold back the tears. For about thirty minutes I sat there crying quietly, wallowing in self-pity until finally, I fell asleep.

I woke up just as the stewardess had come around with refreshments. My father woke up just long enough to down a cup of ice water, ask me if I was okay, then doze off again. I grabbed a Cherry Coke and sipped it slowly. As I watched him sleep, I wondered how he had the patience to deal with me. I wondered why I hadn't inherited his tolerance or calm disposition or any of his other fine qualities. *Surely these characteristics are in me*, I thought. *I have his artistic ability so why not his temperament or his patience or his cunning?*

It occurred to me that I hadn't spent enough time with my father and too much time around my mother. I had managed to absorb all her bad qualities and none of his good qualities. From that point on, I decided that I was going to change my life around. I was going to become a better person. No more inconsiderate and selfish Lonnie. The new me would be thoughtful, considerate, and responsible. I told myself I would stop drinking and doing drugs. And I promised myself that I would only give my body to someone who respected me.

I felt a little bit better stepping off the plane, better than I did when I got on. We walked to baggage claim in silence, with my father leading the way and me trailing the rear. While we waited at baggage claim, I apologized again.

My father snapped.

"I don't want any more apologies," he said, looking tired and fed up. "Your apologies are paper thin, Lonnie. And frankly, they don't carry much weight anymore."

"But I mean it this time, Daddy," was all I could come back with.

"I don't want apologies. I want action."

My father was right. I had said sorry too many times and to too many people. But I was going to change, whether he believed me or not. I was determined to show him that I could be better.

Chapter 24

My father became a different person. He wasn't friendly and fun anymore. He wasn't the cool, laidback, easy-going guy he used to be. Decisions were now made for me instead of by me. He had turned into a micromanager, a hardened and strict disciplinarian, an overprotective and overbearing pain in the ass.

My father came up with a set of rules that he insisted I follow: no smoking, no drinking, no dating, no cursing. I had to remove the *N* word from my vocabulary. But the rule I had the biggest problem with was the curfew. I hadn't had a curfew since I was ten years old. The curfew was in three parts. One, I had to come home immediately after school. Two, if I wanted to go out afterwards I had to tell him where I was going and who I was going to be with. And three, I couldn't stay out past eight on weekdays and nine on weekends.

My father wasted no time and enrolled me in high school. As if the curfew wasn't shocking enough, I had to start out in summer school. Because I had a history of truancy and poor grades, I had to take two remedial classes before I could start as a freshman. It was a math and writing class because those were areas I had the most trouble with. I was not happy going to classes for six weeks out of the summer.

The school itself was great. It was within walking distance of our house, spread out over a large campus with a huge faculty of teachers and staff. There was just one problem—the students were nothing like me. I was one of a handful of black students amidst a sea of white and Mexican kids. It wasn't so much that they were white or Mexican, they just weren't like me. Even the other black kids weren't like me. They walked differently, talked differently, and dressed differently.

After a couple days of classes I did what I had always done when distressed—I called Lia.

Lia was glad to hear from me, but she wasn't the least bit sympathetic to my situation.

"Lonnie," she said, "be glad you have someone who loves you enough to take care of you. Your father is not intentionally trying to ruin your life as you say."

"Then why all the stupid rules?" I pouted.

"Because that's what parents do. They establish rules and guidelines for us to follow. And let's face it, up until now you haven't been following any. You've just been doing your own thing. At least I make a conscious effort to go to school once in a while, and I know when to stop drinking. I try to come home at a decent hour, and I try not to give my parents too much to worry about. You on the other hand, not only do you break all the rules but you make up your own."

"Okay fine," I conceded. "But why California? Why can't he move back to Brooklyn if he wants to be a part of my life?"

"Come on, Lonnie, you already know the answer to that."

Lia sounded frustrated with me.

"What's your problem?" I fired back. "I was just saying—"

"I know what you're saying," she interjected. "But this is what I'm saying. I know California is not like Brooklyn, but surely you can make the best of it. Take advantage of the opportunities your father is giving you. Some good may come out of it. You might actually finish high school, and if you're lucky you might not turn into a statistic."

"A statistic? What are you talking about?"

There was a long pause. I suddenly felt nervous.

"Talk to me, Lia."

"My period was late this month," she finally continued. "For two weeks I was out of my mind with worry, not to mention scared to death. I don't know what I would've done had I been pregnant. Thank God it finally came, but it got me thinking."

"Thinking about what?" I said with a sigh of relief.

"That maybe I've been partying too much, the drinking, the smoking, and the sex without protection. It's just a matter of time before it all catches up to me. I don't know about you, but I don't want to get pregnant. I don't want to drop out of high school so I can become a full-time mom. I don't want to be a *statistic*."

I had heard stories of girls my age getting pregnant and being forced to drop out of school. Lia's words resonated. I didn't want to become a statistic either. Her advice not only helped me regain focus but helped me realize what I didn't want most of all.

After our conversation, I told myself I was going to put Brooklyn and its influences behind me. California was my new home now, and my father and his girlfriend were the kind of role models I needed in my life. I was focused, as focused as I had ever been.

I got up every morning and went to class. But I may as well not have been there. In four weeks of attending class, I hadn't learned anything. I didn't even know my teachers' names. When it came to school, I had the attention span of a carrot. But still, every day after class I'd go straight home and attempted to do homework. I'd add up a few numbers and say that I conquered math. I scribbled on paper and called it an essay. And I'd flip through the pages of my text book and say that I studied. But it was just a façade to make my father happy and my way of keeping my promise to myself.

In truth, I was struggling, holding on for dear life. I wasn't sure how much longer I could keep up the front. I was pretending to care when deep down inside I didn't. I was pretending to be a good kid when really I wasn't. All I thought about all day was getting high, and it was beyond wishing at this point. I craved it physically. I'd salivate at the mere thought of having a cold beer and a joint. I was going to explode if I couldn't find some social outlet or a way to blow off some steam.

Chapter 25

Summer school was a drag and I couldn't wait for it to be over. It was hard trying to pay attention to information I wasn't interested in. But no matter how much I tried, my thoughts continued to drift away.

One day, I was sitting in the back of the class, as I did every day for an hour and a half daydreaming about beer and sex of all things. I had come to love the taste of beer. But since my father didn't keep alcohol in the house, I was going to have to wait until I turned twenty-one to have a beer again.

Sex occupied the other half of my thoughts. I was long overdue and every guy in school was beginning to look desirable. Sometimes I would daydream about Sean. I wondered if he thought about me or if he missed me. Probably not, but I was certain he missed my money. He may have been a jerk, but he sure knew how to throw a good hooky party.

After slapping myself back to reality for about the twentieth time, my math teacher finally put the class on a break. I headed outside to smoke one of the four cigarettes I had left in a pack I smuggled from Brooklyn—my last pack. I knew after this pack I wouldn't be able to get another one. California was not like Brooklyn. I couldn't just walk into the store and purchase beer and cigarettes without an ID. That worried me, but I had bigger problems at the moment.

As I made my way towards the door, the teacher called me over to her desk.

“Lonnie, may I have a word with you,” she said, waving me down with her hand.

I stopped in front of her desk.

“Lonnie, I’m a little concerned about you,” she started. “Are you okay?”

“Yeah, I’m okay”

“Are you sure? Is everything okay at home?”

“Everything is fine. Why, am I in trouble?” I asked nervously.

“No, you are not in trouble. I asked because you seem like you’re having a hard time staying focused. Is there anything you’d like to talk about?”

“No, I don’t need to talk about anything.”

She looked me, nodding her head slowly as if she didn’t believe me.

“Okay,” she said after a brief pause. “But if you ever need to talk to someone, I’m here.”

“Thank you, but I don’t need to talk to anyone,” I told her. “I’m just homesick, that’s all.”

. . .

Outside, the July sun was intense, but it felt good. That was one thing I liked about California. The weather was very pleasant. It didn’t have the humidity of New York.

I walked down the block and away from the school. I didn’t like smoking directly on campus for fear a teacher or counselor might see me. I propped up against a big old eucalyptus tree and pulled out my box of Newports. I lit one and took a long drag. With my eyes closed, I exhaled the smoke slowly, savoring every bit of nicotine. When I opened my eyes he was standing in from of me.

Startled, I dropped my iPod and clutched my heart.

“I’m sorry,” he said with a brilliant smile revealing the deepest dimples.

“It’s okay,” I replied, catching my breath.

"But I was wondering if you could spare a cigarette," he continued as he picked up my iPod and handed it to me.

I responded with a soft, subtle "thank you" while reaching into my pocket for the cigarettes. He took one from the pack and lit it right away. He took a long drag, then blew out a large cloud of smoke. I watched him carefully. He made something as simple as lighting a cigarette seem cool and sexy. He was not the kind of guy I would've ever imagine myself being attracted to. He was older—a lot older than the high school guys I had messed around with.

Standing six foot one, he was lean yet ripped. He wore blue jeans and a snug-fitting T-shirt that revealed his tattooed covered forearms and biceps. Multi-colored tattoos of skulls, crossbones, gargoyles, and other demonic images looked nice against his pale white skin. His wavy, blond hair was slicked back with just the right amount of gel. His smile was brilliant, and his eyes were the kind of blue you'd only see on a clear summer day.

"I'm Richard," he said and extended out his hand.

I shook his hand and replied, "Lonnie."

"It's nice to meet you, Lonnie," he continued.

Richard was gorgeous and he made me nervous. I could feel myself about to do something goofy, so I fought the urge and simply smiled. He returned my smile with one of his own and asked where I was from.

"Just up the street," I replied.

"Where are you from originally? I sense you're not from around here."

"I just moved here from New York."

"New York," he echoed. "How exciting. I've always wanted to visit New York."

"Then why don't you?"

"Because I live a pretty boring life." He shrugged.

"Really? You don't seem boring. What do you do?"

"Nothing right now. I'm in-between jobs so most days I just sit around the house, drink beer, and hang out with friends."

Oh my God, did he just say "drink beer", I thought to myself.

My eyes lit up. The tingling feeling of excitement surged through my body and my mouth began to water. I was elated at the mere thought of having alcohol again. But I had to relax. I couldn't show my excitement. I didn't want to seem too eager or too easy.

"There's nothing wrong with that," I said nonchalantly. "Occasionally, I like to do that too. Come to think of it, I haven't had a cold beer in quite some time."

I couldn't resist. I had to put it out there. I had to let him know that drinking beer was okay. Richard smiled, and then said exactly what I was hoping he'd say.

"Then we should get together one of these days and have some beers."

"I'd like that," I said and smiled.

"Come to think of it," he added, "I have beers at my apartment, so if you're not doing anything later?"

"I'm not doing anything now," I responded eagerly.

We both laughed and before I knew it we were in his apartment.

. . .

Richard's apartment was exactly the type of place you'd expect a single twenty-eight-year-old guy to have. The place was in terrible shape. Empty beer cans and alcohol bottles covered every corner of the tiny one-bedroom apartment. The carpet was dirty and worn from high traffic. Discoloration from cigarette smoke made the walls a dingy yellow. And judging from the lack of furniture in the house, he was either a very simple man or he had no money. My guess was that he was broke.

Inside, we walked through a small foyer and entered the living room. Richard looked around for a brief second and then walked over to the couch. After dusting off the potato chip crumbs and removing the candy bar wrappers from in-between the cushions, he offered me a seat. He told me to make myself at home and then went into the kitchen. I tried to get comfortable and not get grossed out. But as I looked around the room I thought to myself, *How could anyone be so messy? Even my apartment back in Brooklyn wasn't this bad.*

In front of me there appeared to be some sort of homemade coffee table. But what it was really was four cinder blocks covered by a piece of plywood. On it was a dirty ashtray filled with cigarette butts, more empty beer cans, and what looked like dirty laundry. I took a deep breath and reached for the TV remote buried beneath the pile of clothes. I turned on the TV and waited.

Shortly after, Richard returned and cleared the table. He removed the pile of clothes and took away the dirty ashtrays and empty beer cans. I offered to help, but he insisted I relax and do nothing. After tidying up somewhat, he went back into the kitchen and returned with chips, salsa, and two beers. He may have been a slob but he made up for it with hospitality.

"I don't normally drink this early," he said as he sat beside me. "But then again, it's not every day I have such lovely company over."

His comment made me blush, and once again I fought the urge to say or do something goofy.

"How old are you?" he asked.

"Nineteen," I lied.

"You're tall. You must be about five-five, right?"

"Close. Five six."

And so it went. We made small talk for a while, and I began to relax as the beer kicked in. It had been a while since I drank, and I had almost forgotten how much I love beer. I wanted to down the whole can but refrained. I promised myself I wouldn't get drunk. I didn't want to make a spectacle of myself like I had done many times before. But more importantly, I couldn't risk getting in trouble with my father.

After finishing my first beer, he offered me another. I was tempted to decline, but I felt so at ease with him that I couldn't resist.

"Okay," I said, "but just one more. After that I really have to get going."

Richard got up and went into the kitchen. I sank back into the couch and thought about what I was doing. I could not afford to have more than two beers. I was already buzzing from the first one.

A minute later, Richard came back with fresh chips and salsa and two more beers. We drank some more and we talked some more. We had some laughs, and then we smoked the last two cigarettes I had. Afterward, I thanked him for the cold beers and great conversation. I gathered my things to leave, but Richard wanted me to stay and have one more.

He seemed to be genuinely interested in me.

"I can't," I said.

The truth was I wanted to stay. I liked Richard. I felt an instant chemistry and a mutual attraction between us.

"Are you sure," he said, smiling softly while breaking me down with his piercing blue eyes.

I thought it over for a minute. *Stay and drink or leave while I still had a chance.* The choice was obvious. There was little to gain from staying but a lot to lose by not leaving. If my father found out what I did, he would disown me for sure. I knew I had to leave, but I couldn't say no. I had a weakness for beer and an even greater weakness for good-looking men.

I checked the time. It was two-thirty. My father usually got home around four. I figured I could stay a little longer. I drank another beer with Richard, but I kept a close eye on my watch. At precisely three-thirty I took my last sip. Richard could tell I was a little drunk and offered to walk me home. I told him it wasn't necessary and left in a hurry.

Luckily neither my father nor his girlfriend were home yet. I went straight into the bathroom and brushed my teeth, trying desperately to remove the smell of alcohol from my breath. Afterward, I chewed a stick of gum that I found at the bottom of my school bag.

By the time my father got home I was a nervous wreck, pacing my room trying to come up with a good excuse for what I did. But after thinking about it, I realized that all the excuses in the world wouldn't have made a difference. My father would've been furious, so finally I decided to avoid him all together.

I quickly undressed and got into bed. Two hours later, I awakened when I heard knocking at my door. It was my father checking in on me. He wanted to know if I was okay. Not getting out from under the covers, I told him it was my time of the month and that the cramps were really bad. He said he understood and left me alone. Relieved that I had dodged a bullet, I told myself that I would absolutely and positively never do that again.

Chapter 26

I woke up the following morning with a huge smile. For starters it was Friday, and I had always enjoyed when the school week came to a close. But more importantly, I was glad to have met Richard. It was the most exciting thing to happen to me since returning to California.

Later that morning, I sat in class with my chin planted in my palm, looking forward. I was staring up at the teacher but by no means was I paying attention. I could only think about Richard. *Does he like me? Does he think I'm attractive? Will I see him again?*

As I sat there daydreaming, my phone began to vibrate and brought me back to reality. I looked down at the phone number. It was an 805 area code. The only person I knew with an 805 area code was my father, but it wasn't his number. *Could it be Richard?*

Whoever it was, he, or she, left a voicemail. I looked at the clock on the wall. We had only been in class ten minutes and probably weren't going on break any time soon. My heart started racing and my palms got sweaty. I just knew it was Richard, and I wanted to play the message. I raised my hand and got the teacher's attention. She looked at me.

"I need to use the bathroom," I told her.

"Okay, do you need me to show you where it is?" she replied sarcastically.

Chuckles erupted around the classroom. I felt silly. But whatever, I thought, and left in a hurry. I walked swiftly to the bathroom, looking as if I really had to go. I pushed the door open and walked inside. I looked around. The bathroom appeared to be empty so I went into one of the stalls and sat down. I took out my phone and played the voicemail.

"*Hello, Lonnie, this is Richard . . . ,* " the message began.

I listened carefully to the low and heavy tone of his voice. He wasn't quite a baritone, but his voice was deep enough to give me the chills.

"*I just wanted to call and see how you're doing,*" he continued. "*You left in a hurry yesterday and I didn't get a chance to tell you how much I enjoyed your company. I had a great time, and I was wondering if you'd like to get together again. I'm free this weekend. Call me if you want to hang out.*"

Back in the classroom, all I could think about was meeting up with Richard. I wanted to hurry up and call him before he lost interest or before he found someone else to hang out with. I couldn't wait for class to be over. It was torture and perhaps the longest forty minutes I've ever had to wait.

When the teacher finally put the class on break, I went to my usual spot by the eucalyptus tree and called Richard. I could hardly contain myself. My heart raced as I dialed the numbers. My emotions were a mixture of excitement and nervousness.

The phone rang three times before Richard picked up.

"Hello, this is Richard," he answered.

"Hi, Richard, it's me, Lonnie."

"Hi, Lonnie, I'm glad you called. I've been thinking about you."

"Really," I said, shocked at the idea that this guy was actually thinking about me.

"Why do you sound surprised?" he questioned. "I had a great time with you."

My face flushed with redness.

"No, not surprised," I stuttered. "Just glad. I had a great time too."

"Great, then you wouldn't have any objections to doing it again?"

"No, not at all," I told him.

Richard wanted to meet up later in the day, but I couldn't. Not with my father's no dating rule and strict curfew. It really annoyed me that I had so little control over my life. Not being able to come and go as I please got my blood boiling. I liked Richard and I really wanted to see him. So after giving it some thought, I did the only thing I could. I skipped school and went to Richard's apartment.

When Richard opened the door my eyes lit up. He wore blue jeans and a tank top, which made it hard to keep my eyes off his barreled chest and muscular arms. Inside, he gave me a hug and thanked me for coming. As he embraced me, I picked up the scent of cigarette smoke and cheap cologne. This excited me. But as excited as I was, I was nervous about how things might turn out. I had a weird feeling I was getting into something crazy.

Richard was different, a little strange in fact. He had an unusual outlook on the world. Somewhat of a paranoid conspiracist, he was convinced that most events were the result of an alleged plot by either the government or wealthy socio-political figures whose goal was to control the populace. He was unlike anyone I had ever known, and probably not the kind of guy my father would approve of.

Richard was also into drugs, and not the sort of drugs I was used to. LSD, meth, and cocaine were just some of the things he used.

We started drinking around ten and by midday I had a mild buzz. After a few beers, Richard asked if I wanted to try something. I said yes before I even knew what it was. It was ecstasy. At the time, I had no idea what ecstasy was or what it does. In my naive mind, illicit drugs were only those substances such as crack or heroin found mainly in ghettos and used only by the under privileged and the destitute of society. I wasn't comfortable with the idea of doing drugs. I had seen firsthand what drugs did to my mother, and it wasn't a road I wanted to go down.

"Ecstasy is just a mild stimulant," Richard explained. "It will give you a rush and intensify all your feelings, whether good or bad. But I'm sure you will only experience feelings of euphoria, enhanced mental and emotional clarity."

I was speechless. Richard was talking as if he had stock invested in this drug. He convinced me that ecstasy would turn the good time we were having into an even better time. It was a great sales pitch, and after listening to him I became rather intrigued and couldn't wait to try it.

There were six colored pills inside a little plastic bag. They resembled children's daily vitamins and seemed harmless. Richard grabbed a yellow one and I took a purple. I put it on my tongue and then washed it down with beer. Nothing happened at first, we just continued to talk and drink more beer. But after about forty minutes, I felt a rush of energy like never before. My heart started racing, my mouth became dry, and I could not stop grinding my teeth together. I felt anxious and unsure of what to do with myself. Richard, however, seemed fine and unaffected, while I on the other hand was burning up and sweating profusely.

I took off my shirt and staggered to the kitchen. I grabbed a drinking glass from the pile of dirty dishes in the sink and drank some tap water. Overwhelmed with thirst, I drank another glassful as I tried to catch my breath. Richard came into the kitchen wearing a dopey smile. He walked up and started groping me, feeling my waistline and fondling my breasts. I liked Richard, but I wasn't the least bit aroused. There was nothing euphoric about what I was feeling—I felt confused.

I pushed Richard away and drank some more water.

"If you're thirsty, drink another beer," he suggested.

He grabbed two beers from the refrigerator, took my hand, and led me back to the couch. I didn't want more beer but I was thirsty.

"Just try and relax," he told me as he kissed my neck and collarbone.

But it was hard to relax. My heart was beating like a tribal drum. The alcohol and ecstasy made me loopy. And to add to my confusion, Richard continued to touch my body. I got up and started pacing the room. Richard came after me.

"Finish your beer," he told me. "It will help even you out."

I grabbed the can of beer and guzzled it fast. I took several deep breaths and surprisingly a calm started to come over me.

Richard handed me his beer and laughed.

"Don't worry, you'll be fine," he said. "The first time is always a trip."

I just nodded and continued to drink.

"I'll never forget mine," he continued. "I was tripping just like you. But once I got a handle on things, I became incredibly horny. And all I wanted all night . . . "

Richard took off his shirt and walked up to me. His broad chest and firm abdomen, also covered with tattoos, looked perfect. He grabbed me and pulled me close. I could feel his erection against my stomach as he looked into my eyes.

"All I wanted was sex, sex, and more sex," he said.

Richard kissed me. His tongue invaded my mouth without warning. I returned his kiss as we made our way back to the couch. He lay me down and caressed my body. No longer paranoid, I moaned passionately each time he touched me and gasped when he slipped his hand down my pants. Before I knew it we were both naked and Richard was on top of me. I gripped him tightly between my thighs as he plunged into me. Richard did not know the meaning of gentle. He pounded my body aggressively and without concern for my pleasure. I felt suffocated beneath the weight of his body. What started out nice soon became uncomfortable. His jackhammer-like pounding of my loins quickly dried me out and irritated my vagina. I couldn't wait for him to finish. But it would be a while before I found relief. Richard had stamina beyond belief.

By now all sexual pleasure was gone for me and nausea took over. Richard's rocking of my body caused a fluttering of the fluids in my stomach. I hung my head off the couch and puked quietly, while he continued to enjoy himself. I became dizzy and disoriented, slipping in and out of consciousness. All I could do was shut my eyes tight and wait. Finally, after what seemed like forever, Richard's muscles began to twitch and his body stiffened as he released himself inside me. After a few minutes, I rose from the couch and gathered my clothes. Drenched in sweat, I stumbled to the bathroom and shut the door. I climbed inside the bathtub and splashed cold water on my vagina. It offered some relief, but not much. Afterward, I dressed and drank some more tap water. I don't recall ever being so thirsty.

When I came out of the bathroom I checked the time. It was four in the afternoon. My heart sank into my stomach. *How on earth did six hours go by so fast?* I looked at my phone. I had five missed calls from my father. My hand trembled as I listened to his voicemails. He wanted to know where I was and there was worry in his voice.

Richard came over with another beer.

"Is everything okay, babe?" he inquired.

"Ah, yeah, everything is fine," I managed.

But everything was not okay. I had a tremendous headache, and my thoughts were in a whirlwind of worry and confusion. What was I to do, go home and face my father, or stay with Richard and continue the façade? The latter of the two seemed the safest. There was no way I could go home drunk and high on ecstasy. I decided to hang around a little longer—just long enough to come down from my high. I figured I could deal with my father better if I wasn't high.

I sat down on the couch and took a deep breath. Consumed with worry, I began thinking about what I was going to say to my father. But what could I possibly tell him that would keep him from killing me? Things were not looking good for me. I closed my eyes to keep the room from spinning.

I could hear Richard talking to me, but nothing he said made sense. I listened closely, but the more I tried to make sense of his words, the more his voice seemed to fade away. I tried to open my eyes but I couldn't, it was as if my eyelids were stapled to my cheeks. I could feel myself fading away into the deep recesses of unconsciousness until suddenly, everything went black.

Chapter 27

I woke up eighteen hours later face down in a bed not my own. As I struggled to open my eyes, a warm ray of sunlight from the window stunned my pupils. I quickly turned in the other direction and found refuge underneath the pillow. I took a deep breath and began to gather my thoughts, trying desperately to make sense of my situation. The last thing I remembered was drinking with Richard, and that alone was a blur. I wasn't sure where I was, but I figured, or at least I hoped, I was still in Richard's apartment.

After looking around the room, I felt confident that I was still in his apartment. What I thought was a bed was really just an old mattress on the floor. The walls were stained with cigarette smoke, and cheap blinds barely covered the windows. But the thing I found to be most indicative of Richard's style was the dirty laundry and empty beer cans spread throughout the room.

I could not believe I had done it again and in California of all places while under my father's supervision. He had to be sick with worry. I reached into my pocket for my cell phone. It wasn't there, nor were my pants for that matter. Beneath the blanket I was bare from the waist down. I scanned the room looking for my pants. They were on the floor along with my underwear, socks, and shoes. *That's really strange*, I thought.

How did I end up in bed with my top fully intact but my pants and underwear completely off? I began to wonder if I had been raped. As much as I tried, I could not recall anything. There was nothing I could do except dress and talk to Richard, hoping he'd fill in the blanks.

I crawled out of bed and put my underwear and pants back on. I took out my phone and looked at the time. My jaw dropped. I could not believe it was ten o'clock Saturday morning. Shocked that I had slept so long I began to panic. My hands trembled as I looked through my missed calls. There was seventeen voicemails from my father, each one more disturbing than the next. His voice, weeping with a convulsive shortness of breath, begged me to phone home. I held the phone in my palm for several minutes, trying to figure out what to tell him. What excuse could I come up with? What lie could I make up? How could I possibly justify being out all night without as much as a phone call? I felt terrible.

As I stood there contemplating my problem, Richard opened the door and peered inside.

"Hey, you're up," he said, looking surprised. "I thought you'd never wake up."

I smiled awkwardly.

"Come inside," he said and gestured. "I'm making lunch."

As I walked through the door I detected the smell of bacon, something I loved and normally would've made my mouth water. That morning, however, it upset my stomach and caused me to dash to the bathroom. I threw up twice and dry heaved for about five minutes before coming back out.

Richard and three of his friends were in the living room eating bacon cheese burgers of all things.

"Come join us," he said.

I walked over and sat amongst them. I passed on the burger but managed to stomach some french fries. Richard introduced me to his friends whom had been there all night. They must've came after I blacked out. We sat around for a while and made small talk, but I felt uncomfortable the whole time. For some reason they kept smiling at me, and I kept thinking to myself that I should leave. But I was afraid of what my father might do to me, so I stuck around despite the awkward feeling I got from Richard and his company.

As I sat with Richard and his friends, the thought of rape entered my mind again. I was suspicious because all their jokes were laced with sexual innuendos. I had no idea what they were talking about and Richard wouldn't tell me. He'd simply say, "It's nothing babe," and keep laughing. Their jokes ate away at me, and I wished that I hadn't blacked out. Somehow though, I managed to convince myself that I was overreacting. I didn't drink the remainder of the day, and I didn't do any more ecstasy, despite the pressure from Richard and his friends. I just couldn't take a chance.

Richard's friends finally left around midnight. By then he was drunk and high and demanding sex. It was the furthest thing from my mind but I felt obligated. I didn't want to go home and face my father, and I didn't have any place to go. I let Richard have his way with me and got the same drunken pounding that I got the night before.

The next day no one came over. With his last twenty dollars, we got a few things from the grocery store and he made me a terrific spaghetti dinner. I chipped in a few bucks of my own and we got a six pack of beer. We spent the rest of the day talking and getting to know each other. I got to see a softer, gentler side of Richard. He told me about his strengths and weakness, his likes and dislikes, and his goal to one day open his own business. I was beginning to fall in love with him.

...

In the morning, while my father and Lorna were at work, I snuck into the house and got some of my belongings. I had never placed a value on clean underwear before until I went three days without. After gathering my things and stealing some canned foods from the pantry, I sat down to write my father a letter. I felt obligated. I had put him through a lot of worry. He at least needed to know that I was alive.

With pen in hand, I sat down to collect my thoughts. I began, *Dear Dad*, and stayed there. After about fifteen minutes that was all I could come up with. Although I tried, I could not articulate how I felt. I could not find the words to express how bad of a daughter I had been for putting him through such an ordeal. I continued to rack my brain and all I could come up with was, *Sorry*. Frustrated, I got a fresh piece of paper and tried again. But still, nothing came to mind. Finally, I became annoyed. I crumbled up both pieces of paper, threw them in the waste basket, and left.

On Tuesday I skipped school again. At this point I had made up my mind that I wasn't going back. There was just no point. I didn't have any friends. I hated being there, and the teachers may as well have been speaking Japanese because I had no clue what was going on. I was certain to fail. I also made up my mind not to go back home despite the bombardment of phone calls I received from my father. He left message after message, and each time I listened to one my heart bled a little more. Ironically, however, each day that passed I seemed to care a little less.

. . .

Nearly six months would go by before I would see my father again. From July to about late November, I lived with Richard and about half a dozen or so of his friends that routinely spent the night. Living with him, I soon learned that he was not as ambitious and goal oriented as I first thought he was. All the talk about opening a business was just that—talk. Richard made a living peddling cocaine, ecstasy, and a little bit of marijuana. He was a small-time dealer, but he was also a big-time user. He made just enough to get by, and any profit he made usually went up his nose. Richard loved cocaine, and he tried his best to sell me on it. But after my trip on ecstasy I was scared to try anything else.

The time I spent with Richard was a lot like my time with Sean. Very rarely were we together alone. He had a lot of friends, many of whom were his customers. Most times that they came to make a purchase they ended up staying, and it seemed like every day was one big hangout party in the tiny apartment.

Living with Richard was great. Alcohol flowed freely on a daily basis. Marijuana and other drugs were also available. I avoided anything in the form of a pill or white powder. Not that getting drunk every day was any better. But frankly, some of the things Richard and his friends were into were frightening.

I didn't know what a crystal meth junky was until I met Amy. She reminded me of the crack addicts in Brooklyn—she reminded me of my mother. Once a sane, attractive young girl, now she was a rapidly aging, delusional addict chasing an unattainable high. She only came around once or twice a week, but each time she came around she looked worse than the last time. Her obsessive skin-picking exacerbated her acne and left her face with several open sores. She was frail and undernourished. The muscle tissue and facial fat fading from her face gave her a gaunt, hollowed-out appearance. Her teeth and gums were a nightmare, a decaying mess that would scare away most dental hygienists.

Amy started using socially when she was twenty. Three years later, she was hooked, consumed by the drug, and unable to cope with life on life's terms. Amy's story was enough to keep me from doing drugs. But it didn't stop me from drinking or having the occasional joint.

What started out as fun quickly got out of hand and things began to fall apart. Within a few months my drinking had become unmanageable, even more so than before. My days, nights, and weekends were spent drinking. I drank so much that I had gotten to a point where I needed a drink in the morning just to feel right. Each time I drank I found myself strung out, lost, and confused. But the thought of stopping scared me, because being drunk had become normal to me.

The truth was I liked drinking. Alcohol removed my mental filters. It made me think less before talking, and I felt less pressure to be charming. Alcohol lowered my inhibitions. Under the influence, I would do things that normally I might not do without booze in my system. This included playing strip poker, making out with girls, and casual flings or group sex. But that's putting it mildly. I basically became the apartment slut, a human mattress for Richard and his friends.

All my experiences with Richard were guided by alcohol. Just about every night I would find myself in a variety of sexual situations that I'd always regret in the morning. But the regret, the guilt and self-pity, was usually short lived. Once I got more alcohol in my bloodstream it was easy to forget my problems. Alcohol was all I needed to stay in routine. This went on for several months until I finally got caught.

Chapter 28

Every time I talked to Lia she told me to go back home.

"You are being really reckless right now," she said.

"I can't go back," I told her. "Not after everything that's happened. My father would kill me."

"You have to go back. In fact, this is beyond reckless. It doesn't even sound safe."

"I'm plenty safe. Richard looks out for me."

"Come off it, Lonnie. You are not safe," Lia insisted. "You live in a house with a drug dealer and a bunch of drug addicts."

"I'm fine. Everyone here is real chill."

"Come on, Lonnie. Just go home. Your father is worried about you. He calls here all the time asking me if I've heard from you."

"You haven't said anything, have you?" I asked in a worried tone.

"Of course not, but I can't keeping lying to him. You know, if you go home, he'll probably be so happy that you're alive he won't care about what happened."

"Yeah, he will. He'll make more rules for me to follow. He'll probably start driving me everywhere. I'm not going back."

I knew my father was worried about me, but I couldn't go

back after everything I did. So instead, I decided to give him a call to let him know that I was okay.

When he picked up the phone he was in shock, I could tell. His voice filled with worry and despair, he begged me to come home.

"Oh my God, Lonnie. Is that really you?" he asked.

"Yeah, Daddy. It's really me."

"Are you okay? Where are you?"

"I'm fine. I'm with some friends."

"What friends? You don't know anyone in California."

"I met some people. Don't worry, Daddy. I'm fine."

"How can I not worry? Please come home, Lonnie."

"I'm sorry, Daddy. I can't."

"Where are you? I'll come get you."

"I'm sorry, Daddy. I have to go. I promise I'm okay."

I knew he was dying inside, but it still wasn't enough to make me go back. I had been too liquored up to want to care. I wished him a happy belated birthday and hung up.

After talking to my father I couldn't help but feel sad. Lia was right, I had gone too far, and I had no idea how to get off the train to nowhere that I was on. Every so often my emotions would get the best of me, and that day I felt overwhelmed with guilt and emptiness. To remedy this I decided to get drunk. That was usually what I did whenever I found myself feeling down.

Around the apartment the usual cast of characters were sprawled out sleeping. I maneuvered around the sleeping bodies and made my way to the kitchen. I opened the refrigerator praying that all the beer hadn't been consumed. But as luck would have it there wasn't a single beer left over. Frustrated, I slammed the refrigerator door shut and went into the bedroom. Richard was sleeping face down on the bed. I grabbed his wallet off the dresser and took a twenty dollar bill.

Since running away, I had always made it a point to stay in the apartment during the day in case the cops were looking for me. I mostly went out at night, and it was usually just down to the convenience store for beers, cigarettes, or snacks. That morning, however, I couldn't wait because my hangover was too much to handle.

Outside, a cool November breeze ruffled the tree leaves as I walked swiftly to the 7-Eleven two blocks away. Inside, I went to the back and grabbed a case of beer. It was the no-frills brand that Richard liked, and the kind that I had gotten use to drinking. Then I went down the next aisle and got a home pregnancy test. My period was two weeks late. I placed everything on the counter and asked for a pack of cigarettes.

Ashim, the young man from New Delhi who worked at the convenience store, gave me an uncharacteristic blank stare. He had a look of worry on his face, and I wasn't sure what to make of it.

"I'm sorry, Ma'am, but I'll need to see your ID," he said, looking incredibly nervous.

"What are you talking about?" I replied with a chuckle.

Ashim was one of Richard's customers. He worked at the 7-Eleven part time while attending medical school. He wasn't a hardcore drug addict like many of Richard's other clients. He was only into marijuana. He's been to the apartment many times. I'd had several conversations with him, and I'd even smoked with him on many occasions. Needless to say, I had purchased beer and cigarettes from him before. I thought his behavior was a little strange.

"Your ID, please," he continued, this time his eyes moving to the corner of the store.

I turned slightly and followed his stare across the store. Standing by the magazine rack, a middle-aged, white man wearing blue jeans and a polo shirt was flipping through a magazine. I could tell he wasn't really interested in the magazine. He had been listening and staring at us the whole time. As soon as I looked over at him his eyes fell back into the pages. I turned back and looked at Ashim. He was smiling uncomfortably and sweating profusely. My mind started racing.

"On second thought," I said, now feeling nervous myself. "It's a little early to be drinking. I won't be needing this after all."

I turned and started walking towards the door. My heart started racing. My first instinct was to run. But I was kidding myself thinking I could get away as hungover as I was. I took a deep breath and kept walking towards the door. I prayed his sudden departure was purely coincidental and that he wasn't coming after me. But it wasn't and he was. I was about three feet from the door when he grabbed me and showed me his police badge.

"Let me guess, you're not twenty-one," he said.

I looked up at him. His blue eyes were cold. His unshaven face was leathery and hard. I didn't reply. I couldn't. I didn't know what to say.

"How long did you think you were going to get away with this, Lonnie?" he asked.

I was shocked that he knew my name. But how?

I shook my head in disbelief.

"My name is not, Lonnie," I lied.

"Are you sure? Because the girl in this picture ID looks a lot like you."

I don't know how but he had a copy of my school ID. He also had a picture of me posing with Mickey Mouse. I remembered taking the picture when my father, Lorna, and I all went to Disney Land several months back. I was speechless.

"Yeah, I thought so," he said smartly as he spun me around and put handcuffs on me.

I had never been arrested before. I broke into tears.

"Please don't do this," I begged.

"Sure," he said, wearing a condescending smirk as he dragged me through the door.

Outside, he put me in the back of a black Ford Crown Victoria. I sat in the unmarked police car for several minutes while he looked through some paperwork in the front seat. Finally, he got on the radio and contacted the station. He told the dispatcher that he had me and he was on his way back.

...

When we arrived at the police station I was handed off to a female officer who processed my case. She was very nice and answered all my questions.

"What's going to happen to me?" I asked. "Am I going to go to jail?"

"I don't know," she said. "What did you do?"

"I didn't do anything."

"You had to do something. They wouldn't have brought you here if you didn't do anything."

"I was trying to buy some cigarettes. That's not a big deal, is it?"

"It is if you're a minor."

I started crying.

"I put the cigarettes back though," I told the officer.

Sensing my worry, she told me that I wasn't in any real trouble. She said they were just going to hold me until my parents came and got me.

After filling out some forms and plugging some information into her computer, she had me take off my belt and shoelaces. She made me empty the contents of my pocket into a bag and then placed me in a holding cell.

The cell was about six-by-eight feet, made entirely of concrete with a steel door and a small window. Inside was a stainless steel table mounted to the wall and a couple of stainless steel stools bolted to the floor. The cell reflected my mood—cold and depressing. I had picked the wrong day to be hungover. I paced the tiny cell for an hour before I got tired and took a seat on the hard concrete. I tried to nap but there was too many thoughts bouncing around in my head.

. . .

About three hours later, my father and Lorna showed up at the police station and signed for my release. I followed them to the parking lot and got in the back seat of his car. I chewed my fingernails down to the stubs. I stared out the window, anxiously waiting for one of them to say something. But nothing was said. They didn't even talk to each other. I knew he was going to go off on me, I just didn't know when. When we got to the house my father finally spoke.

He wanted to know where I was and who I was with. I wasn't sure what to say, but I had to say something, so I told him the truth. He was shocked.

"Boyfriend?" he said, looking surprised and confused.

"Who is this boyfriend?", "Where does he live?", and "How old is he?" were just some of the questions my father expected answers to.

I looked away. Afraid that he'd want to confront Richard, I decided not say anything further. If he knew that Richard was thirteen years older than me he would've been furious. I didn't want Richard to go down for statutory rape, so I told him that it was none of his business and stormed upstairs to my bedroom. My father came charging after me.

"It is too my business," he replied. "If someone is dating my fifteen-year-old daughter I have a right to know."

We were now standing in my room.

"Come off it, Dad. This isn't about you."

"I'm your father, Lonnie. You're my responsibility."

"I don't need a father right now," I exploded.

I had a terrible headache and was not in the mood to be lectured. I needed a drink badly. All I could think about was Richard. *He's probably up by now and wondering where I am. I have to get back to the apartment. I need to talk to him. I need to tell him that I missed my period.*

"Can we please continue this later?" I asked, trying to regain my composure. "I have some unfinished business to tend to."

"Absolutely not," my father yelled. "You are going to tell me right now where you've been for the last six months. Why would you put our family through this?"

I folded my arms and rolled my eyes as tears came streaming down my face. I was on the brink of a nervous breakdown. I was trying to keep it together, but each time my father yelled it brought me closer to catastrophe.

"Answer me damn it," he barked.

"No," I yelled back. "Just go away. Leave me alone."

Lorna finally appeared after being absent the whole time. She grabbed my father's arm and told him to stop yelling. She said it was not the way to get things resolved. She got him to stop yelling, but he was still very angry.

"Okay, we'll pick this up later," he conceded. "But you will answer my questions."

"I have to go, Dad."

"Go where?"

"There is something really important I need to do."

"Like hell you do. You are going to sit here and think about what you did."

He walked away. Lorna remained in the doorway and looked at me. I could tell she wanted to say something but didn't want to undermine his authority. She didn't understand either that I needed to see Richard. I was emotional and edgy with rebellion. I stood there crying, getting angrier by the minute.

"Can you talk to him, please?" I said desperately.

"I think your father is right," she replied in a shaky voice. "You should stay here awhile."

"What is wrong with you people?"

Anger finally got the best of me. I snapped and grabbed the chair in the room. It was the same chair I sat in six months ago when I tried to write my father a letter. Without thinking, I threw it through the bedroom window. Lorna's eyes lit up in shock. My father ran back in the room. He too was shocked as he walked towards the window for a closer look. I didn't wait for him to respond. I took advantage of the opportunity and made a run for it.

I blew by Lorna who was still standing in the doorway with her mouth open. I ran down the stairs, out the front door, and down the street as fast as I could.

. . .

I ran to Richard's apartment but he wanted nothing to do with me. The police had paid him a visit and scared him real good. They knew that I had been living there thanks to Ashim, who squealed when the police interrogated him. Richard now knew everything. He knew that I wasn't nineteen but, in fact, a fifteen-year-old runaway who incidentally he'd been harboring.

"Come on, Richard. Please let me in," I begged.

"No way, man," he replied, standing in the doorway. "The cops said that you're fifteen, is that true?"

"Yeah, but I can explain."

"What's to explain. You lied."

"I know, and I'm sorry. I just thought that if I told you I was fifteen, you wouldn't want to talk to me."

"You damn right," he said, rolling his eyes. "They also said you ran away from home, is that true too?"

I nodded.

"What the hell, Lonnie," he exploded. "You know what I do here. Do have any idea how much trouble I could be in right now?"

I didn't say anything. I just stared at him with watery eyes.

"Man, I cannot believe this," he said, plowing his fingers through his hair. "Why did you come back here anyway? What do you want?"

I would've preferred to talk inside, but Richard wasn't going to let me in.

"I haven't gotten my period yet," I said.

"So, what are you telling me for?" he said, suddenly looking nervous. "We didn't do nothing. I just gave you a place to stay, man."

What?

"Look, Lonnie," he continued. "I can't talk to you anymore. Please leave. I don't want any trouble."

Richard slammed the door shut. My heart shattered into a dozen pieces. Unsure what to do next, I stood outside his door crying until the police came and got me again.

I never stepped foot in my father's house again after that day. When the police brought me back I made a huge scene at the front door. I was uncontrollably emotional, so much that as soon as the handcuffs came off I tried to attack my father. I ran towards him with every intention to do him harm. As far as I was concerned he was the enemy and the reason Richard wouldn't talk to me. I cursed him and wished him dead as the two policemen took me down and cuffed me again. My father tried to talk to me, but I wouldn't listen. I spat on him.

"I hate you," I said.

"You have to calm down, Lonnie."

"I don't want to calm down. I don't want to be here, don't you get that? I'd rather be dead than live here with you."

"Lonnie, please."

"I mean it. I will kill myself if I have to stay here."

After that there was a brief silence. One of the policemen pulled my father aside and talked to him. I don't know what was said but shortly after they put me back in the police car. My rage quickly turned into fear.

"Where are you taking me?" I asked.

"Someplace where you can't hurt yourself," one of the policemen said.

I had no idea what that meant. For all I knew they could've been taking me back to jail. I turned to my father.

"Okay, I'm sorry. Please don't do this, Daddy."

My father didn't say a word. He just watched as they hauled me away in the back of the police car.

. . .

They took me to the psychiatric ward at St. John's Regional Medical Center and put me under suicide watch. I had no desire to kill myself. I only said it out of anger and to make the point that I wanted to go back to Brooklyn. Had I known the consequences of my words I would have never opened my mouth. I had no idea that when I woke up that morning my day was going to go from bad to worse. By the evening, I was on a gurney in the ER waiting to be admitted to the psych ward.

After three miserable hours in the ER, I was finally admitted. When I left the ER, I sat down with a crisis counselor.

"Why do you want to hurt yourself?" he asked me.

"I don't want to hurt myself," I said defiantly. "Can I just go home now?"

"I'm sorry, but you can't go home right now. We need to keep you here a while to make sure you're alright."

"For how long?" I asked, suddenly feeling faint.

"That depends on you," the counselor said.

Afterward, a nurse showed me to my room. She gave me a towel, a bag of toiletries, and one of those ugly hospital gowns to sleep in. There were three other girls in the room talking amongst each other. When I walked in they all stopped and stared at me. I said hello and gave a half smile. Assuming the empty bed in the room was mine, I walked over and lay down. A few minutes later, the nurse came around and turned off the lights.

I barely slept that night. My body adjusting itself to a lack of alcohol gave me a serious case of night sweats and tremors. Forced by my circumstance, I had no choice but to struggle and fight through the withdrawal symptoms. It was difficult. Nausea, headache, rapid heartbeat, and anxiety came in fierce waves throughout the night. I needed a drink so bad I could taste it.

I cried silently throughout the night wishing that I could go back to Richard's apartment. Finally, around three that morning, I decided I couldn't take it anymore. I went in the lobby and found the nurse on duty. She looked me over, called a doctor, and then gave me a sleeping pill and a mild tranquilizer. I got back into my dormitory-style bed and fell asleep about thirty minutes later.

Chapter 29

I woke up around seven panicking, unsure where I was. I thought that I dreamt the whole thing, but as I looked around, I quickly realized the reality of my nightmare. For breakfast, we got a cold egg sandwich, a small carton of milk, and two pieces of hard toast. I skipped breakfast and stayed in bed, hoping I could get a little more sleep. It was pointless. About twenty minutes after I closed my eyes, the nurse came back around and collected everyone's trash.

"You didn't eat any of your breakfast," she said. "Are you okay?"

"I'm not very hungry," I replied. "I just want to go home."

"Don't worry about going home right now. Try to eat something, and focus on getting better."

"But I'm fine."

"You're not fine, honey," she insisted. "You're having serious withdrawal symptoms, and your mind is clouded with bad thoughts. You have to stay here until you get better."

"How long am I going to have to stay here?"

She said the same thing the counselor said.

"That depends on your recovery."

Frustrated, I climbed back in bed and cried some more.

Shortly after, I attended group therapy. We had two sessions a day, one in the morning and one in the afternoon. The conversation mostly revolved around stress and how to deal with it. Other than a brief introduction, there was no pressure to talk or share feelings so I just listened to the others. There were a total of twelve patients, including me. Not counting myself, ages ranged from nineteen to around fifty. They were all seriously suicidal and I remembered thinking that I did not want to be there.

One of the girls, a petite blond with scars on her arms, threw a temper tantrum about thirty minutes into therapy. I watched in fear as two hulky guards and a nurse dragged her out kicking and screaming.

“Where are they taking her?” I asked a middle-aged woman sitting next to me.

“The Time Out room,” the woman said.

“What’s going to happen to her?”

“They’ll sedate her if she doesn’t stop acting crazy.”

At the time, I didn’t know what sedate meant.

“It means they will drug her real good,” the woman explained.

Therapy continued shortly thereafter, even though we could still hear her scream violently in the other room. Her screaming sent chills down my spine. It went on for several minutes and then finally, it stopped. The conversation resumed as if nothing had happened. It was hard to sit through therapy after that. I was scared.

For lunch, I sat with the girls from my room. On the surface they all seemed very nice, but deep down inside they were clinically disturbed. One was a twenty-two-year-old college student who tried to kill herself over her professor. When their love affair became a threat to his marriage he dumped her, and soon after, she tried hanging herself. She showed us the rope burns around her neck. My other roommate was a thirty-year-old mother who suffered from postpartum depression. Her severe mood swings and crying spells made her want to hurt her baby, and she too had tried to kill herself. The last roommate had a mood disorder in which she experienced extreme highs and lows. She was on three different types of anti-depressants and remained loopy throughout the day.

After lunch we had a little time to ourselves before the next group session. I wanted to be alone so I went back to the room. I could not get the image of the petite blond girl being dragged away out of my head. I realized that I could not afford to lose my temper or I too would suffer the same fate. I had to behave if I wanted to go home. I could not say anything was wrong, be seen as unhappy, or mention anything about hurting myself even as a joke. I told myself I was going to participate at group therapy, chat with the nurses and other patients, try to smile more, and tell them whatever they wanted to hear.

The second group therapy went well. There wasn't a single incident of patients going ballistic. The second session was followed by visiting hours. When I learned we could have visitors I became excited. I thought for sure my father would come see me, but he didn't. He didn't even call. With nothing scheduled for the next two hours, I found myself alone with only my thoughts. I became sad, wondering why he hadn't come. *Perhaps he had enough?* Maybe he was finally tired of my behavior and wanted nothing more to do with me. And who could blame him? I certainly couldn't. Convinced that I had been abandoned, I wept.

After visiting hours I met with the psychiatrist. As my goal was to go home, I offered my brightest smile and put forth my best attitude. Like the crisis counselor, he also asked why I wanted to hurt myself. I told him I was merely acting out of anger. I had no intention of killing myself, especially considering that I could be pregnant. I went on and told him about Richard and the events that followed but left out the details about the illegal drugs and group sex. I talked for nearly an hour while he listened and took notes. It felt good to vent and unload my frustrations and concerns. Afterwards, he ordered me a pregnancy test and said good night. The night, however, was anything but good. I could not sleep to save my life. Night sweats and tremors kept me up again, and this time the nurse could not prescribe anything on account that I could be pregnant.

My second day at the ward was exactly like my first, and I imagined every day from then on would also be the same. I could not fathom the thought of being there two or three weeks as some of the other patients had been. If they didn't release me soon, I truly would've went crazy. On day two, I got the results of my pregnancy test. I was relieved to learn it was negative, but couldn't understand why my period was almost three weeks late. The nurse explained it could be a number of things: stress, a poor diet, lack of sleep, and heavy consumption of alcohol can affect hormone levels in the body. I was guilty of all the above.

As I figured, day three at the ward was no different. The petite blond girl was finally back in group therapy. But she didn't participate in any of the discussions. Looking abused and defeated, she just sat with her head down the whole time. She was obviously numb from medication and there seemed to be no sign of life left in her. I didn't know what her situation was, but I couldn't help but feel sorry for her.

I still hadn't seen or heard from my father. Without a cell phone or money to buy a phone card I couldn't call anyone. I feared that I would be stuck at the hospital. No one except my father knew where I was, and he wasn't coming to get me.

Later, I met up with my psychiatrist.

"So, Lonnie, how are you feeling today?" he asked.

"I feel pretty good, actually. I'm starting to sleep a little bit better."

"Awesome," he replied with a smile. "And I see the result for your pregnancy test came back negative. How do you feel about that?"

"Super relieved," I replied. "That is not something I need right now."

"That's good." He nodded. "Now, talk to me about the therapy. How's that working for you?"

"Well, I didn't like it at first because I didn't want to be there, but once I starting talking, it was nice. I like that I could talk and not worry about anyone judging me or telling me to grow up or be responsible. It's cool that they just listen. Sometimes, I feel like no one listens to me. So, yeah, therapy is cool."

"I'm going to write that down, *therapy is cool*," the psychiatrist said.

We both laughed.

"Are you still having thoughts of hurting yourself or others?"

"No, I don't want to hurt myself, and I could never hurt my dad. He's been really good to me and really patient with me up until now. I feel bad for putting him through all this."

"What would you say to your dad if you could speak to him right now?"

"That I'm sorry. I don't mean to be so bad. It's just that when I start drinking, I do stupid things. I screw everything up. I'd ask him to forgive me and help me stop drinking."

I started crying. The psychiatrist placed a box of tissues on the table in front of me.

"But I know he's not going to forgive me," I continued. "He hates me, that's why he hasn't come to visit me."

"I don't think your father hates you, Lonnie. But these things take time to fix. Are you willing to do what it takes to fix things between you and your father and your family?"

"Yes, I'll do anything," I replied, balling like a baby.

At the end of our meeting, the psychiatrist told me that I was making excellent progress and that he didn't think I was a threat to myself anymore. He authorized my release. He told me my father would be by in the morning to pick me up. I didn't know they had been in contact, and I was a little hurt that my father didn't want to talk to me. I figured he was angry, but to leave me in the dark the way he did seemed wrong. In fairness, I suppose it was no different than what I did when I ran away. I didn't sleep a lot that night but it wasn't because of tremors or night sweats. It was the anticipation of finally leaving the hospital.

. . .

In the morning, I found my father waiting in the lobby. Our first encounter after that fateful night was awkward to say the least. I didn't know what to say. I could barely look him in the eyes. We walked to the parking lot and drove off without saying a word to each other. Finally, after about twenty silent minutes on the road I broke the ice.

"I'm sorry, Dad."

"Don't be," he replied with little reaction, still staring at the road ahead.

But I was. My father didn't deserve what I put him through. I wanted him to know just how bad I felt.

"Look, Lonnie," he continued. "You don't want to be here. You've never wanted to come to California, and I shouldn't have forced you."

"You were just trying to do what you thought was best for me, and I appreciate that."

"Well, you have a funny way of showing it," he said, letting out a small chuckle.

I sighed. What could I say? He was right.

"I really am sorry, Dad."

"I'm sorry too. I'm sorry I dragged you out here. But don't worry, I'm going to send you back to Brooklyn."

My father never once looked at me. He just stared dead ahead at the road. I couldn't have felt any guiltier. I wanted to go home but not under these circumstances, not with this hanging over my head. I turned and looked out the window. That was when I realized we were heading towards LAX airport. *He didn't waste any time*, I thought. Tears ran down my face instantly. I knew right then and there that my father was finished with me.

. . .

I thought about him a lot on the flight back to New York. He did not deserve what I did to him. I kept thinking what if someday I have a kid and he or she did something like that to me. How would I react? What would I do? I had to change my ways. I realized I couldn't keep going on the way I was.

With guilt eating away at me, I told myself I was going to stop drinking and smoking. I was going to stop giving myself to men who weren't worthy of me. I had said it before, but this time I meant it. I didn't need a man to validate my character. My father's love was all I needed. I felt like a fool for pushing him away.

After my plane landed I called him. I wanted to tell him again how sorry I was, but he didn't answer his phone. Instead, I left him a message saying that I had arrived safely and to call me once he got the message.

When I arrived my grandfather greeted me at La Guardia Airport. I couldn't say that I was happy to see him because I hated being around him. I would've preferred to walk home than to listen to him ramble on in the car. As usual my mother wasn't home. She came and went for days at a time while my grandmother looked after her son. Once again I was alone, without any supervision and free to do anything I wanted.

Chapter 30

The first two months that I was back I stayed home and tried to be good. I helped out around the house by watching my little brother while my grandmother cooked and cleaned and did other things. I stopped smoking weed and getting drunk. I promised to go back to school once the year ended and the new semester started. But once I actually looked into it and realized just how far behind I was I got discouraged. Most of the kids my age were now sophomores or juniors. Technically, I was still a freshman. I would have to do a lot work, and the humiliation would be too much. I was done with school.

Lia was doing great, earning straight A's. She was definitely college bound and destined for success. I tried my best to leave her alone and not influence her when I felt the need to have a drink. I held out for as long as I could. But it didn't take long before I got bored and broke every promise I made to myself.

First, I tried to be a social drinker, only having one or two drinks, but that quickly escalated into binge drinking. I started smoking weed again, too. By the time the New Year came around I was back to my old ways—partying without caution or regret. And although I tried not to involve her, Lia slowly found her way back to the dark side. I didn't feel bad, because Lia was her own person, and there was no persuasion on my part. The fact was, she loved to party just as much as I did. We picked up right where we left off. It was as if we never stopped.

. . .

My first winter back was rough. I had gotten spoiled living in California and forgot just how bitter cold New York gets. Winter came and went, and I had nothing to show for it except good times at Marlboro Housing Projects. Lia and I started hanging out there again. Sean had gone away to college, but Lia and I made new friends. They were from the same messed up crowd of truants, drunks, and stoners, just different people.

Nine months passed and I still hadn't heard from my father. I called and left numerous messages, but I never received a call back from him. Finally, I stopped calling. I was convinced that he had given up and wanted nothing to do with me. Over time, I gave up too. As I became more and more self-absorbed in my own reckless behavior, I learned to accept the fact that I wasn't going to have a father figure in my life anymore.

One day in July, after a long weekend of partying in the projects, I got a call from Lia. I was dead to the world, sleeping off a hangover when my grandmother woke me up and gave me the phone. Lia was upset, crying uncontrollably because her period was late.

"You have to calm down," I told her. "A late period doesn't necessarily mean you're pregnant."

"How do you know that?"

I reminded her about my experience in California and what the nurse told me about a late period.

"Yeah, but it's been two months," she argued. "I don't care what some nurse in California told you. I really think I'm pregnant."

"Two months," I echoed in shock. "When were you going to tell me? And still, how can you be so sure? Are you having symptoms?"

"What kind of symptoms?" Lia asked after a brief pause.

But the truth was I didn't know the difference between a cold symptom and pregnancy symptoms.

"Okay, never mind that," I said. "There's only one way to be certain. You'll just have to take a pregnancy test."

Lia and I went out and got a home pregnancy test. We went to my apartment and she took it. Lia was pregnant. The positive icon on the test strip was clear. I just about died when she showed it to me. Lia got up and splashed water on her face then plowed her hands through her hair.

"This can't be happening," she said, looking at herself in the mirror.

I could only imagine how she must've felt. I couldn't believe it either.

"Is it possible we did it wrong?" I suggested.

"I don't think so," she replied. "It's a pretty simple procedure."

I started rereading the directions to make sure we did the test correctly.

"Let's see," I began. "Step 1—wash hands with warm water and soap."

"Okay, we did that," Lia said, looking over my shoulder reading along.

Step 2—remove the testing device from its foil wrapper. Step 3—sit down on the toilet. Step 4—place the absorbent side of the test stick in your urine stream with the 'result window' facing up and pee on it for five to ten seconds. Step 5—place the testing stick on a flat—"

"Oh, forget it," Lia said in frustration and walked away.

"Hold on, let's see if we missed anything," I said.

"There's no point, Lonnie. We followed the instructions to the letter. Let's face it, I'm pregnant."

Lia started crying, her voice choking, frantic with fear.

"My parents are going to kill me," she said.

I was speechless. I had no idea how to console her. But her parents were the least of her problems. They had their own issues going on. Lia's father was still seeing his mistress and supporting the love child they had together. Her mother had taken on a lover of her own. Perhaps to be spiteful or maybe because she stopped caring, I wasn't sure. But the two stopped talking to one another, even though they lived in the same house. If they did for some reason talk, it usually turned into a fight. It made for a very tense household and I hated being there.

I smiled, though it wasn't easy. She didn't need to see that I was afraid too.

"It's going to be okay," I said, trying to comfort her. "We'll figure something out."

Lia was silent for a moment. Tears still running down her face, a frown between her eyebrows, she looked at me very seriously.

"I can't keep this baby," she said. "I have to get rid of it."

"What do you mean get rid of it?"

"I'm going to get an abortion."

"An *abortion*," I echoed. "But why, how, where? Where does one go to get an abortion?"

"I don't know." She shrugged. "But like you said, we'll figure something out."

A couple of days later, Lia called me. She seemed to be in a better mood from the last time I talked to her. She told me she had information on how to go about getting an abortion. A girl in her English class who's had two of them recommended a place—a clinic across town. She said it cost three hundred dollars and no questions asked.

"Oh my goodness, that's a lot of money, Lia."

"I know, but I already have two hundred of it."

"Where'd you get that kind of money from?"

"It's money I have saved up from when my parents were fighting and they were trying to buy my love."

"Okay, that's great, but where are we supposed to get the other hundred from?"

"I don't know. I was hoping you could help me out with that part."

"I don't know either. The only person I know who has that kind of money is my father, and he's not talking to me."

There was brief silence.

"Can you ask your grandfather?"

"No way. I couldn't," I said without hesitation.

"Please, Lonnie, I really need your help on this."

I pictured Lia on the other end of the phone, her facial expression hovering somewhere in a zone between weariness, disappointment, and desperation.

"Okay, but what will I tell him it's for?"

"Tell him you need it to enroll in a GED program."

"Wow, you came up with that awfully fast," I said. "You've already had this planned out, didn't you?"

Lia just laughed. It was the first time I had heard her laugh since we found out that she was pregnant.

Chapter 31

The clinic was on the first floor of a four-story, dilapidated brownstone in Bedford-Stuyvesant, Brooklyn. We got off the A train and walked towards Tompkins Avenue. The place was a little misleading. Other than the sign hanging over the door which read, *Dr. Emmanuel Brown, Medical Practitioner*, it looked more like someone's apartment.

We got there early in the morning. We were the first to arrive, as Lia wanted this done as soon as possible. We both took a deep breath and then Lia rang the doorbell. A minute later, we were buzzed in. We stared down a long, dark hallway with rooms on both sides. Unsure what to make of it, Lia and I just looked at each other, when suddenly a woman appeared at the opposite end.

"Come on down," she bellowed and walked into one of the rooms.

The floorboards squeaked as we walked down the long corridor. I never felt more nervous in my life. The room we entered was probably once a bedroom that had been turned into a waiting room. There was an unusual stench in the air that made me nauseous—a combination of rotting wood and body odor. With all the blinds drawn shut, the room was cold, dark, and eerie. Inside was a file cabinet, a wooden table, a dusty looking old couch, and some single chairs lining the walls. The middle-aged white women, whose facc we had yet to see, had her back to us as she rummaged through some papers in the file cabinet. Feeling uneasy, I turned to Lia.

"What kind of clinic is this?" I asked beneath my breath.

"It's supposed to be under the radar," she whispered back.

"What the hell does that mean?"

"It means they'll do the procedure without a parent's consent."

"I don't know, Lia. I have a bad feeling about this place."

Lia sighed and looked away. When I turned, the woman was staring at us, waiting with her arms folded over breasts. This woman was hideous. Her face was hard and leathery, like she had been exposed to second-hand smoke since birth. She had a huge bump on her nose and beady, rat-like eyes. And if her hair was any greaser, you'd think it was wet.

"Which one of you is this for?" she said with an attitude.

Lia raised her hand and walked over to the table.

"How far along are you?" she asked.

"Nine weeks," Lia told her.

"Do you have the money?"

She snatched the money from Lia's hand and began counting it. Then she sat and wrote something down in her ledger log. When she finished, she got up and told Lia to follow her.

"Wait, I want my cousin to come with me," Lia said.

"No, your cousin can wait in here," she declined.

"Please, you have to let her come. I need her support."

The ugly woman let out a hard sigh and rolled her eyes.

"Whatever," she said and walked out of the room.

Lia grabbed my hand and dragged me along.

We followed her into another room that led off the long corridor. As we entered the room a heavy, pungent, almost putrid smell of rotting meat invaded my nose. I glanced around at the deplorable state of the examination room. Dust and dirt covered every surface in the room, and the floors, walls, and furniture were spattered with blood. If that wasn't enough, baby body parts in huge mason jars lined the shelves like game trophies. It took everything in me not to vomit.

There was a chubby, freckled-face black man with a receding

hairline at the sink washing his hands. Beneath his thick, bifocal glasses, his eyes were cold, dark, and untrusting. He had a mouth full of yellow teeth that I couldn't help but stare at when he talked. His voice, deep and scratchy, he told Lia to undress from the waist down, get on the exam table, and place her legs inside the stirrups. As Lia was undressing, the ugly woman brought in some instruments on a tray and set them down by the exam table.

The instruments didn't look like anything I had ever seen in a doctor's office—they looked ancient. I did recognize a speculum, but that was about it. There was a long metallic rod, a set of surgical knives, some type of small hook with an extension at the end, and one or two other metal implements that looked like they were out of a 1930s horror movie. There was a mason jar with a black rubber seal around the brim with a thin piece of tubing protruding from it. It was connected to what looked like an ordinary shop vac. The doctor's utensils were so low-tech and obscure, I just knew in my heart we were making a terrible mistake. I grabbed Lia as she was getting on the exam table and pulled her aside.

"I don't think you should go through with this," I warned. "It feels wrong."

"I have to," she replied.

"No, you don't," I challenged. "Just bite the bullet and tell your parents. What's the worst that can happen?"

"No, I cannot keep this baby," she insisted. "I don't even know whose baby it is."

"Really, you don't?"

I don't know why that was so hard for me to comprehend. I was in the exact same predicament just a few months ago when I thought I was pregnant.

"Come on, don't look so surprised, Lonnie. As much as you and I sleep around."

Lia sighed.

"So, tell me, how will I explain that to my parents?" she continued. "Ah, Mom and Dad, I'm pregnant and I haven't the slightest idea who the father is."

"Okay, sarcasm noted. But you don't have to do it here. This place gives me the creeps."

"Then where?"

"I don't know. But we'll find another place."

"No, we're already here, and I just want to get it over with."

I continued to plead with her, but Lia wouldn't change her mind. She was anxious to abort the baby. But I had a bad feeling about this place and this doctor, who was now standing in front of us.

"Are you going to stand there and argue all day?" he asked.

Lia didn't hesitate. She climbed on the exam table, pulled the white sheet over her mid-section, and placed her legs inside the stirrups. The tiny exam room was hot, humid, and the offensive odor just hung in the air choking me the entire time. The doctor must've been immune to the smell because it didn't seem to faze him. I tried to think positive thoughts and tell myself it's going to be okay. But still, I was shaking like a leaf.

The doctor grabbed his stool and sat between her legs at the foot of the exam table. I braced myself as my knees began to buckle. Lia on the other hand gasped when he picked up the long metallic rod.

"Hold my hand, Lonnie," she called to me.

The doctor promised it would be painless.

"I'm just going to take a sounding of your uterus," he said. "I need to see how much fluid I'll have to drain out."

With the speculum in place, he started forcing the tip of the rod into her cervix. Lia let out a cry of agony. The pain was unbearable, I could tell. She started sweating instantly from the overwhelming white-hot, radiant pain cooking her from inside. I stroked her hair, as she strained against the undeniable urge to pull away. Her squirming was breaking his concentration as he too began to sweat.

"It will be over soon," I told her. "Just hang in there."

"I don't know if I can," she mumbled. "My insides feel like they're ripping apart."

"Just hold on," the doctor echoed. "I've almost got it where it needs to be."

He leaned forward, placed his hand on her pubic bone, and shoved the rod deeper into her uterus. Lia screamed and dug her fingernails into my hand as tears came streaming down her face. The pain was excruciating, but the doctor wouldn't let off.

Unable to fight it, Lia turned and threw up on my lap. I could feel her slipping out of consciousness. I continued to stroke her hair and talk her down while the doctor inserted the long piece of tubing into her cervix and up her uterus. Then he removed the rod. It was saturated with blood, but there was nothing on it that looked like a fetus. That's what the next device was for—the tiny hook with the extension at the end.

"Are we done?" Lia asked, inches away from unconsciousness.

"Not quite," he replied and inserted the small hook inside her cervix and up her uterus.

Lia snapped back to reality, screaming in pain when he began scrapping her uterus. She shook violently while he waited for blood, fluid, and tissue to pump into the jar. Not satisfied, he scrapped harder. Still quaking and crying, she winced from the pain.

I held her tight and prayed for it to be over quickly. But still, he continued to scrape inside her. She was in pain and became disoriented.

"Please, no more," she cried.

"It's okay now," the doctor said with confidence. "I got it, finally."

I looked down, the jar was filled with blood, fluid, and tissue. Satisfied, he began removing the instrument from insider her. Lia screamed and squirmed under my hold. Her eyes flickering in the back of her head, I just knew something was wrong. The instrument was stuck.

"It's okay, everything is fine," he assured me. "This happens sometimes."

Frustrated, he jerked aggressively on the hook until it came out, followed by a stream of thick crimson blood. The doctor then stood up and tossed the instrument back on the tray. He said he was done and told us the nurse would be in shortly to give us discharge instructions. I asked Lia if she was okay. Barely conscious, she nodded and asked me to take her home. I told her she was brave and helped her sit up. A few minutes later, the ugly nurse came in with a bowl of warm water and some wash cloths. After helping Lia clean up, she gave her a menstrual pad and told her to stay off her feet for a few days.

. . .

We left the clinic and walked into a heat wave. Outside, the August heat was unbelievable, and the humidity wasn't any better. Thank goodness the train station was only a few blocks away. As we started walking, Lia asked if we could take a cab instead.

"I don't feel so good," she complained.

A cab would've been ideal, but I didn't have enough money and neither did she.

"It's not that far," I told her. "We'll walk slowly."

We managed to walk a block before Lia started complaining again. She wanted to sit. She said she was in a lot of pain and felt dizzy. I tried to take hold of her but failed. Before she could take another step, Lia collapsed face first onto the concrete. Thirty minutes later, I was on the phone with Aunt Pamela.

"Auntie Pamela, you have to come now. It's bad, it's really bad, and I'm afraid."

"What are you talking about, Lonnie?"

"Lia fainted, and now she's in surgery, and I'm scared she's not going to make it."

"That doesn't make any sense."

"I'm sorry, Auntie, I tried to stop her, but she wouldn't—"

"Lonnie, you have to calm down. I'm putting you on speakerphone. Lia's father is here too. Take a deep breath and tell me what happened."

"So, we went to this clinic to get an abortion—"

"Abortion, what abortion?"

My aunt and uncle couldn't get their brain around the fact that Lia had gotten pregnant.

"Yes, Lia was two months pregnant. She didn't want to tell you guys, because she was afraid you'd disown her or something."

"Is this some kind of cruel joke, Lonnie?"

"No, Uncle Skyler, it's not. Anyway, the place was really creepy, the doctor was even creepier, and I just knew it was a bad idea. I tried to stop her, but she wouldn't listen. She insisted on going through with it. When it was over, she said she was in a lot of pain. Next thing I know she passed out."

"Okay, don't move a muscle. We're on our way."

I sat in the waiting room at Woodhull Medical Center, waiting for my aunt and uncle to arrive. My head throbbing with pain, I shut my eyes, trying to figure out where it all went wrong. *Why was my life constantly upside down? Why was I always in some kind of trouble?*

Not very long after I hung up, my aunt and uncle arrived at the hospital. They had gotten there awfully fast, and it made me wonder if they'd even stopped for any traffic lights. I cannot adequately describe the emotional state I was in when my aunt and uncle walked into the waiting room. It was a strange mixture of apprehension, nervousness, and throat-clogging terror.

My aunt was hysterical, and my uncle Skyler did all the talking. He went straight to the nurses' station and demanded a status on Lia's surgery. The nurse didn't say much, except that Lia was still in surgery having a hysterectomy. It turned out that abortion doctor's relentless scrapping of her insides had ruptured her uterus. By the time we got to the hospital, Lia was hemorrhaging severely. The trauma team had no choice but to remove her uterus.

This was the first time I had heard the status of Lia's condition. Up until now, no one would tell me anything because Lia was a minor. In fact, they weren't even supposed to operate on her without a parent's consent. But because there was such a profuse discharge of blood, her injury was considered life threatening. They had to, and I had no choice but to call my aunt and tell her.

Standing six foot three, my uncle was towering over me demanding answers.

"What the hell is going on, Lonnie?"

I told him everything. I had to. Through whimpering tears, I told him everything, not leaving out a single detail about the drinking, the smoking, and hooky parties. Uncle Skyler never looked away from my face. When I finished he just hung his head, rubbing the bridge of his nose. He forced himself to draw a deep breath. I could tell he was fighting the urge to snap.

"I'm so sorry about all this," I said, hoping to make things a little less tense. "I really did try to stop her—"

"Shut up," my uncle stood up and yelled. "Shut your mouth and don't say another word, as a matter of fact, just leave."

"Skyler, calm down," my aunt interjected.

But he wouldn't and continued yelling at me.

"I don't want you around Lia anymore," he said, towering over me once again with his index finger in my face. "You're no good for her. I know what you did in California, and you're not going to do that here. I'm not going to let you take Lia down with you. So just leave. Here's five dollars. Find the train station and get the hell away from this family."

He crumbled up the five dollar bill and threw it at me.

"Okay, that's enough, Skyler," my aunt said, finally getting in between us.

"I'm not kidding, Pamela. I don't want her around this family anymore."

"Oh, will you just go and sit down. Lonnie is not entirely to blame. Lia is not an angel either, and God only knows, all this fighting we've been doing probably hasn't helped her much."

My aunt took me in her arms and hugged me tight.

"Please, Auntie, don't make me leave," I cried. "I care about Lia too."

. . .

After three and an half hours, Lia's surgery was finally over. The doctor came into the waiting room and introduced himself. My aunt and uncle couldn't wait to talk to him.

"Tell me, Doctor, how is she?" my uncle asked anxiously.

"She is well," he said with a smile. "The procedure was successful. Lia had a supracervical hysterectomy, also known as a sub-total hysterectomy, meaning we removed the uterus without removing the cervix. We went the abdominal route as opposed to vaginal to prevent any further damage to her cervix.

"What exactly does that mean, Doc?" my uncle interrupted.

"Well, simply put, vaginal means we remove the uterus through the vagina, whereas with the abdominal procedure it comes out through an incision on the abdomen—similar to the size and location of a C-Section."

My uncle just sighed and shook his head, as if the information was too much for him. But the doctor did reiterate that the procedure went well. Lia was going to be okay, he said.

"So, what exactly happened?" my aunt asked further.

"Your daughter was a victim of a botched abortion. These

types of abortions are not at all unique. These horrendous procedures and the doctors who perform them are prevalent in many abortion facilities around the city. They tend to attract people, mainly underage girls, who may not have the money for a safe abortion or who wish to keep it from their parents such as in this case. Sadly though, death of the mother is sometimes the result of these unsafe abortions. Lia is very lucky to be alive, thanks to your quick thinking, Lonnie. You were wise to call an ambulance."

Finally, I had done something right. Auntie Pamela put her arm around me and kissed my forehead. My uncle gave me a soft, gentle stare. I could tell he was thankful, and he probably regretted yelling at me. After talking to the doctor, we went into the recovery unit to see Lia.

She was lying on her back, motionless and pale, with an IV tethered to each arm. Her young life had been forced to near death, but thank goodness it wasn't taken. With a white sheet pulled to her chest, she was breathing lightly but steadily. The side of her face was still badly bruised from when she had fallen, and her hair was tangled wildly around her face. She didn't look very good. Auntie Pamela's eyes swelled up with tears instantly as she leaned over her and kissed her cheek lightly.

Lia's eyes opened slowly, unfocused and unaware of what had occurred.

"Mom, Dad," she whispered, still groggy from the anesthesia.

"We're right here, honey," my aunt replied, squeezing her hand.

"Where am I?" she asked, slowly adjusting her eyes to the lights in the room.

"You're in the hospital."

"What am I doing in the hospital? The last thing I recall . . . "

Still weak, she paused between her words to collect her thoughts.

"Lonnie and I were walking, and then suddenly everything went black . . . Where is Lonnie?"

"Lonnie is here too, honey."

I came forward and gently massaged her shoulder. Lia reached up and felt my face.

"You okay?" she asked.

"I'm fine," I said, trying to hold back tears.

"Are you okay?"

Lia cracked a flat smile.

"Everything hurts."

Hearing that, the nurse came around and picked up the morphine plunger. She turned up the dosage on her intravenous line and told Lia she would start feeling better in a few minutes. She was in a lot of pain, just talking seemed like a mere struggle, so we just let her relax and enjoy the relief the medication brought her.

I visited her every day that she was in the hospital until she was finally released three days later. Subsequently, that was the beginning of the end of our friendship.

Chapter 32

After Lia's discharge from the hospital, her parents became extremely overprotective, and I saw less and less of my friend. The incident hit them both very hard. My aunt and uncle blamed themselves for what happened, convinced their fighting left her feeling neglected. They vowed to never put their problems first and to seek help from a marriage and family therapist.

I had always thought Lia had the best of everything. My uncle worked hard to provide for her and he was generally nice. My aunt was loving, caring, and compassionate. Lia's life was grand in my opinion. Even when conflict increased in the marriage, they stayed together and didn't abandon her.

Lia admitted she was lucky to have them and was grateful that they were attending therapy. There was no longer a dead silence in the house. They started talking about their feelings without getting angry or shouting at each other. They both stopped their affairs and promised to give the marriage another go.

While Lia and her parents were trying to improve their relationship and home life, I found myself alone with no one to talk to or hang out with. For the first couple of days, I sat around my apartment and dwelled in my own disappointment, sleeping in well into the afternoon simply for a lack of desire to get up. Once again, I had reached a point in my life that I could not make sense of. This admission pains me for the simple fact that I was now sixteen-years-old, and the last four years of my young life were spent chemically altering my brain in a futile pursuit to feel good. In the process, I had fell victim to the tight grip of alcohol dependence and didn't even know it.

I needed to drink, but I knew enough not to go back to the housing projects, even though alcohol and drugs flowed freely. I had come to realize that when I drink I cannot keep my legs closed. After what happened to Lia, I refused to put myself in situations where I was having unprotected sex with guys I hardly knew. Getting pregnant had now become my biggest fear.

Instead of going out, I stayed home and drank warm vodka from a water bottle. I snuck beer as much as I could around the apartment for as long as I could tolerate my grandmother's mouth. When I couldn't take it anymore, I'd go up to the roof of my building and drink there.

Drinking by myself was depressing. I hated being alone with my thoughts. I missed the peer culture of adolescents like me who thrived in having a good time. When I found myself overwhelmed with boredom I'd call Lia, but there was always some reason why she couldn't hang out. She said she needed time to heal, which I understood. But after five weeks, I was beginning to think she wanted nothing to do with me, or perhaps her parents wanted that. I was desperate for mischief and adventure.

One day while roaming the neighborhood, I befriended a girl in the area. I had seen her before, jumping in and out of cars, most of which were luxury imports and assumed she was a prostitute.

Her name was Astrid. She was an immigrant girl from Haiti who came to the states at age ten. Now twenty-five years old, her Haitian accent was camouflaged beneath a New York City dialect with mild street slang. Astrid was a drug runner who moved cocaine and heroin by the pound. I was drawn to her right away for what I thought was arrogance at first. But to my dismay it was pure confidence. After my experience with Richard and his drug addict friends, she was the last person I needed to be around. In fact, I should've ran from her when she told me what she did. But instead, I embraced it with intrigue and curiosity.

Lia's near-death experience should've been a wakeup call, a defining moment for me, and a reason to finally get off the path of self-sabotage. But it wasn't. I had not hit rock bottom yet. My descent to the bottom was just beginning.

I met Astrid in a convenience store one Friday morning while standing behind her waiting to pay for my beer and pack of cigarettes. She was nicely dressed, wearing a short, black mini skirt with a butter-yellow blouse and matching low-heeled stilettos. With her hair back in a bun and no makeup but just a soft-colored lip gloss, she looked naturally beautiful.

"I like your bag," I said.

It was a black, Chanel, vintage, quilted shoulder bag that sold for about fifteen hundred dollars retail. She turned and looked at me.

"I've never seen such a pretty bag," I said. "Did you get it in Manhattan?"

I felt a little weird for being nosy, but she was nice.

"No, it was a gift," she replied softly.

I nodded and left it at that.

"What's your name?" she asked.

"Lonnie."

"Do you normally drink this early, Lonnie?"

"Yeah, usually when I'm bored."

"If you're bored, you should consider getting a hobby."

"This is my hobby," I said and laughed.

She laughed too, then turned and paid for her Snapple Ice Tea. On her way out, she smiled and told me to have a good day. When I finally walked out of the store myself, I found her standing out front sipping her ice tea, staring at me as if she had been waiting for me.

"Where are you going?" she asked.

"Nowhere, really," I replied with a calm shoulder shrug.

"Would you like to come with me to run some errands?"

She turned and opened the passenger door of a sporty, BMW 318i and motioned me over. I had no idea who this woman was, and I knew better than to get in a car with a perfect stranger. But there was an alluring presence about her. The choice was obvious. Go to the roof and drink by myself or take a drive in a nice car and have a conversation with a real person.

The car was a stick shift that she operated with ease. As I watched her release the clutch and pull away from the curb, I flashed back to California when I had the accident with Jenna's car. I thought to myself, *Okay, so that's how it's done.*

She handled the five-speed transmission like a professional race car driver, swerving in and out of lanes at high speeds. I was impressed and couldn't help but stare at the defined muscles in her legs as she shifted from one gear to another. I didn't even know where we were going, but it was nice just being out and doing something. We drove in silence at first, so to break the ice I decided to be nosy again.

"You have a lot of nice things," I said, looking around the car. "So, what do you do?"

"Let's see." She chuckled. "Last year, I graduated from college with a bachelor's degree in business. Afterwards, I tried to get a job in my field. I filled out numerous applications and sent out dozens of resumes, but no one would hire me. When my bills began piling up, I became desperate and took a job at a delicatessen in Bay Ridge. I worked long hours doing laborious chores—cutting up meat, stocking shelves, taking out trash, you name it."

I sipped my beer slowly as I listened. I remembered looking at her, thinking, *I wouldn't want to do that type of work if I had a fancy business degree.*

"One day, I was working at the counter and a man in a suit came in," she continued. "He wanted a pound of sliced turkey. I had just finished slicing some ham for a previous customer. As I was removing the block of ham from the meat slicer, he told me I had to break down the slicer and clean it before I sliced his turkey. I asked him why and he replied very smartly, 'Because I'm Jewish, I don't eat ham,' and rolled his eyes, as if I was supposed to know that."

"What a dick," I interjected.

"Tell me about it. Anyway, I said I'm not giving you ham and proceeded to slice the turkey. He didn't like that. He went off and started shouting at me. By now a line was forming behind him and I was becoming increasingly embarrassed. Within seconds the owner, my boss, came out, and surprisingly, sided with the Jewish man. I was pissed. I came from around the counter and threw the sliced turkey in the man's face. Then I took off my apron, tossed it at the owner and walked out. As I hurried to the train station, blinded by rage, I bumped into a man and accidently spilled his coffee. I quickly apologized. He asked if I was okay. He could tell I was angry and needed to vent. He turned out to be a great listener, and when I finished running my mouth he asked if I wanted a job. Nine months later, I'm still working for him."

"Doing what?" I asked, still clueless as to what she did.

"Okay, we're here," she said, as she pulled in along the curb.

Astrid turned off the engine, pulled up the emergency break, then looked over and told me that she was a drug runner. Unsure what to think, I just stared at her. She smiled, stepped out of the car, and told me to come along. Reluctantly, I opened the door, still clutching the beer in my hand. She told me to leave the bottle, we weren't going to be long. I walked around to the truck where she was standing. Astrid handed me a bag of groceries.

"What is this?" I asked, confused and still unsure what to think.

"The groceries are just a front, the drugs are at the bottom of the bag," she replied.

She grabbed a second bag, closed the truck, and told me to follow her. Suddenly, everything went silent, and all I could hear was my heart pounding. My eyes nervously darted back and forth, fearful someone might be on to what we were doing. I followed her into one of the restaurants in the commercial district in Bay Ridge. We went to the back of the restaurant, through the kitchen, and into a small office. She knocked and walked in. Inside, a man was sitting at a desk going through receipts.

"Astrid, I wasn't expecting you so soon," he said as he rose from his chair.

He came from behind the desk, took the bag, and kissed her on the cheek. He set the bag down then they talked quietly for about ten minutes while I stood there holding my bag. I didn't hear anything that was said because they whispered. But I had a strange feeling they were talking about me. Finally, when they finished he came over and took the bag from me. He told me his name, shook my hand, and said he was glad to meet me. I just smiled and said, "Likewise."

Still very nervous, I watched as he emptied the bags, tossing the groceries aside to retrieve four big blocks of cocaine wrapped in clear plastic. I had never seen so much drugs in my life, except for in the movies. My heart started racing. I kept thinking that at any second, FBI, DEA, or SWAT was going to burst in the room with guns blazing and put us all on the floor. After examining the product, this man handed Astrid an envelope full of money and we left.

Back in the car, I downed the rest of my beer with trembling hands as Astrid pulled away from the curb. I asked her if it was okay to smoke and lit the cigarette before she could even reply. She smiled and told me to light one for her too. I took a long drag, sunk back in my seat, and waited for my nerves to settle.

On the drive back to my apartment, Astrid gave me a little more insight into her life and her job. I hung on her every word. When we pulled up in front of my building, I didn't want to get out of the car. I wanted to stay with her longer and talk more.

"Yes, this is where I live," I hesitated.

Astrid asked to see my phone. She took it and punched in her number. Then she pressed a fifty dollar bill inside my hand.

"What's this for?" I asked, completely surprised.

"It's for your part in today's delivery. Call me next time you're bored."

I stepped out the car and closed the door. Then I watched with an open mouth as she made a broken U-turn and sped off down the street.

Chapter 33

I could hardly contain myself. Meeting Astrid was the most excitement I had in the ten months since I'd been back. I called Lia, thinking she'd be excited about my news. But instead, she chastised me and said I was being foolish once again. Deep down inside, I knew she was right but what was I to do? I had no one to talk to, no one to hang out with; I was bored out of my mind. We got into a huge argument over the phone.

"That's easy for you to say," I fired back. "You have everything, parents who care about you, a great big house, you go to a good school, and you get good grades. As for me, I have none of these things. I live in a run-down, roach-infested apartment, and I have a drug-addicted, prostitute for a mother and a father who won't talk to me. So excuse me if I'm not thrilled about my life right now."

"Lonnie," she said, after listening to me rant. "What happened in California is nobody's fault but yours. But it's done and you can't undo it. What you can do is change your ways, stop drinking and partying so hard. Stop sleeping around so much. Get on the right path. Hanging out with this Astrid person doesn't sound like the right path for you."

Lia was right, but I didn't want to admit it.

"When did you become so self-righteous?" I asked. "You used to love drinking and partying too."

"When I was laid up in the hospital," she replied in sobering tone. "I realized I could've died because of the poor choices I made. Thank God you were there. But regrettably, I will never be able to have kids now."

There was a brief pause.

"I'd hate for something like this to happen to you. Be smart, Lonnie, learn from my mistake."

I hung up the phone, feeling pretty lousy. To cheer myself up, I got my hair done and my nails painted with the money I earned. The rest of it I used to buy booze. As I was leaving the convenience store with a six pack in my hand I ran into Astrid. She was in an awful hurry and told me to call her on Monday. With nothing to do and no one to talk to, I decided to get drunk the remainder of the weekend.

When Monday came around, I called Astrid. She was happy to hear from me and asked if I wanted to come along on a few deliveries. I was in front of my building, sipping a beer when she pulled up around a quarter to twelve. With excitement surging through my veins, I ran over to the car and jumped in. We drove up the road and got on the freeway towards the Oceanside neighborhood of Brighten Beach. We made small talk at first, mainly about what we did over the weekend. She said she liked my hair, I told her I liked her shoes, and then we got down to business.

"I never did get to thank you for taking me with you last week," I told her.

"So, I take it you enjoyed yourself."

"I sure did. Matter of fact, I wanted to ask you, how can I get a job like yours."

Astrid chuckled.

"It's funny you ask, because I was actually thinking that I could use you, but . . . "

Astrid took her eyes off the road momentarily and looked at me.

"But what?" I asked with worry.

"I'm concerned about your drinking, Lonnie. So far, every

time I've run into you, you've had a beer in your hand. It's barely twelve o'clock and you're already drinking. I bet you haven't even eaten yet, have you?"

Shamefully, I shook my head.

"No, I haven't."

"To do this type of work, Lonnie, you have to be sober. You have to stop drinking. Can you do that?"

I replied yes without hesitation. Nothing good ever came out of my drinking. Every time I drank I made a fool of myself or I got in trouble. I wanted to stop and now I had an incentive to do so. Astrid was offering a chance to be responsible for something and I liked that, even if it was something illegal.

"I only drink because I have nothing else to do," I told her. "If you take me on, I promise I won't disappoint you."

Astrid looked at me and smiled. She seemed satisfied with my answer.

"Where are we going by the way?" I inquired.

"Well, the first thing we're going to do is get you something to eat. Drinking on an empty stomach is not healthy."

We got off at Ocean Parkway and turned left onto West Brighton Avenue where we had lunch at a small sandwich shop. I ate an oven-roasted turkey on wheat while Astrid went through her business proposal. She seemed excited about the prospects, for she had thought about it for some time. I was equally excited. This woman, who had known me for only seventy-two hours, was willing to include me in her business venture. Her plan was simple and indicative of how most businesses get started.

After running drugs for nine months, she'd saved enough money to go into business for herself. Her plan was to sell weed and cocaine to college kids. My part was to hang around campus, blend in with the students, and sell them drugs. We would then split the profits equally after she recouped her initial investment. She was certain we'd make lots of money, because according to her, "College kids love to party." My only concern was blending in, but she was confident I could pass for a college student because I looked older than I really was. I was excited and couldn't wait to start.

After lunch, we made her scheduled deliveries—two in Brighton Beach and one in Coney Island. For my part, I was paid one hundred and fifty dollars. Following Astrid's advice, I purchased a backpack and a couple trendy outfits for my new role as a pretend college student.

Staying sober was harder than I thought. Drinking was all I thought about for two days. It had become my routine and physically I didn't feel right without it. But despite the difficulties, I fought through the cravings and stayed clean. Finally, a couple of days later, Astrid picked me up and we drove to Brooklyn College. I didn't have to sell anything. I was there only to make friends and learn their drug habits. Still though, I was a nervous wreck.

I stepped out of the car shaking like a leaf. Ironically, I thought about drinking a beer to calm my nerves, but then I remembered my promise to my new employer. Instead, I decided to have a cigarette and walk around. Once I started making my way around campus and people watch, I started to feel a little bit at ease.

It didn't take long before I started drawing attention. But it was mostly from guys trying to hook up with me. As tempting as it was, because they were cute, I had to turn them down. I was there on business. Finally, after walking around for an hour, I met up with a clique of girls—four total. We got to talking when one of them asked me for a cigarette.

"What's your name?" she asked, as she lit the cigarette.

"My name is Lonnie," I replied.

"I'm Kim."

The other three were Jessica, Heather, and Nikki.

"I haven't seen you around, are you new here?" Kim asked.

"Yeah, this is my first semester."

"That's nice. So what's your major?"

I paused for a second, I didn't think I'd have to answer questions like that.

"Umm, I'm in the arts department," I replied.

"Cool," Jessica said. "So, you like paint pictures and shit?"

"A little bit. I mostly do illustration."

"No shit, so can you design me a tattoo?"

"Ah, yeah, I'm sure I could."

Then suddenly, the other two girls expressed their interest in a tattoo design. We continued talking then the conversation shifted when Kim mentioned that she couldn't wait for the weekend to arrive so that she could party. That caught my attention. When I inquired, I learned they were into all sorts of drugs, thus becoming my first customers.

The next day I came prepared, carrying with me five dime bags of marijuana, which sold for ten dollars, and five baggies of medium-grade cocaine, one gram each, which sold for fifty. Meeting that group of girls was a blessing. Not only did they purchase my product, they also introduced me to other students hungry for drugs. By noon I had sold out of everything that Astrid had given me, and I had orders for more.

I called Astrid right away. Thirty minutes later, she pulled up in the BMW and we drove off. She was pleased that I was able to move the merchandise so quickly. And when I told her I had requests for more she became ecstatic. The next day she gave me twice as much, and I sold it just as fast. The following week, I doubled up yet again and had the same success. Every week after that we would raise the bar just a little, and every week we expanded. Four months later, we had about a third of the student body on our clientele list. Business was booming and we were raking in the dough. Cash was coming in faster than I could spend it. Fortunately, I had Astrid to mentor me. She gave me three guiding principles to live by.

"One, only buy things you need," she said. "Two, save as much of your earnings as you can, and three, never tell anyone how much money you have. In this business, you're going to have but few friends."

In four months of doing business together, Astrid and I had gotten to know each other and became good friends. During the week, we'd hang out for a couple of hours after work and just talk or she would give driving lessons. I really enjoyed driving the car. But more importantly, it was the first time anyone had actually taught me how to do something. On the weekends we'd do girly things like get our hair and nails done or we'd go shopping. At this point, Astrid was slowly replacing Lia as my best friend. But Astrid was better than a best friend. She was a mentor and a teacher too, always teaching me about finances and how the drug business works.

"The drug business is no different from any other business," she explained. "They both work the same way. You start at the bottom, working very hard, hoping for a better position at the top. As you move up, you get people under you, people you train while you get paid more to make sure the job gets done. The more you move up, the less you do, and the more you make. The same principles apply when it comes to selling drugs. You start out peddling the drugs yourself. But you work hard and save until you can get others to peddle for you. The more peddlers you get, the more money you make. The more money you make, the less drugs you touch."

It sounded really good and I ate it all up. I could've listened to her talk for hours. But at the time I didn't see the big picture. I thought Astrid was teaching me all these neat things because she liked me. And granted, she may have, but that wasn't the real reason.

Chapter 34

By Christmas of 2007 I was sober, I had a substantial amount of money saved up, and I found a great friend in Astrid. But despite these new experiences, I couldn't help but feel sad during a time when the rest of the country found joy. It started the Friday before Christmas when I received a phone call from Lia. I had just gotten home from another profitable day on campus. Astrid was hosting a Christmas party later in the evening, and she wanted me to attend. The weekend was off to a good start and I was elated.

Lia was the last person I expected to hear from, considering she hadn't called me in months.

"Hi, Lonnie, is this a bad time?"

"No, not all," I replied.

"So, how are you? What have you been up to?" she asked with hesitation.

It had been so long since Lia and I talked, I wasn't sure what to say. I wanted to tell her everything, but I knew she wouldn't approve. I refrained from telling her about my business venture with Astrid and all the money I'd been making. I did, however, tell her that I stopped drinking. That I knew she'd be proud of.

"So, what have you been up to?"

"I've been spending a lot of time with my parents," she replied. "In fact, that's really why I called. After the abortion, Mom and Dad were pretty hard on themselves. They strongly believed it was their fighting that pushed me away and caused me to behave so inappropriately. As a result, they've become more attentive to my needs, and they're a lot closer now that we've been attending family therapy. It brought something out in them that for a while I thought was lost. I have to admit, we're much closer as a family now than we've ever been."

Listening to Lia talk about how close her family had become was depressing me. I didn't have anyone in my life who cared for me the way her parents cared about her. It made me envious, and I wanted to get off the phone. Even though I missed my friend, I listened only to be polite. I was about to change the subject and get off the phone when Lia got to her point.

"Anyway," she continued. "My father's company has offered him a promotion, but the new job is in West Hartford, Connecticut. My father and my mother both think it would be a good idea to leave the city. They agree there are too many negative influences around us. 'City life can be challenging when it comes to raising a family' my father said."

"Are you serious, Lia?"

"I don't like it either. But they've already made up their minds. While we've been attending therapy, my father was simultaneously pursuing a lawsuit over my botched abortion. He hired a very good lawyer, and we were able to settle out of court for a handsome amount. They want to take the settlement money and buy a house in some suburb in West Hartford. In fact, after the holidays we're driving up there to look at some properties."

Lia may as well have shot me in the chest. I had assumed this therapy thing would eventually pass and we'd go back to hanging out again. I never imagined it was going to end up with Lia moving out of state. After that I lost all interest in the conversation. I pretended to listen for a little longer and then rushed off the phone.

Later on, I was standing in front of my building waiting for Astrid to pick me up when my mother and Sharon of all people showed up. I could tell the two of them were high by the way they were laughing and carrying on. It was 29 degrees out and neither of them had on a winter jacket. *Only crack cocaine could make someone immune to freezing temperatures*, I thought.

"Lonnie, is that you?" my mother said, shouting into the night.

Her eyes were bloodshot and glazed over. I could smell the alcohol on her and prayed Astrid didn't pull up at that moment to see my poor excuse of a mother. I took a deep breath and tried to remain calm.

"Where are you going, looking so nice?"

"Nowhere special, just out."

"Maybe she's got a hot date," Sharon chimed in and started laughing.

"What, you got a boyfriend?" my mother asked, feeding into Sharon's nonsense. "Does he have money? He better have money, don't be hooking up with no broke-ass niggers, okay."

"I don't have a boyfriend. And thank you for the motherly advice."

If sarcasm could kill, she would've dropped dead right then and there. I looked up the road and saw the headlights of the beamer. Astrid parked in front of the building. I quickly pushed passed them and jumped in the car.

I had never been to an upscale social gathering before. Everyone looked so sophisticated in their expensive clothes, walking around with mixed drinks in hand. I didn't look half bad myself, sporting a backless, tight mini dress with matching three-inch pumps. My makeup was a soft shade of lipstick and a hint of eye shadow. I wore my hair back in a ponytail to expose my collarbone and neck, showing off my over-sized hooped earrings. Every guy in the place had their eyes on me.

Afraid to venture off on my own, I followed Astrid around most of the night. I didn't talk much and tried my best to remain unnoticed. It was hard though because I was the youngest person there. But at the same time, it was flattering having a bunch of thirty-five and forty-year-old men checking me out. I had no idea what to do with myself or how to fit in. At one point, I considered leaving because I felt so out of place. Seeing that I was somewhat uncomfortable, Astrid took me to the bar and ordered me a beer.

"What are you doing?" I asked her.

"Isn't this your favorite brand?" she replied, as she placed a Heineken in front of me.

"Yeah, but I thought you said I couldn't drink."

Astrid chuckled.

"Yes, when you're on the job. Right now we're at a party. It's okay to have a drink or two when you're in a social setting."

Astrid picked up her glass of cranberry and vodka and took a sip.

"See, I'm having a drink."

Astrid then walked off and said she was going to talk to some business associates. I stood at the bar for about five minutes, staring down at the green bottle with icy condensation trickling down the sides. I placed my hand around the cold bottle, and suddenly, my heart started racing. The medium malt and barley aroma invaded my nose. I salivated looking at the pale, gold hue from within. I wanted to bring the bottle to my lips and taste the bitter, fresh flavor, but I was torn and confused. *Why did she order me a beer? First she tells me not to drink, then she tells me it's okay*. For a minute, I thought she was messing with my mind. *But Astrid wouldn't do that*, I told myself. *She's my friend. I'm analyzing this way too much. She's right, it's okay to have a drink or two in a social setting. And besides, it's been four months since I had a drink. I deserve this.*

It was just as I remembered. Light bodied and full of flavor, a lively carbonation with a crisp finish. I could've downed the whole bottle in one shot but I didn't want to appear unladylike. I sipped it slowly and with each sip, the endorphins and pleasure sensors in my brain started to come alive. By the time I finished the bottle, which didn't take long, I felt relaxed, uninhibited, and ready to socialize. With Astrid gone, many of the men at the party began to approach me. I smiled and shook more hands than a politician on a campaign trail. I gave my phone number to every guy who asked for it. I couldn't help myself, they were all so good looking, and I was suddenly hot for sex.

By the time Astrid returned from whatever she was doing, I had already drank three beers and working on a second Red Bull and vodka that someone had given me. Having been sober for four months, my tolerance had lowered significantly. But what hadn't changed was my insatiable appetite for alcohol. I was already feeling drunk when I made my way back to the bar for another drink.

The tall, handsome man I'd been throwing myself at for the last twenty minutes was standing behind me, caressing my thighs when Astrid finally reappeared. She gave me a peculiar look and him as well. I don't know what she whispered in his ear but he left in a hurry afterwards. Astrid looked at me. A shameful blush warmed my cheeks. I quickly straightened my dress and fixed my stockings.

"I'm glad you're finally feeling comfortable," she said, staring at the drink in my hand. "But try not to overdo it."

"No, of course not," I assured her.

Astrid took my hand and led me away from the bar. We went over to the couch and sat down. My heart was racing. I thought she was going to lecture me about my drinking.

"You've been doing a great job pushing out product," she started. "But I worry over the long run we won't be able to sustain these kinds of profit with just you on the job. We need to get you some help."

I nodded as I sipped my drink.

"What I'd like to do is put someone else at Brooklyn College. Have them continue where you left off. Then in a couple of months when that person has enough capital, we'll start selling to that individual directly as much as he or she needs. Meanwhile, I want to move you to New York City Tech, downtown, so that you can set shop there. Basically, do the same thing you did at Brooklyn College until we can find someone to succeed you, and then we'll move on to the next college. Are you with me so far?"

"I think so," I replied. "And if I understand you correctly, you're saying that over time I won't have to handle the drugs myself. I'll simply supply the distributors, therefore making money off them."

Astrid chuckled.

"I've trained you well," she boasted. "Now, all we have to do is find you a replacement. Is there anyone you know that would be interested in our business, someone you can trust?"

"Actually, I do know someone who may be interested. I met her around the second week that I was dealing. Her name is

Courtney, and she doesn't do drugs. She is currently working her way through college, and she's always complaining about how expensive school is. She says she never has money for anything. I might be able to bring her onboard."

Astrid approved. She told me to try my best to bring Courtney in and plan on relocating to New York City Tech if she decides to come onboard. When our conversation was over I had another drink, my last one for the night. I wanted more but I was afraid I'd get entirely drunk and make a fool of myself as usual. But more importantly, I stopped because I didn't want to embarrass Astrid and ruin the trust I had built up with her. So the remainder of the night I drank water and made small talk with the people I came across. Finally, around midnight, I told Astrid I was getting tired and she drove me home. After she left, I walked down to the all-night corner store and bought a six pack of beer. I wasn't ready to stop drinking.

Chapter 35

My senses for alcohol were re-stimulated the night of Astrid's Christmas party. I finished up the weekend with more beer and more vodka. That year the weekend rolled right into Christmas, which for me, was lame and uneventful. To keep things interesting, I drank more beer and more vodka. In the days that followed, I received a phone call from Roberto. He was the tall, handsome man from the Christmas party who Astrid had chased away.

Roberto was incredibly good looking, so much that it made me wonder why he picked me when he probably could've had any woman of his choosing. He was six foot two inches of muscle with very little body fat, tan skin, and beautiful, animal-brown eyes that revealed coolness and confidence. His bright smile and perfectly formed, white teeth were behind a neatly framed goatee that matched his silky, wavy black hair.

He asked if I was really sixteen because I looked much older. I told him that I was, in fact, sixteen but he didn't seem to care. He wanted me and I wanted him to have me. He asked me to spend New Year's with him and I gladly accepted. We hung out for about two days at his very fashionable condo in Park Slope, Brooklyn.

Upon first sight, I was wowed by the lavish décor of his place. Beautiful frescoes adorned the walls of the foyer and huge living room. A big leather sectional and ottoman took up most of the space in the L-shaped living area. A contemporary-style chandelier hung from the ceiling of the dining room that sat off the open kitchen. And all around the place, expensive-looking vases and other accessories pulled everything together for a modern and clean look. Roberto's place was indeed nice, but he didn't invite me over to view his place. I went there to have fun and that I did.

We spent the entire time drinking and having sex. At one point, Roberto suggested I try some cocaine. I didn't want to at first. After my trip on ecstasy, I had written off anything in the form of a pill or powder. But somehow, I let Roberto convince me that it was nothing to be afraid of.

He spread the coke out onto a tray and then cut it into neat little lines with a razor blade. He went first, snorting an entire line in one shot. Then he pulled me onto his lap and handed me the rolled up twenty dollar bill. He told me to do a line. My heart thumping, I leaned over and sniffed an entire line just as he had done. The coke whizzed up my nostril and brought tears to my eyes. He told me to hold my head back and pinch my nose to make sure none came out. Within a few minutes, the coke was trickling down my throat and I needed a drink. After having a beer, I began to feel the first flush of the cocaine high—anxiety, giddiness, excitement, and alertness rippled through my body. I loved the way the coke made me feel. I was hooked instantly.

. . .

When I left Roberto's place, he made it clear that nothing serious could ever come of us. Because he was significantly older than me—eighteen years to be exact—he said our relationship could only be physical. He added that he trusted me to be mature and not discuss our arrangement with anyone, especially Astrid. I don't know what his relationship with her was, but he was adamant that his name never come up in my conversations with her.

I didn't mind his request. In fact, I welcomed it. After my relationship with Sean and then Richard, I decided to stop falling for guys who didn't give a damn about me. I had a track record of allowing whoever I was dating to shape my life and make decisions based on their needs, rather than what was best for me. I decided I wasn't going to do that anymore. I was going to take a page from Lia's playbook, which was, *Trust no man and never confuse love with sex*. I thanked Roberto for a good time and then called a cab. He offered to drive me home, but I told him he didn't have to. He appreciated my independence and was glad he didn't have to babysit me.

The following week I was at City Tech, walking around trying to set up shop like Astrid and I had discussed. But it was not a good day to begin work. I was hungover from the drinking binge that I'd been on since Astrid's Christmas party. However, despite my fatigue and lack of motivation, I managed to drag myself around campus and do what I was sent to do, which was to make friends and learn their drug habits.

Despite the assurance I gave Astrid, alcohol continued to plague my mind as I walked through campus. After about two hours I became frustrated. The headaches were starting to get the best of me and I gave in. I left campus and got a beer. An hour later, I was back to my old self and ready to meet people. With the pep back in my step, I returned to campus and as luck would have it, I connected with some potential clients. Before I called Astrid to come pick me up, I decided to get lunch and have another beer. Afterwards, I got some gum and candy to freshen my breath while I waited for my ride.

Not before long, Astrid and I were driving along Flatbush Avenue heading towards Brooklyn College to check up on Courtney. After the Christmas party, I had contacted Courtney and proposed to her the idea of selling for us. The conversation was brief and I didn't have to do much convincing. She was more than willing to do it.

Earlier that morning, I dropped off a package with Courtney. It was the same thing I started out with a few months back five dime bags of weed and five baggies of medium-grade coke. I thought it was strange that Astrid didn't want to meet Courtney. She made me get out a block away and walk the package to her. Later, I realized why. The less people that knew her, the harder it would be to identify her if something were to ever go wrong.

Courtney did well. She sold out in record time too. The next day, I supplied her with more drugs and then went to City Tech to begin making an impact there. After Astrid drove off, I took a couple of sips from my water bottle, which was filled with vodka, to get rid of my developing headache. The night before, I had partied pretty hard with Roberto and I needed something to take the edge off. Once I had some sense of normalcy, I met up with my clients. I dumped off my drugs, took more orders, and made new contacts.

The time flew by and the drugs flew out of my hands even quicker. Within a month's time, I had an extensive clientele list at City Tech. And the business was so good at Brooklyn College, we hired two more girls so we could keep up with demand. Astrid insisted we only employ women. Her reasons: "One, men cannot be trusted. Two, men are greedy. And three, women are usually less suspected of being drug movers."

. . .

By the time spring came around, Astrid and I had a mini enterprise with three girls at Brooklyn College, two at City Tech, and two at Kingsborough Community College on the edge of Brooklyn in Manhattan Beach. Everything was unfolding exactly how Astrid had described.

I was working less because I had recruited and trained others to take my place. Astrid turned the car over to me with complete confidence to drive around and manage our different drug sites. My job now was to simply supply our distributors. I'd show up, hand out the drugs, collect our profits, and make payroll to our workers. In the interim, I was making money from their hard work, and because business was good, my personal wealth was growing commensurately.

My day started usually around nine or ten in the morning, depending on how much I partied the night before. Hanging out with Roberto was always a guaranteed good time. He loved sex, he loved drinking, and he loved cocaine. After a night with him, I had to have a fix before I could get my day started.

Noon was usually about the time my stomach would settle and I could have a sandwich or slice of pizza, along with more alcohol. My evenings were spent either alone drinking or with Roberto drinking. Occasionally, I'd do some girly stuff with Astrid on the weekend. But whatever I did, alcohol was always included.

I was proud to call myself a businesswoman whose managerial ability for weighing time, personnel, and money allowed me to be a functioning alcoholic. Despite Astrid's orders not to drink on the job, I continued to do so while managing seven people and coordinating the movement of several pounds of drugs and thousands of dollars. It wasn't hard to do. The more Astrid used me to move up her own ladder of success, the less she was involved in the day-to-day activities. This afforded me the freedom to manage at my level or do things how I saw fit and come and go as I pleased.

This routine went on for months. I was moving drugs, I was making money, and I had a commitment-free, guilt-free affair with an older man who seemed to enjoy my company. I thought I had everything under control. But Astrid was right, you have to be sober to do this type of work. When you're on drugs, you're not in control of anything. Unfortunately, that was a lesson I had to learn the hard way.

It was a cold, breezy morning. Spring showers prevalent through the night left the city wet and the roads slick. I had been up all weekend, drinking and snorting coke off every part of Roberto's rock-hard body. I had never done that much blow in one sitting before, and my body ached all over. My brain was fried and I was sleep deprived. This was not a good day to be on the road. But duty called. I was now doing Astrid's job too, running kilos of coke to various points throughout the city on top of my other duties.

I drove from Roberto's place back to my apartment. I needed to put myself back together the best I could after a weekend of overindulgence before I met up with Astrid. Upstairs, I took a hot shower then drenched myself in perfume so Astrid wouldn't smell the alcohol emitting from my pores. After I dressed, I fixed myself a stiff drink. I brushed my teeth, popped in a piece of gum, and left.

The rain had been on and off all morning. Another down pour hit just as I stepped out of my building. There were numerous accidents on the road. So I drove to her place with caution. When I finally arrived, I blew out a long breath and popped in another piece of gum before I went in to see Astrid.

She was pleased with the way things were moving along. She

wanted to hire more girls and branch out to other schools.

"But I'm a little worried about you," she said with concern on her face. "You seem overwhelmed."

I paused for a second to compose the right answer.

"No, not at all," I finally said. "I have some family issues I'm dealing with right now, that's all."

Perhaps it was guilt eating away at me, but I felt as though she could see right through me. I felt empty and naked under her intimidating stare. The room suddenly got hot. My palms became moist and clammy with perspiration as we locked eyes in a mini stare down. Feeling uncomfortable, I quickly looked away. I thought at any second she was going to call me a liar and force me to come clean. But she didn't. Instead, she smiled and offered her sympathy.

"Alright then, if you insist that's all it is."

I could tell she wasn't convinced but the time wasn't right. There was work to do. There were drugs to deliver and money to collect. I couldn't wait to get out of there. Astrid filled up the trunk with the day's deliveries and told me to be careful. I nodded and left in a hurry. I had to. The physical effects of withdrawal were starting to take a toll. I left her place shaking like an old man with Parkinson's disease.

I got in the car and turned on the engine. I put the car in gear but then waited for a moment. I didn't feel good. I took the car out of gear and cut off the engine. With trembling hands, I lit a cigarette then tossed the box aside. Desperate for relief, I reached under the seat and grabbed my water bottle filled with vodka. I had gotten in the habit of keeping readily available liquor for when times got hard. I took a long swallow then reclined back in the seat. I closed my eyes and exhaled slowly. My head was still throbbing, but I started to feel the warm sensation in my chest right away. Relief was just another swallow or two away. With jittery hands and all, I put the bottle to my lips and took another big gulp. I smoked the remainder of my cigarette before turning the engine back on. *There has to be a better way than this*, I thought, as I put the car in gear and drove off.

I needed to deliver three kilos of cocaine to three different locations. I left Astrid's one-bedroom condo in Brooklyn Heights and got on the Brooklyn Queens Expy towards Sunset Park to make my first delivery. Twenty minutes later, I made my first drop off with no problem. My only issue was that I was still hungover and coming down from my three-day cocaine binge. My body needed sleep. But like a fool I kept taking sips of vodka, thinking that would pick me back up.

As I was leaving Sunset Park, the sky opened up and more rain came pouring down. It was a miserable day and I felt awful. At this point I just wanted to hurry up and make my deliveries so I could go home and crash out. I got back on the expressway and floored the pedal to my next destination. The in-line, six-cylinder engine roared as I accelerated to seventy miles an hour.

Thinking a little nicotine would help keep me awake, I looked around for my cigarettes. They weren't in my pocket. The box was on the floor on the passenger side of the car. With one hand on the steering wheel, I leaned over and tried to pick up the cigarettes. But I couldn't, my arm wasn't long enough. I scooted over and leaned in even further, but still, I couldn't reach. Frustrated, I unbuckled my seatbelt and reached down for the cigarettes.

When I sat back up and finally looked in front of me, I was about thirty feet from a stalled car in the number one lane. I panicked and I slammed on the brakes. The wheels locked and the car went into a skid. Realizing I wasn't going to stop in time, I turned the steering wheel to get into the next lane. The car spun out of control. The backend clipped the stalled vehicle and I spun again in the opposite direction. The car flipped onto its side and slid down the freeway.

The last thing I remembered was being thrown from my seat, my limp body bouncing around the cabin like a pinball several times over until finally the blackness of unconsciousness enveloped me entirely.

I was lucky to be alive and even luckier to have only suffered minor injuries—four cracked ribs, a broken left arm, and a whole lot of bruises. I left the hospital under heavy guard and went straight to the police precinct for processing. I was in terrible shape and I just wanted to go home, but I knew that wasn't going to happen. I was terrified of the situation I had found myself in. This wasn't like anything I had done in the past. Skipping school, getting drunk in public, crashing Jenna's car, and running away from my father were all petty compared to what was happening at that moment. Drug possession carried a hefty penalty in New York, and I had two kilos of cocaine in the trunk of my car. And I was driving under the influence. *What was I thinking?*

At the precinct, I asked for my one phone call and called the only person I could. I had burned everyone who tried to do right by me and Astrid was the only friend I had at this point. I assumed she would make things better or at minimum give me sound advice and guide me through this unfamiliar ordeal. But that was not the case when Astrid got on the phone. She only seemed to care about one thing.

"Where the hell are you?" she barked. "I've been calling you all day. And why haven't you delivered the coke?"

"I was in the hospital."

"The hospital," she echoed. "What are you doing in the hospital? What the hell is going on, Lonnie? And where is the coke for the last time?"

"I don't know. I assume the police have it."

Astrid was angry and frustrated. I could hear her breathing hard on the other end of the phone. I could tell she was about to snap. I backed up and started from the beginning. I told her everything—my involvement with Roberto, my cocaine binge over the weekend, the drinking and smoking, and what led to the accident. There was an uncomfortable pause. I could almost hear Astrid's mind processing my words on the other end of the receiver. To break the tension, I added that my injuries were minor and that I was okay.

"I don't give a damn about your injuries," she snapped. "Do you have any idea what kind of predicament you've put me in?"

I could only imagine. I assumed she had a boss too, and she was going to have to explain to someone that the coke was in police custody.

"I know. I messed up and I'm really sorry."

"Shut the fuck up!" Astrid screamed over the phone. "Just shut up and listen to me. Do not say a word about where you got the coke. Don't mention my name or where I live or anything about me. Do you understand?"

"I haven't said anything," I assured her.

"I'm not kidding, Lonnie," she continued, talking through her teeth. "If you drag me into this, I promise, you are going to wish you were dead when my people get through with you. I was a fool to have trusted you. I should've known better."

I listened to Astrid threaten me and chastise me at the same time. She made it perfectly clear that we were not friends. This was an unforgivable mistake and no matter how long it took, I was going to have to pay back the money I cost her. Otherwise, she'd make my life miserable. But my life wasn't that great to begin with. Astrid was my last friend, or so I thought. Like all the others, she had turned on me and then abandoned me.

She went on and on about the money, until finally, I got fed up and told her that I would pay for the coke. When I told her that I had fourteen thousand dollars saved up, she laughed and said that wouldn't even pay for one kilo. She was right. The street value of a kilo of cocaine in New York City was about twenty-three grand.

I was in bigger trouble with this woman than I thought. If the state didn't lock me away for good, I was going to be working off my debt to Astrid and her people for the rest of my young life. Feeling defeated, I begged her to cut me some slack. I told her not to worry, I would give her everything I had and find some way to make up the rest. After that I couldn't listen anymore and hung up the phone.

After my depressing conversation with Astrid, I sat on the floor of my holding cell and went to sleep. A couple of hours later, I was wakened and taken to NYPD's Central Booking and held until my arraignment. Central Booking is a wretched place.

I entered into a horseshoe passageway of holding cells filled with alleged offenders. There were about twenty offenders per cell. The cells were small with cement floors and only a few wooden benches. There was a toilet in the cell, which didn't work so the entire cell reeked of urine. I made my home in a vacant corner of the cell and tried to go to sleep. But I couldn't. It was too hot and noisy from the many conversations going on at once. To pass time, I read every single piece of graffiti on the wall. Finally, I grew angry and flagged down a guard. I wanted to know exactly how long I was going to be there. He told me that I should be arraigned within twenty-four hours. But with a limited staff of four officers per every twenty offenders, it ended up being more like forty-eight hours.

Chapter 36

After two days without food, because it was that bad, and because I didn't want to have to use the toilet in front of twenty strangers, I was finally sent up to be arraigned. Eleven girls, including myself, were shackled together and taken through a maze of corridors that led to the courthouse. We were placed in another holding cell filled with people from the previous night also waiting to be arraigned. Finally, after several hours of standing around I met with a public defender in a tiny room behind a plexi-glass divider. Here, I learned of the evidence the state had against me and what the district attorney's office wanted to charge me with. The public defender read the charges: underage drinking, operating a motor vehicle without a driver's license, and driving under the influence . . . But the most serious of the charges, possession of cocaine with intent to sell carried some pretty severe fines and penalties. I was facing years in prison.

My lawyer briefly explained how the next sequence of events was going to play out. Once called upon, I would have to go in front of the judge to be formally charged for the alleged crimes. After that I would have to enter a plea of either guilty or not guilty. He made it a point to say that because this was my first offense things could actually work out to my advantage. If I cooperate with the district attorney's office, meaning if I told them who I got the cocaine and the car from, I could receive a significantly reduced sentence, or maybe even probation, along with some community service and substance abuse treatment.

Court ordered treatment and community service sounded so much better than prison. I didn't want to go to jail, but I was terrified of what Astrid would do to me if I snitched. She sounded dead serious over the phone. I realized that I didn't know her as well as I thought. I knew she was a heavy mover of drugs. But then I learned she stole cars too. There was no telling what else she was into or what she was capable of and I wasn't willing to find out.

I sat back in my chair and looked up at the ceiling. I didn't want to cry, but I couldn't stop the tears from springing to my eyes. I choked as air rushed out of my lungs and feelings of dread and worry twisted in my stomach. I told the public defender that I wasn't ready to make a plea. I needed time to think about it. He looked at me and shook his head dramatically.

"You don't have a lot of time," he said and leaned forward into the plexi-glass. "And you don't have many choices. Possession of eight ounces or more of cocaine is considered criminal possession in the first degree, an A-I Class felony punishable by eight to twenty years in prison. You had two kilos in the trunk of the car. Do you have any idea what that means?"

Math was never my strongest subject, but basically, I had more than eight times that amount. He looked at me for a moment, his eyes revealing tenderness and compassion. I had a feeling he genuinely cared. But he wasn't about to go out of his way and do more than what the state of New York paid him to do as a public defender.

"If you don't cooperate," he continued, "there isn't much I can do for you. This is a federal offense. They will process you as an adult and you could very well suffer the full force of the law."

He continued to stare at me, waiting to see if I'd say something, perhaps hoping his speech would've made my choice easier. But despite the evidence against me, I wasn't ready to decide. Unsure what to do, I got up and went back into the holding cell.

Four hours later, with the public defender beside me, I was standing before the judge as he went through the long list of charges. After reading the charges, the judge asked me to enter a plea. I plead guilty.

In order to accept my guilty plea, the judge spent about thirty minutes going through a series of questions to make sure I understood the rights I had relinquished. After my guilty plea went on record, the public defender tried to get me out on bail. But I declined a bail hearing and told him it wasn't necessary. Frustrated, he took me aside and said that I was making a big mistake. He told me to reconsider and cooperate with the district attorney.

"It's not too late to make a deal," he said. "If you plead guilty, you do so not knowing in advance what the sentence is going to be."

"That's okay, I still don't want to make a deal."

I didn't want to go to prison either, but I had a strong feeling something much worse than jail was waiting for me on the outside.

Astrid knew that the most money she could get out of me was fourteen thousand dollars—less than half of what she lost. She had no real guarantee that I wouldn't turn her in. So what better way to close the loop on this problem than to take me out? I didn't want to believe that Astrid would kill me. But she had been using me the whole time—using me to sell her drugs while she stayed clean and made lots of money off my hard work. It was exactly how she had explained it to me. After considering everything that was at stake, I decided the safest thing to do was to stay in jail.

Chapter 37

The next day, I was transferred to the Metropolitan Detention Center in Brooklyn, a nine-story, two-sided county jail that housed about three thousand prisoners, many of whom were pretrial inmates waiting for a court date. Others were like me, just waiting to be sentenced. And then there was a whole host of prisoners in various statuses. Some were in transit, awaiting destination to federal prison, and some were awaiting release. There was even a small number of INS detainees awaiting deportation. The detention center became my home for the next ninety days. After about a month into my stay, I got a visit from the last person I expected to see—my father.

I met him in the institution visiting room, located on the first floor of the building. He walked up and hugged me, holding me tightly for several minutes. Most of my bruises had faded by then but my arm was still in a cast. I couldn't hug him back fully, so I patted him lightly on the back with my good hand. He was choked up and misty eyed when he finally let go. We moved to an empty table, sat down, and made small talk at first.

"Hi, how are you?" I started.

"Good," he replied.

"And Lorna, how is she?"

"Good," he replied again with no follow up.

"How's work?" I asked, trying to keep the conversation going.

My father didn't respond. He looked at me for a long moment then let out a long breath.

"What are you doing here, Lonnie?" he finally asked.

"It's a long story, Dad."

"I like long stories."

"I don't even know where to begin," I said, not really wanting to talk about it.

My father just sat there staring at me. He had traveled a long way to see me and to find out what happened. I knew I wasn't going to get off that easy. I figured I might as well talk. And besides, I had some questions for him too—like why hadn't he called me or taken any of my calls in over a year?

"I guess it all started when Lia got out of the hospital."

"What happened to Lia? Why was she in the hospital?"

"Well, that's an entirely different subject, but long story short, Lia got pregnant. She and I went to a clinic so she could have an abortion. The doctor turned out to be incompetent and ruptured her uterus during the procedure. Lia was rushed to the hospital, where she had an emergency hysterectomy."

My father was speechless. I could tell he was surprised, everyone was, because they all thought Lia was a good kid.

"After that, Lia and I didn't hang out anymore. Her parents kept her on a short leash. With nothing to do, I began drinking heavily, which was slowly making me depressed. Then one day I met a girl and we hit it off, so much that I started working for her . . . "

"Doing what?" my father interjected.

"Selling drugs," I replied, looking down at the floor.

I didn't want to see the disappointment on his face. I had seen that look too many times before.

"It started out small, but then it got big. We could barely keep up with demand, and the money was coming in faster than we could count it. I was having the time of my life. In the beginning, I had stopped drinking, but then I somehow started again and that's when things got away from me."

My father didn't speak for the remainder of my story. He

just listened in disbelief, disappointment, and disgust. When I finished I waited for him to say something, but he seemed to be at a loss for words. Feeling the need to say something, I told him that I was sorry.

"No, don't be sorry," he said in a sad voice. "I'm the one who needs to apologize. I failed you as a father, Lonnie. I blame myself for all of this."

What the hell is this? I thought. *That was the exact same thing Lia's parents told her when they found out that she had been screwing every guy in Brooklyn and got pregnant. Why is it that when kids mess up, parents tend to blame themselves?* I was surprised to hear my father say that, and I wasn't going to let him blame himself.

"No, Dad, you're not to blame," I said, putting my hand over his.

"Yes, I am," he argued. "I abandoned you when you needed me the most. There isn't a day that goes by that I don't think about that Richard ordeal. Thinking back, there were so many things I could've done differently. I could've been a little less strict. I could've taken off from work and spent more time with you. Or we could've gone to counseling. When you ran away, I just figured you didn't want me in your life. I was very hurt."

My father stopped and wiped his eyes. But I had been in tears long before he was.

"I'm sorry I didn't try harder."

"No, Dad, you did what you could. None of this is your fault. I did those things because I wanted to and for no reason other than that. I did not want rules in my life. You were a great parent. You gave me everything I could ever ask for. But I was a lousy kid. I repaid you with grief, heartache, and despair. I'm the bad guy in this story, Dad. Please don't blame yourself."

My father nodded. We both took a minute to compose ourselves. After a couple of collective deep breaths he looked at me again.

"Why did you plead guilty?" he asked.

I took a moment to collect my thoughts. I didn't want to tell him about my conversation with Astrid and how she threatened me. I didn't want to give him something else to worry about. I had done enough of that.

"Because I'm guilty," I replied.

"We can fight this, Lonnie. I'll get a lawyer. We can talk to the district attorney."

"Dad, I don't want to fight this," I said, cutting him off in mid-sentence. "I need to be here. I need to reflect on the things that I have done. I've been slowly going through the pain and difficultly of self-examination. And as I examine myself, I realize that the journey to recovery is not a short one. I can't simply tell myself that I've learned my lesson when I haven't suffered yet. In order to appreciate what I had out there, I need to be in here a little bit longer. I don't want to continue hurting the people around me. I'm sick and I need to be here so I can get better. I know this is true because I'm not as sick as I was when I first got here, and I'm getting a little bit better every day."

What I told my father wasn't exactly a lie. Astrid's menacing threats wasn't the only reason for my decision. I truly believed that my life had become unmanageable. I was constantly making bad decisions. I was doing coke and drinking a lot more than I needed to, and I didn't know how to stop. I wanted to be in jail because I hated who I had become—my mother. I may not have sold my body for money, but I did do regrettable things for less. Still, no matter how I looked at it, I was no different than she was—an unreliable, unpredictable, untrustworthy, selfish drug addict.

I don't hate my mother, although at times I did. She made me. Her blood runs through my veins. I can't be mad at her any more than I can be mad at my father for giving up on me or Astrid for turning on me. I blame myself for what happened. And I wanted to be in jail because I was far from recovered. I knew that once things blew over and the dust settled, I'd eventually start drinking and using again. I was lucky to have survived a car crash with no seatbelt on. Next time, I might not be so lucky.

"Sweetie, you have to rethink this," my father pleaded one last time. "They could lock you up for a long time."

"I know, but hopefully not too long. Will you promise to write me?"

My father started crying again. I got up and walked around the table. I threw my arms around his shoulders and hugged him as tight as I could. After about five minutes of holding him, I finally let go and kissed him on the forehead. He looked up at me with wet eyes as if he was about to say something. But I didn't give him the chance.

"Promise me you'll write," I said.

He just nodded and smiled.

"I promise."

CPSIA information can be obtained
at www.ICGtesting.com
Printed in the USA
LVOW11s2349050317
526231LV00001B/114/P

9 781633 932289